Was it Love? or was it Paris?

A Novel

MJ BACHMAN

In loving memory of my mother

ALSO BY THE AUTHOR (WRITING AS MJ ROË)

The Seven Turns Trilogy

As Darker Grow the Shadows, A Novel of the French Résistance

The Blue Amulet

The Seven Turns of the Snail's Shell

The Heat of the Desert Wind

L'amour vient—jetant un sort

Est-ce qu'il vous chantera une chanson?

Est-ce qu'il vous dira adieu?

Qui peut le dire?

Love comes along—casting a spell

Will it sing you a song?

Will it say a farewell?

Who can tell?

-Jacqueline Bouvier, Paris 1950*

* From *Dreaming in French: the Paris Years of Jacqueline Bouvier Kennedy, Susan Sontag, and Angela Davis* by Alice Kaplan. Note: Jacqueline Bouvier's bi-lingual poem was a translation of the Johnny Mercer/Hoagie Carmichael song "How Little We Know" performed by Lauren Bacall in *To Have and Have Not* (1943).

Normandy, France
July 1945

Chapter One

The war had ended; the hated Boches were gone. Paul Delacroix was finally able to return to his family's château. He had asked his son Georges-Henri to accompany him. They'd taken the morning train from Paris.

It was a hot day. The air in Paris had been stifling when they left Hélène's apartment in the sixteenth. The two had been glad to get out of there. The new baby, Charlotte, had kept the entire household awake during the night.

"What do you suppose it will be like after all that has happened?" Georges-Henri asked as the countryside sped past the window.

Paul looked over at him. "I don't know. We shall see." He didn't want to share his worst fears.

His son was the spitting image of himself at the same age. Tawny gray eyes, curly hair, a quick smile. But now he walked with crutches, and his face was haggard and ashen, his sunken eyes surrounded by dark circles. He was only twenty years old, but he looked fifty.

They had heard stories about the ravages the war had wrought in Normandy. For all they knew, the château had been completely destroyed, bombed, gutted by fire, as the last months of the war dragged on. Paul had tried to find out, but none of the old villagers he knew had answered his letters. That, too, had him worried. Were they all dead? Did the village even exist anymore?

He couldn't think about that now. Father and son would deal with whatever had happened when they arrived.

The train chugged through the countryside, passing villages and farms. Where once cows grazed peacefully in a lush green landscape, only burned-out skeletons of houses and outbuildings were left. Entire villages had been reduced to rubble. The fields lay barren and ravaged.

Paul surveyed the devastation and wept. Little remained of the Normandy he loved.

"Maybe the château has been saved, Papa," Georges-Henri said. "We know the Boches lived in it. They wouldn't have destroyed it when they fled." He rubbed his chin. "Or would they?"

"Anything is possible. We can only hope for a miracle."

"In this war," his son said, a sad look in his eyes, "miracles rarely happened."

Paul nodded, then he patted his son's shoulder. "You are here with me, *mon fils*, that is enough of a miracle for me."

Georges-Henri smiled at him. He said, "If it is necessary, you and I, we will rebuild together, Papa. Marielle will help us, too, when she returns."

Paul stared out the window. He wouldn't tell him. Not just yet.

The train pulled into the station and came to a screeching halt in a cloud of steam. Paul stood and picked up both their valises. Whatever was left of Normandy, he was home.

The château was eerily quiet. No dog to greet them. Paul wondered what had become of old Napoleon. The loyal shepherd was getting on in years when they had had to flee from the château.

He looked out to the pasture. The donkey was gone, too, as were the two horses. Come to think of it, there were no birds singing in the trees. The only sound was the quiet susurration of the wind as it swept through the trees and across the gray, barren meadow. Nothing looked as it might have this time of year. The war had stolen the surrounding countryside and robbed it of its lushness.

He sighed over the appearance of the château. Smashed and broken windows. The ancient stones chipped and pitted with bullet holes. One of the turret wings had been severely damaged, most likely by a bomb. There was a crater in the side yard where another bomb had destroyed the outbuilding where he had once stored his car. The large garden behind the barn had been neglected, vegetables left to rot, roses to fend for themselves over too many harsh winters. What the Nazis hadn't destroyed when they retreated, the Americans had pulverized as they pushed their way to defeat Hitler.

Wiping a tear from the corner of his eye, he said, "We can restore all this. It will take time. I'm thankful the old girl didn't let them completely destroy her."

"Come on, Papa," Georges-Henri said. "The back door has been left open. Let's go inside. Maybe they kept the interior better than the exterior."

"Careful, *mon fils*," Paul warned, putting his hand against his son's chest. "We don't know what or who might be lurking." Thieves and poachers had most certainly invaded the deserted buildings after the war had done its damage. "Trust nothing."

Georges-Henri gave him a knowing look as he stepped over the threshold.

They walked wordlessly from damaged room to damaged room. The devastation went beyond theft: flowered wallpaper hung in damp strips and a heavy smell of rot and mold filled the air. A thick layer of dust coated everything.

The kitchen had been scavenged of dishes and pots and pans; the rugs and curtains had disappeared. Upstairs, they found more of the same. The beautiful old floors were pockmarked from the constant pounding of jackboots. The wardrobes were empty. Much of the furniture had been carted away.

In the dining room, the long table in front of the ancient fireplace had obviously been used as a command post. Broken shards of china plates and the château's crystal wine glasses were scattered everywhere. Paul picked up a stem from a goblet next to the hearth. Holding it to the light, he imagined a German commandant taking a sip and smashing the glass against the fireplace.

"Come see this, Papa," Georges-Henri called from the salon.

Paul went through the foyer, where once two statues of medieval knights had greeted visitors. The statues, both smashed, lay in pieces against the far wall. "What is it?" he asked as he entered the salon.

Georges-Henri stood in the middle of the room. "It's been left intact," he said with a broad grin on his face. "Can you believe it, Papa?"

The salon had been Paul's favorite room in the entire château. He patted the desk, a much-treasured antique Bartholdi with black lacquer diamond inlay on its center. He smoothed his fingers over the beautiful gold-tooled leather writing surface. "This is where they must have signed the documents of surrender," he said softly.

"*Oui*," Georges-Henri said. "We are very fortunate our château was chosen."

Paul bent down and ran his hand behind the desk's right front leg until he found the catch. When he pressed it, a seamless door opened to reveal a velvet-lined hollow that, like the hollows in the other three legs, was filled with gold pieces. The family treasure had remained undiscovered for all those years. He stood and shook his head. "They didn't find them," he said. "They used this desk, but no one suspected the secret it held."

He put his hand on Georges-Henri's shoulder as they descended the spiral staircase. "We will make the château beautiful again." There was hope. He would be able to return it to its original glory.

"*Bonjour? Y a quelqu'un?*" Is anyone there?

Someone was in the kitchen. Georges-Henri felt in his pocket for his pistol.

"*Qui est là?*" Paul called. Who is it?

A man entered the foyer, carrying a rifle. He was dressed in ragged, tattered clothing, and he held his old farmer's hat to his chest. "*C'est moi.* Jacques. Don't you recognize me?"

If the man had not told him who he was, Paul would not have recognized his former gardener. He was gaunt, his eyes sunken, and his skin like parchment. He looked as if he'd aged twenty years. "Jacques?"

The man came forward. He leaned the gun against the wall and shook Paul's hand, then Georges-Henri's.

"How are you, *mon vieux?*" Paul asked.

"Half the village is destroyed. The church misses its roof." Jacques shrugged. "But we survived. *Dieu merci,*" the old man blessed himself and shook his head. "So much loss; so much destruction. I thought it would never end."

A woman peeked cautiously from the kitchen, brandishing a meat cleaver in one hand. "Who is it, Jacques?" she asked.

"*Ça y est, Mathilde*," Jacques said, assuring her that all was okay. "Paul has arrived."

"Oh," she lowered the cleaver and came forward, tears glistening in her eyes. "Monsieur Paul," she said taking his hand. "I thought we'd never see you again after…"

"It's all right, *ma chère*," Paul embraced her. "Like you, I survived. And look," he pointed to Georges-Henri. "I've brought my son."

Mathilde put her hand to her mouth and tears filled her eyes. "*Mon Dieu!*"

Georges-Henri leaned against a crutch and smiled. He'd grown up during the war. The last time he'd been to the château was for Christmas when he was fourteen. The next year Hitler smashed through the Maginot Line and brought France to its knees. "I remember your *bûches de Noël*, Mathilde," he said. "My favorite was the chocolate."

Mathilde smiled.

"There is much to be done," Paul said to Jacques. "Do you think you can help me make the needed repairs?"

Jacques rubbed his chin and thought for a moment. "There are men in the village who might be willing to provide assistance. Some have lost a limb or two; others are wounded…here." He pointed to his temple. "Every day, someone shows up who we thought dead. You never know." He smiled. "It will do everyone good, Paul, to see the château restored."

Mathilde spoke up. "I'll set to work immediately on the kitchen. Such a beautiful kitchen it was, too. A shame the way they left it." She shook her head and put her hands on her hips. "But there is still the ancient fireplace. Heaven knows, with a pot and a fire, I can make soup from practically nothing."

"And she can, too," Jacques said.

Paul rubbed his forehead. "We still have our land. If we replant the garden soon, maybe we can even get some fall roots harvested before winter."

Jacques and Mathilde nodded in unison. "It's good to have you back," Jacques said.

Paul looked at the two of them. The old château was damaged, his beloved country was in ruins, and his son had returned a cripple, but they had survived. They would rebuild.

That evening, Paul and Georges-Henri sat at the kitchen table eating a watery potato soup Mathilde had prepared for their dinner with two potatoes she'd managed to dig up from the *potager*.

"Jacques said he would bring a small crew to begin work tomorrow," Paul said. He looked at his son and shook his head. "There is much to be done."

Georges-Henri nodded. "Where to begin?"

"Food is our first priority," Paul said. "We should try to get some chickens. There is an old coop at the back of the property. We could raise them for eggs."

Mathilde poked her head out from the pantry where she'd been salvaging whatever hadn't been pillaged. "The first chicken you bring goes into the soup pot!"

Paul whispered. "We had better find more than one hen, then."

"That is a good idea," Georges-Henri said. "Maybe we could find a milk cow, too. It's been so long since we've had cream."

"That it has. What I wouldn't have given for even a drop these past few years. Now that we can get coffee with our ration cards..." Paul stared into space. "Just the thought of a *café crème* makes me delirious."

Georges-Henri nodded. "My mouth is watering already just thinking about chicken soup."

Jacques came through the back door with a baguette tucked under his arm. "What's this about chicken soup?"

Mathilde came from the pantry. "We were just planning to fill the coop," she said. Then her eyes grew wide. "Where did you get bread, Jacques?"

Jacques smiled. "The village boulangerie has reopened. The Duclos are back, but they won't tell us where they've been."

The bread, crusty on the outside, soft on the inside, tasted better than anything they'd had in months.

Paul and Georges-Henri slept on the floor on mildewed cushions that first night. The next day, they would set about putting plans in place to return the château to its original glory.

The village was a pile of rubble. Entire houses were leveled, the church gutted and burned, its spire destroyed. It was worse than Paul had expected.

"How did you survive?" he asked Mathilde who was standing behind him.

She made the sign of the cross. "We hid, Jacques and I, in the basement every night. It was a miracle that our house stood when so many others…" She wiped tears from her eyes. "So many killed in their sleep. We took in the survivors, you know. So many mouths there were to feed! There was never enough. We were all starving." She smiled. "*Dieu merci.* Somehow, we managed."

They found the village livery stable intact. Inside the centuries-old stone barn, the air was cool and the smell of manure was strong. A good sign, Paul thought. There would be animals.

Jean-Pierre, whose family had lived in the attached farmhouse ever since Paul could remember, was in one of the stalls. He came forward. One of his arms, Paul noticed, was missing. The sleeve of his shirt was pinned to his shoulder.

"Paul, *mon ami!*" With his good arm, he pulled Paul to him in a crushing hug.

Paul couldn't speak immediately. Jean-Pierre was the same age as he was, but he looked ninety. He'd been in the first war, survived Verdun, and returned to the village. Paul knew only that he had returned to the Army after the Nazis marched on Belgium.

"I've come to see about my animals," Paul said. "Jacques told me you might know if any of them survived."

Jean-Pierre wiped sweat from his forehead with the back of his hand. "There's an old donkey in the pasture behind the barn," he said finally. "It may be yours. The horses were all taken by the Germans. After that, my stable hand ran off. No one ever saw him again." He stared into the barn. "All we have now are two cows and a goose that somehow escaped being eaten."

Mathilde stood next to Paul. "I didn't have the heart to kill the goose," she said with a sigh. "None of us did. We always said that we'd save it for the village feast on the first Christmas after the war." She threw her arms in the air and let out a little chuckle. "I wager, come December, the goose will be cooked."

"I'd like to see the donkey," Paul said to Jean-Pierre. "It might be Rue." He held up an apple he had plucked from a tree on the way. "He likes these. Are the cows for sale?"

"You'll probably want to take a look at them first," Jean-Pierre said. "Only one gives milk."

Mathilde spoke up. "We'll take it," she said.

Paul snorted a laugh. "Sight unseen?"

Mathilde's eyes widened. "Why not? How bad off can it be?" She shrugged. "If it gives milk, it will do."

In the end, Jean-Pierre offered to give them the donkey in exchange for a weekly delivery of milk from the cow. Paul agreed. He would never know for sure if the animal was his old Rue, but the cow would need company, and he was certain it would be happier in the pasture than in the livery.

"Now, if I could just find a horse or two," Paul said.

Jean-Pierre said he would promise to keep a lookout.

Two days later, the cow and Rue were lazily grazing in the patchy grass that had begun to grow again in the pasture behind the château. As he stood in the window watching them, Paul thought about all that had taken place since the last time he'd been in Normandy.

After the sad winter day in 1941 when the château was requisitioned by the Boches and he was forced to vacate, Paul had sought refuge in Paris where his daughter Hélène had a spacious apartment on the avenue Mozart. Her husband had been called up, and she lived in fear that the Nazis would take over the residence. She offered her father the large bedroom on the front side of the building and moved herself and her baby to one of the back bedrooms.

A third bedroom was supposedly rented, but Paul discovered the truth almost immediately. It was being used by the Résistance. British and American airmen who had been shot down were shuttled through on a regular basis. Hélène fed them, provided clothing, identity papers, and cigarettes, then sent them on their way.

Eager to be of use to his country, Paul joined up.

The leader of the clandestine network was known to them only as *DocteurYves*. His medical practice was located in an isolated townhouse not far from avenue Mozart.

Paul had felt uneasy about him from the first time he'd met him. "He's a know-it-all," he told Hélène. "A braggart. I don't trust him."

"It's not our place to judge. He's doing good things."

"Like what? Prescribing sleeping pills?"

"I hear his patients adore him."

"Pfftt."

In the early evening of a dreary Saturday in March 1944, Paul was moving the *Signalé* in place just inside the open window of his room to alert the network that an imminent handover was required.

Glancing toward the dark silhouette of the Eiffel Tower in the distance, he noticed the chimney of a house spewing a great fiery plume of smoke. Suspicious, he hurried downstairs to the foyer.

"I'm going out for a short walk," he called to Hélène in the kitchen as he grabbed his beret and left the apartment to investigate. In minutes, his suspicion was confirmed: it was the same house on the rue Le Sueur where the Résistance made their drops. It was also where the man they knew only as Docteur Yves had his office.

The dilapidated townhouse was located on a very narrow and isolated street with the Eiffel Tower just visible in the distance between the buildings. Paul had never been invited inside. Messages were always dropped in the slot at the front door, and instructions delivered later to their apartment via courier. As he drew closer to the neighborhood, the smoke grew thicker. A sickly stench permeated the air. It made him want to vomit.

He watched as two *flics* arrived on bikes and began pounding on the front door. When a fire brigade showed up, he realized the police would surely begin a search of the neighborhood. He made a quick turn into an alley and returned to the apartment.

Hélène was sitting in the darkened salon smoking one of the black-market Gauloises they supplied to the airmen.

He sat on the sofa next to her. "I fear we've been compromised," he said. "Have you had any word?"

"*Non.*" She pushed the pack of cigarettes in his direction.

He picked it up, shook one out, and lit it with hers.

"It's been over thirty-six hours. Not good. He's still upstairs. We will have to move him soon." She took a drag on her cigarette, snuffed out the glowing tip with her fingers, and stuffed it in her apron pocket.

Paul reached over to cover her hand with his. "We need to be careful from now on. I'll try to find out what's going on tomorrow."

The next day, Paul went back to the townhouse. The street was deserted. He pounded on the front door and waited like he always did before dropping a message in the slot. A knock from inside meant to leave the note; the sound of a bird chirping meant there was danger and to come back later. This time, there was no response at all.

"No use, Monsieur. The place has been condemned." The voice startled him, and he swung around. An elderly man was standing on the threshold of the townhouse next door with a broom. He was a neighbor; Paul recognized him. He'd wondered whether he was a member of Docteur Yves's network.

The man began to sweep his step. "The firemen broke the bolt on the door last night," he muttered without looking at Paul. "They found the bodies."

"What bodies?" A sickening feeling grew in the pit of Paul's stomach.

The man stopped sweeping and scratched his temple. "The smoke," he said. "That's what caused the stink. A large number of bodies were being incinerated in the furnace." He made a disgusted face and spat into the street. "The *Boches* have to get rid of them somewhere." He shrugged and tilted his head toward the end of the street. The Gestapo's security and intelligence service was just around the corner on Avenue Foch.

Georges-Henri's fiancée, Marielle, and her family had disappeared at the same time.

Paul pinched the bridge of his nose. He knew he would have to break the sad news to Georges-Henri eventually.

Paris, France
September 1950

Chapter Two

Jacquie stood in her slip in front of the mirror. Turning this way and that, she eyed her figure. Satisfied with what she saw, she picked up her brush and ran it through her shiny dark brown hair. This year abroad was going to be the adventure of a lifetime for her. Maybe she'd even fall in love. After all, she was young, and she was in the most romantic city in the world.

What if she had already met the man of her dreams and didn't know it? Or maybe it would be a chance meeting, what the French called *un coup de foudre*, a lightning bolt. Love at first sight. A little shiver of excitement ran through her.

"I think I'm in love, Claudie," she said aloud.

From her perch by the window, her roommate snorted. "Already? How is this possible? We've only just arrived in France!" She raised her eyebrows. "Tell me more."

"I'm in love with Paris."

Claudine's jaw dropped dramatically. "His name is Paris?"

Jacquie laughed. "Not a man, silly." Their eyes met in the mirror. "Though I wouldn't mind if a man with that name suddenly came into my life." She swirled around. "It's this city I'm in love with. La Ville Lumière. The City of Light."

Claudine sighed and turned to stare out the window again. "Not that we can see any of it from here. Hélène promised us a room with a view of the Eiffel Tower. I was really looking forward to that. Instead, what do we get? A room looking into a courtyard! I think we should complain."

Jacquie joined her. "We have nothing to complain about," she said, leaning out the window. "We are in the most romantic city in the world. There's a gorgeous tree, and, down below, a beautiful rose garden. You can smell the scent from way up here. You're just tired, Claudie. After you've had some dinner, you'll feel differently."

"There's no central heating. And a single bathroom we have to share with at least six other people. I just know there won't ever be enough hot water for a decent bath."

"We have to be open minded." Jacquie returned to the vanity and applied a touch of color to her lips. "We should just be happy to have a room. Madame is one of the few whose grand apartments weren't taken over and trashed by the Nazis during the war. Housing is scarce for American students coming to Paris to study. If my mother hadn't found this, we might be in a dormitory."

Claudine scoffed. "That might be better than this."

Jacquie retorted, "The accommodations there, I'm told, are not at all nice. Just look at this room Madame gave us." She walked over and sat on one of the two beds. "Try yours," she said patting the thick down comforter. "Mine's really soft and comfy."

"It should be for what we're paying her for it."

"Oh, Claudie, she's a war widow. This is a big apartment, and she has children. My mother thought the price was quite reasonable, given that we're going to be here an entire year."

"Admit it, Jacquie. Your family's rich. Money's no object for you." Claudine sniffed again. "Not the same in my case."

Jacquie smiled and lay back against her pillow. Seeing Paris in 1950 made her realize how lucky she was to be American. The city still bore the scars of the war. It looked shabby; even the grandest buildings were dirty on the outside and dark inside.

"Well, I'm twenty years old, and I'm not going to let anything ruin my excitement," she said, sitting up. "I'm here to learn how to be French." And perhaps fall in love. She rose from the bed, rummaged through her trunk until she found her favorite yellow dress, slipped it over her head and twirled in front of the mirror once again. "*Voilà*. I'm ready to begin. Come on. Let's go downstairs. Maybe we can take a walk through that rose garden before dinner." She held the door for her roommate. "Don't forget Madame la Comtesse's rule— we're supposed to only speak French from now on."

"What a beautiful courtyard! *Quelle belle cour!*" Jacquie exclaimed, careful to enunciate each syllable in French, as she and Claudine entered the salon through French doors.

The countess smiled. "*N'est-ce pas!*" she replied.

Hélène de Montmorency was rail thin but beautiful. Her chestnut-colored hair was cut short and waved, and her amber eyes shone like gemstones in her pale face. The only visible makeup was red lipstick. She wore a simple flower print cotton dress, a red striped apron, and red high-heeled shoes. She looked, Jacquie thought, elegant.

"It's so peaceful out there. I shall spend a lot of time reading by that fountain, I think."

"You have come at the right time of the year, *ma chère*. The roses are at their peak," the countess replied as she scurried through a door that led into the kitchen. "Until the winter arrives."

Jacquie made a little moue and turned to Claudine. "I don't want to think about that now. Winter is a long way off."

"I would be happier," Claudine mumbled under her breath in English, "if we had the Eiffel Tower to look at when the bad weather arrives."

Jacquie shushed her. "We can't do anything about that now, Claudie. What's done is done, as my mother always says."

Claudine glared at her. "I wonder if your mother would be satisfied with a room with no view."

"Go into the dining room," the countess ordered from the kitchen. "After tonight, we will eat dinner at eight, but, today, we're eating early. I'm sure you are famished from your voyage, and, besides, I wanted the children to meet you."

As if on cue, they filed into the room in the well-behaved manner of French children. "First, the oldest, Christine," Madame said as she herded them in.

Christine's eyes glistened, and her light brown curls bounced as she gave them a little curtsy. "*Soyez les bienvenues, Mesdemoiselles*," she said, glancing at her mother for approval. "I am excited to learn all about America," she added. "Will you teach me to drink Coca-Cola and straighten my hair?"

"*Tais-toi,* Christine," her mother said, shushing her. "Jacquie and Claudine are here to study French culture. I'm sure they will be drinking *picon citron* instead of that dreadful cola you're so set on trying."

Christine frowned. "But all the other kids…"

"*Suffit!*" The countess held up her hand. "Allow me to present my other children."

Jacquie suppressed a giggle.

"*Voici* Théo," the countess continued, proudly pushing a reluctant little boy forward. He bowed, whispered a soft "*Salut,*" and looked at his mother. "*Maman*, can I be excused now?"

"Don't you want any dinner, *chéri*? We have chicken and *frites*." She waited for a reaction. When there was none, she added "and *mousse au chocolat* for dessert."

The dessert got the little boy's attention. He ran to the table and sat.

"Last, my youngest," the mother said patting a red-headed little girl on the head, "our *petite* Charlotte."

"Last born, but not to be ignored," a raspy male voice said behind them. "Watch out for her. She's a real trouble-maker, she is."

The child swung around and jumped into the old man's arms. "Papy!" she cried, nestling her head in his shoulder.

"Ah, my father has decided to join us after all," the countess said. "Come, Papa, meet our new arrivals."

The old man was distinguished, very thin, with baggy trousers and large tawny gray eyes that peered from under bushy white eyebrows. There was something childish in those eyes, but not the childishness of senility. "My name is Paul," he said as he shifted Charlotte to the floor and extended his right hand for the Americans to take.

"Do I say *enchantée* when I'm meeting a man?" Jacquie asked. "I don't believe I ever learned that rule."

"Oui, but only if you mean it," he said with a wink. "Otherwise…"

"Papa," the countess scolded, "not that joke now. Wait until they understand you better."

The old man's eyes twinkled. He pressed Jacquie's and Claudine's hands lightly and went to sit down at the head of the table. "I'm starving. Come, children. Time to eat."

The three children took one side of the table, Charlotte closest to her grandfather, Théo in the middle, and Christine at the end. Jacquie and Claudine were directed to sit opposite them.

In front of them was a soup tureen and a baguette. While her father ladled bowls of clear broth for each of them, Madame went back into the kitchen and returned carrying a platter of roast chicken and fried potatoes. "*Attention!*" she said clearing her throat as Théo picked up his spoon. "What is it we do first before we begin?"

Théo set the spoon down. "*Prier au Dieu, Maman,*" he said, bowing his head, folding his hands in front of him, and shutting his eyes tight.

The countess nodded. "*Très bien,*" she said. She took her place at the end of the table opposite her father.

Jacquie, who had been raised Catholic, blessed herself.

"What am I supposed to do now?" whispered Claudine. "I'm not, you know…"

Claudine had told Jacquie she didn't attend any church, but she hadn't given a reason.

"Just bow your head," she said in a low voice.

Claudine put her hands in her lap and slowly lowered her chin.

Christine, the oldest, was asked to say grace. After she had delivered a perfectly memorized prayer, the three youngsters quickly blessed themselves, grabbed their spoons and began spooning their soup.

"How old are the children?" Jacquie asked. "My little brother and sister at home seem about the same age, but they're not quite as well-behaved."

"Ten, seven, and five," the countess said. "They are not always this polite. You will see."

"Oh, Hélène," her father said with a wink, "you know they are absolutely perfect." He shoved his soup bowl aside and pulled the platter of chicken and fries toward him. "Hand me your plates, everyone. I'll serve *la pièce de résistance* tonight." He looked at Jacquie and Claudine and raised his bushy eyebrows. "We can say *Résistance* again, now that the war is over. I was a member, you know?"

"Really?" Claudine asked, wide-eyed. "What was it like?"

"Not now, Papa," the countess admonished her father. She looked at Jacquie and Claudine. "He'll tell you eventually. Make sure you have some time, though. Once he gets started on his stories, he keeps going."

Her father chuckled. "Jacqueline *et* Claudine, *dites-moi, les filles,* what sights in Paris are you planning to see first?" He tore off a piece of the baguette for each of them. "I have some suggestions for you."

With that, he unleashed a torrent of information: what to see, when to see it, how to use the Métro, how to get rid of the beggars, what to look for in the bookshops. When he had ended his monologue, he made an announcement. "When I return from Normandy, I'll take you to a few of the more, shall we say, interesting out-of-the-way places."

"Papy is going to the château," Christine said.

Her grandfather nodded. "*Eh oui,* it is a beautiful old thing in Cotentin. It's been in my family for several generations. Parts of the building date from the fifth century. The original owners, my ancestors, were a family of knights. Over the centuries, it has been transformed." He wiped crumbs from his mouth. "Unfortunately, the Boches found it so agreeable they requisitioned it during the war."

"My father has begun a major renovation since the war ended. His hope, to bring it back to its original grandeur, has yet to be realized," Hélène added with a sigh.

"What is it called?" Jacquie asked.

"Ah, *ma chère,*" Monsieur smiled, "it is known as the Château Delacroix."

"Does it have turrets?" Claudine asked.

Théo laughed out loud. "Of course, it does! It's a castle, Mademoiselle. Don't you know what a castle looks like?"

Everyone at the table stared at the youngster.

"*Ça suffit, petit,*" his mother said sternly. She wagged her finger in his face. "Remember what I told you."

"*Oui, Maman,*" the boy said. "Children should be seen, not heard."

Jacquie smiled. She'd heard that one herself.

A handsome young man who must have been in his late twenties entered the dining room. He limped slightly, and used a cane.

"Ah, *te voilà enfin,*" Madame said as he kissed her cheek and then slipped into the empty chair next to Jacquie. "You are late, *mon frère.*"

He reached over and shook his father's hand, then picked up his napkin and put it on his lap. "*Bonsoir,* all." A shy nod. "*Pardon* my tardiness. I was delayed at the University."

Paul said, "Meet my son, Georges-Henri. He is a professor at the Sorbonne."

Jacquie perked up. "Really? I am to attend classes there. What do you teach?"

Georges-Henri raised his eyebrows. "*Philosophie,* Mademoiselle. But I'm not yet a full professor." He looked at his father. "Now, if my father would hand me a plate. I'm famished, and the food smells wonderful." He gave Jacquie a quick smile. She noticed the scar that cut across his cheek. "You Americans are in for a treat," he said. "My sister is a very good cook."

Madame said, "I prefer to do my own cooking. Besides, my brother has taken the maid's room permanently."

"And quite agreeable it is, Hélène. Just right for a bachelor."

Claudine discreetly dug her elbow into Jacquie's side.

"Papy's room has a view of the Eiffel Tower," Théo piped in.

Jacquie and Claudine shared a knowing look.

Hélène gave her little boy a stern warning; he slapped his hand over his mouth and mumbled, "Sorry, *Maman*."

"Now, where was I?" Paul said. "Ah, oui, I was explaining all the sights in Paris our charming guests should see."

Jacquie was lying on her bed. "Did you see the look on old Paul's face when he suggested we go to the Moulin Rouge?"

Claudine sat at the vanity brushing her short blond hair. "Do you think it's advisable? Two girls alone."

"No harm in peeking inside, is there? It's famous."

"But why did Monsieur advise us to go there, of all places?"

"I rather suspect he was joking with us. Did you see that twinkle in his eye? Maybe he was hoping to escort us."

"I'd rather he didn't," Claudine said.

Jacquie shifted onto her side and propped herself up on one elbow. "To change the subject. What did you think of the son, Georges-Henri?"

Claudine quit brushing her hair. She looked into the mirror and locked her eyes on Jacquie's. "I found him a bit stuffy, and rather rude. He mostly stared at his plate, as though he were preoccupied by something. Then he excused himself, said he was tired and announced he was going to his room."

"Well, I thought he was kind of cute." Jacquie shot Claudine one of her sly winks. "In a sad way. Do you suppose he got that limp during the war?"

"His father did say something about being in the Résistance."

"Perhaps we should ask the son to escort us to the Moulin Rouge."

"You've got to be kidding." Claudine rolled her eyes.

Jacquie grinned. "He seems nice enough. Besides, what can it hurt to ask?" She paused and added, "Did you notice his eyes?

Claudine shook her head.

"Soft. Hazel. Grayer than hazel, actually," Jacquie said dreamily, "with delicate flecks of gold around the pupils."

Chapter Three

When Jacquie awoke the next morning, Claudine was already dressed and writing in her journal.

"You're up early," Jacquie said, rubbing her eyes.

"It's not so early," Claudine said, looking up at her. "You overslept. You even missed breakfast."

"Why didn't you wake me?"

"I knew you were tired from the trip. Besides," Claudine laughed, "I wanted to get to the bathroom before anyone else."

"Was there hot water?"

"Warm. I'm not sure they have hot water in this country. I didn't have much time, though. Théo pounded on the door and yelled that he had to pee."

"I guess we'll have to get used to that."

Claudine sighed. "The worst part is the toilet paper. I just can't get used to using those little brown squares of tissue paper."

"When I write to my mother, I'll ask her to ship us some from home," Jacquie said. "I know my request probably will sound absolutely ridiculous to her, but it's a genuine need."

"The plumbing is so temperamental, too. You'd think we were back in the Middle Ages when baths were something that happened when you fell into a river."

"They used perfume." Jacquie swung her legs over the side of the bed and stretched. "Which reminds me. Mother wants me to send her a bottle of her favorite scent."

"And that would be?"

"Chanel, of course. Number five."

Claudine closed her journal and rolled her eyes. "Of course."

Outside the window, they could hear church bells ringing the morning angelus. Jacquie dressed quickly and, in no time, was ready for her first full day at the Sorbonne. Gray cashmere sweater, navy blue woolen skirt. She sighed. "No Parisian woman would be seen dead in these white ankle socks."

"They do seem kind of out of place in Paris," Claudine agreed. "Especially the color. It doesn't go with that outfit you're wearing."

"It's a requirement for participation in the program I'm in. The Oxfords make it worse, though, don't you think? Ugly shoes, if you ask me, and they aren't even that comfortable." Jacquie twirled around, checked her figure in the mirror. At least she looked good from the knees up. "Maybe I'll start a revolution."

"You do that, *ma chère*, you do that." Claudine picked up her school bag and slipped her nylon-stockinged feet into a pair of plain leather flats. "Well, I'm off to the Polytechnique to study science and technology. Do I look all right? My outfit isn't too, oh you know, American, is it?"

Jacquie stood back to study Claudine's subtle dark green tweed wool skirt and V-neck sweater. "Not at all. That color looks great on you, Claudie."

"Okay then. *Merci.* Ta ta for now." Smiling, Claudine waved her fingers in the air and opened the door.

"Art History for me," Jacquie mumbled to the closed door as she quickly ran a brush through her hair. The class was on Twentieth century art. She couldn't wait to study the impressionists up close.

Georges-Henri was just coming up the back stairway from his room when Jacquie stepped out into the hall humming "*La Vie en Rose.*"

"*Bonjour,*" he greeted her.

Startled, she smiled and nodded politely. "*Bonjour,* Monsieur."

"No necessity to call me Monsieur," he said. "I prefer to be called Georges-Henri."

Jacquie followed him downstairs to the salon. "Then, to you, I am Jacquie," she said. "Are you going to the Sorbonne today?"

"Oui." He checked his watch. "And I am late." He grabbed a well-used leather briefcase sitting in the foyer by the front door and turned to her. "Shall we meet for lunch after morning lectures are over?"

"W-well, sure," she said in surprise. "That would be nice."

"Brasserie Balzar, rue des Écoles. It's two steps from the Sorbonne. Best *soupe à l'oignon* in Paris. À bientôt." And, just like that, he was out the door.

Jacquie took in a deep breath and pulled on her coat, all the time repeating to herself, "Brasserie Balzar, rue des Écoles."

Claudine came from the kitchen with a piece of baguette in her mouth. "I found left-overs from breakfast in a sack behind the door, if you want any." She took the bread out of her mouth. "What? You look like you're in shock? Something happen?"

"Georges-Henri has just invited me to have lunch with him after class today."

"Really?" Claudine giggled.

Jacquie opened the door and they walked out. "It's only lunch, Claudie," she said.

Once they were outside, Jacquie gazed up at their apartment building with its green-glazed roof. The building at 28 avenue Mozart was one of those lovely structures built in the mid-1800s as part of Haussmann's grand redevelopment plan. In the tranquil and refined sixteenth arrondissement, it retained, even as France was just coming out of two devastating wars, the reputation as an area where the nouveau riche liked to live. Unfortunately, a layer of soot now coated the beautiful stone structure.

"You know what I just realized, Claudie? Think about the layout of the apartment. All the bedrooms, including ours, are on the courtyard side. Except for one." She pointed to an open French window on the second floor. "The only one that could have a view of the Eiffel Tower is that one – old Paul's."

Claudine looked up. "You're right. I guess we couldn't expect him to give up the only room with the view, could we?"

"*Non*, I guess not," Jacquie said.

Above them, the French window closed.

Jacquie and Claudine walked down the street to the Jasmine Métro station. They passed a newspaper vendor. The headlines read "U.N. Forces Land at Inchon." For the first time since Jacquie had arrived in France, she thought about the affect a war had on the people's lives.

The first lecture of the day ended. Jacquie rose from her chair and shouldered her bag. It was time to meet Georges-Henri for lunch. She wondered if she really should have agreed to his request. She didn't know him very well; she'd just met him the evening before at dinner. What had she been thinking when she'd said yes? She left the building and crossed the street.

The rue des Écoles in the fifth arrondissement was the center of the Latin Quarter. Book stores and antique shops, one after the other, were interspersed with the usual stores: a boulangerie that smelled like heaven, a charcuterie with an entire pig's head displayed in the window, and a boucherie next to it with whole plucked chickens. There was a pâtisserie with a display case full of mouth-watering tarts, a fromagerie that emitted pungent smells and reminded her of the time she'd tried Roquefort cheese, a quincaillerie that she presumed from the window display sold tools, and a vintage clothing store. She had just passed a poissonerie with its display of fresh whole fish when she spotted the Brasserie just across.

Georges-Henri was standing outside on the terrace next to a table.

She gulped, gave him a quick wave, and ran across the street.

"You didn't forget," he said with a quick smile.

"I'm famished," she said with a grin.

"Well then, have a seat. I've saved us this table." He held her chair and beckoned to the waiter. Then he sat down facing her.

"How was your class?" he asked after he'd ordered *soupe* à l'oignon for them both.

"It was okay," she said. "French language. I'm not sure I'm going to learn anything new."

He shrugged.

"But this afternoon, I have the history of twentieth century art. Now, that I'm looking forward to."

"Of course," he said.

He looked bored. She decided to change the subject. "What were you lecturing on this morning?" she asked.

"Existentialism in Modern Society," he said. "Are you familiar with the theory?"

She shook her head. "I've heard of it, but I don't know anything about it, other than our French teacher talked a lot about Camus."

"It's an interesting topic, really. A new theory for a relatively old way of thinking. How can life be truly joyful and worthwhile when it is always shadowed by enigma? I draw a question mark on the chalk board before each lecture."

"I...I don't quite understand."

"Camus insists the world is absurd, but he is wrong."

Jacquie raised an eyebrow. "Wrong? But my teacher said *L'Étranger*..."

He didn't let her finish. "I am a great admirer of Sartre. His particular version of the philosophy emphasizes freedom and responsibility. For him, the heart of existentialism is not gloom or hopelessness but a renewed confidence in the significance of being human." He stared out the window. "To be human, to be conscious, is to be free to imagine, free to choose, and responsible for one's life." His eyes sought hers. "That is the essence. His book is required reading for my students."

"I see," she said, feeling a little overwhelmed. "I should like to learn more."

He was quiet for a moment. Finally, he said, "The title is *L'Être et Le Néant*. I shall lend you a copy, if you're interested." He looked at her. "Though it's in French. The English language translation has not yet been published, I believe."

"No matter. I am supposed to totally immerse myself, anyway."

He smiled. "We can only guess where our world will go from here. Sartre's central thesis — that humans are essentially free— is something you Americans believe in strongly, if I'm not mistaken."

"Yes," she said, "we do." She sighed. It hadn't occurred to her until then that Americans took their personal freedoms for granted.

The bowls of steaming soup topped with bread and melted gruyère arrived. Georges-Henri picked up his spoon. "Your country is so young compared to France," he lamented. "It has a spirit that I admire. I would like to visit it someday."

"You should," Jacquie said. "New York, where I'm from, is quite exciting." She scooped a spoonful of the soup from the bowl.

He watched her struggle with the gooey, stringy melted gruyere.

"I gather that," he said, a tinge of coldness in his voice.

Perhaps he had misunderstood her comment. "I don't miss it, though," she said quickly. "Here I'm totally immersed in French, unable to speak English." She tasted the hot spoonful and stopped to blow on it to cool it a bit. "I like that my parents are at home and can't tell me what to do every hour of the day. In Paris, I'm free to do as I want." She stopped herself. "That is, except when your sister, la Comtesse, is around. She has her rules, you know."

He chuckled. "You like France, then?"

She nodded. "It's been my dream to spend a year here, and it's finally come true thanks to a wonderful study program my college sponsors."

"Why did you choose now to come?"

"Why not now?"

"Paris is not the way it was." He sighed. "Before the war, it was vibrant, full of artists and lively. Now, sadly, it is damaged."

She started to say something reassuring, but he cut her off.

"My country," he went on, "was drained by the German occupation and scarred by the memories of the camps. The monuments are dark. All people can think about is how hard life was, how the betrayals and deceptions changed relationships. So many families made huge sacrifices."

"I think France is still beautiful."

"It will take time. For now, we rebuild the country, and, with the help of American funds from the Marshall Plan, the economy." He shrugged. "To return to what we once had, I'm afraid, is a long way off." He looked down and repeated himself. "A long way off, I fear."

They ordered tarts for dessert and then coffee. Georges-Henri seemed unhurried. He put his face to the sunshine. "You have a French name. Is your family originally from France?"

She laughed. "Well, the answer to that question is *oui, et alors non.*"

He raised an eyebrow.

"Here's the short story: my relationship to France began as a fantasy. A family story passed down from my grandmother. She claimed her immigrant parents were descended from French royalty."

He leaned forward. "Really? Royalty?"

She laughed. "Not really. Far from it, as it turns out. My grandmother liked to embellish the truth a bit." Jacquie lifted her demitasse and took a sip.

"I don't understand. Your *grand-mère* lied?"

"Let's just say she had a good imagination. The true story, as I understand it, is that my great-grandfather who emigrated was a commoner, a cabinet maker from Provence who had been conscripted into Napoleon's Army. After the defeat at Waterloo, he fled to America in fear for his life. He speculated in land rich with coal, married up in social class, and settled his family in a brownstone mansion on the smartest street in the city."

She looked up at him. When there was no reaction, she shrugged. "That's how the tale goes anyway. The immigrant carpenter, Charpentier, became a successful American real estate tycoon."

They had finished their cafés. Georges-Henri rose from the table. "I'm sorry," he announced. "I have a meeting this afternoon. I'm afraid I have to cut this delightful conversation short."

Jacquie picked up her bag, suddenly realizing she hadn't asked him a thing about himself. "I'm afraid I've been rude," she said.

He looked at her, his face full of confusion. "Why did you say that?"

"I don't know anything about you," she said.

He looked at his feet. "Well then, we can remedy that with a few more lunches, can't we?"

She smiled at him. He seemed so down-to-earth, so easy to talk to. "I'd like that," she said.

They walked silently together until they reached the entrance to the Sorbonne. He opened the door for her and stood to the side. "Au revoir," he said. A little bow. "I won't be seeing you at dinner tonight. I have an engagement." He chuckled to himself. "Plus, I try to avoid my sister's rather obnoxious children as often as I can."

"Actually, I think they are charming. Especially Théo. He has spirit."

He made a face. "He's the worst of the lot. Perhaps you've already noticed he talks out of turn. Always getting into trouble with his maman."

"All in all, they're better behaved than American children," she looked at him, "really." When he didn't respond, she said, "*Merci* for lunch. The soup was delicious."

"Until next time, then," he said. "Enjoy your lecture."

She watched him walk down the street. That limp. How did he get it? And that scar across his cheek? Perhaps she'd ask him the next time.

Chapter Four

It was a warm fall day. The sun was shining brightly, and the leaves of the trees that lined the boulevards were beginning to turn golden. After Jacquie finished her Nineteenth Century Literature class, she took the Métro back to the sixteenth.

Claudine was sitting at the window staring out at the courtyard, her elbows perched on the desk and her chin resting in cupped hands. "There's a note for you," she said. "I found it slipped under our door when I returned this afternoon."

"Who's it from?"

She shrugged her shoulders. "I don't know. It's sealed." She giggled. "Otherwise, I might have been tempted to snoop."

Jacquie picked up the envelope and studied it. It hadn't been posted through the mail. Her name was clearly written on the front. Mademoiselle Jacqueline Charpentier.

"Nice stationery, I might add," Claudine said.

Jacquie agreed. The writing was handsome, too. Using her thumbnail, she pried it open, unfolded the note, and read aloud.

"Louis Jouvet is starring in a Jean Giraudoux play at the Athénée Théâtre this evening. Would you care to attend with me? I shall be at my sister's early for dinner. À *toute à l'heure*." She smiled. "Well, well, what a surprise."

Claudine got up and stood behind her with her hands on her hips. "Who's it from?"

"Georges-Henri."

"Lucky you," Claudine said. "I suppose you're going, too."

"Why shouldn't I?"

Claudine pranced back to the desk, heaved a sigh, and sat down. "I'd do the same in your shoes. I'm just jealous, that's all."

"Did you like it?" Georges-Henri asked after the performance had ended and the lights came up.

Jacquie held her breath. "Oh my, yes," she exclaimed. "This theater is breathtakingly beautiful, and the stage sets were so enchanting." She sighed and looked over at him. "But I could barely understand any of the dialogue. I guess my French isn't quite as good as I thought."

"That's why it's good to go to the theater. Molière's *Fourberries de Scapin* is coming next. Jean-Louis Barrault. If you like, I'll get us tickets."

"That's very nice of you," she said, studying his face, "but I think I should pay my own way after this."

He chuckled softly and nodded. "You Americans," he said. "I admire that." He checked his watch. "It's still early. Would you like to stop for a *chocolat chaud* before we catch the Métro? The café Madeleine is a short walk from here."

She nodded, not wanting to end the evening.

"So, how was your date?" Claudine asked the next morning.

"We had a lovely time." Jacquie picked up her book bag. "But it wasn't a date. It was just to see a play. We're going to another one next week."

"Already?"

Jacquie glared at her. "Oh, Claudie, he's so much older than I am."

Claudine clucked her tongue. "He can't be over twenty-five. That's not that much older, Jacquie."

"Well, anyway, it's not like that." Jacquie opened the door and nearly tripped over a book on the floor in the hallway just outside their room. "What on earth?" She picked it up and turned the thick volume over to see the title.

"What is it?" Claudine asked.

"It's the philosophy textbook Georges-Henri teaches." She studied the cover. "It's by Jean-Paul Sartre."

"Who?"

"The author. Georges-Henri said he'd lend me a copy to read." She thumbed through it and stuffed it in her book bag.

Right behind her, Claudine whistled. "He moves fast, that one."

Jacquie skipped down the hall. "We're having lunch at the Brasserie Balzar again today," she called over her shoulder.

"You do that every day?"

"Most days. He's explaining existentialism to me. Want to join us?"

"*Non, merci*," Claudine said as she headed into the kitchen. "I'll just eat my cheese sandwich in the park and think about you," she chuckled and added with a hint of sarcasm, "and your *philosophe*."

"Okay, then. *Dommage*. Maybe some other time. It's going to be a beautiful day," Jacquie said. "See you this evening."

Claudine watched her trip happily down the front steps and turn up the sun-drenched avenue Mozart to the Métro station.

"She lives a charmed life," she grumbled, shaking her head.

Chapter Five

"*Merci* for the book," Jacquie said as she approached their usual outdoor table at the Brasserie Balzar.

Georges-Henri was already seated. He rose to greet her. "Keep it as long as you like," he said, holding her chair. "It's an extra."

"I'm afraid it will take me forever to read," she said, smiling at him as she sat. "Four hundred pages in French will be a challenge for me."

He was smiling, too. "The *spé*cialité is croque monsieur today," he said. "With *frites*."

"*Magnifique.*" The French version of a grilled cheese and ham sandwich. She was starving.

"The weekend is ahead," he said after he had ordered for them both and the waiter had departed. "What do you like to do in your free time?"

"I like to ride horses," she said, "at least I did at home. Until Danseuse threw me. That's my horse's name. Unfortunately, I broke my arm. After that, my father told me I was never to ride again."

He lifted his chin. "And did you comply with his request?"

She gave him a coy look. "He thought I did."

Georges-Henri smiled. "I thought so."

Was he mocking her? "Why do you say that?"

"You don't seem like a girl who obeys."

He was mocking her. She decided to let it go.

The luscious-looking sandwiches arrived.

Georges-Henri wished her "*bon appétit*."

Jacquie was about to pick up her sandwich when she realized that Georges-Henri was using his knife and fork to cut his. In that instant, she had forgotten she was in France. She grabbed her utensils and hoped the handsome Frenchman across from her hadn't noticed.

"We could go riding in the Bois on Sunday, if you like," he said, spearing a fry with the fork in his left hand and holding it in place with the knife in his right.

Jacquie tried her best to follow his example. "The Bois de Boulogne?"

He nodded. "Have you been there?"

She shook her head. "To ride? *Non.*"

"I mean to see the park. It's rather beautiful. A perfect way to spend a Sunday afternoon. There are many things to do, riding a horse included." He stuffed the piece of potato into his mouth and chewed.

"Actually, I'd like to get back on a horse. I've missed riding."

"I haven't been on a horse myself in a while. I won't tell your father if you decide to mount up." He winked at her. "As long as you don't fall off and break something again."

"I promise not to."

"Sunday it is, then."

Her class having ended early that afternoon, Jacquie made her way back to avenue Mozart. All was quiet. Apparently, Claudine hadn't returned yet, though she was normally back from classes by then. Jacquie grabbed the book Georges-Henri had given her, intending to read it in the park nearby.

As she exited, she glanced up at the apartment building. Something caught her eye. A figure wearing a beret and a scarf stood in the shadows just inside the open window of Paul Delacroix's room. She waved, but it didn't move. "Strange," she thought as she walked on. "I thought he was in Normandy."

That evening, Paul wasn't at the dinner table. Neither was Georges-Henri. The children, however, had been allowed since there would be no school the next day.

"Has your father returned from his château already?" Jacquie asked.

"Oh *non*," Hélène said. "He plans to spend the entire month there."

"Really? I thought I saw him in the window of his room just this afternoon."

Christine stared at her plate. Théo opened his mouth as if he were about to say something, but his mother gave him a stern look.

"No doubt you mistook the window and saw one of the other residents, *ma chère*," Hélène said. "I assure you. My father is not here."

Later, as they were getting ready for bed, Jacquie said to Claudine, "I know I saw someone in that open window, Claudie. It had to be him. Who else could it be? Did you see Théo's face when Hélène shushed him? She set her brush on the vanity and picked up a bobby pin. "If you ask me, there's something strange going on. Maybe I'll ask Georges-Henri about it on Sunday."

"Sunday?"

Jacquie smiled. "He is taking me riding in the Bois de Boulogne."

"Riding? As in a horse?"

"Yes. I can't wait. It's been so long since I've ridden." She picked up the framed photo of her parents that sat on the dresser. "My father would kill me if he knew." She put the photo back where it had been and picked up the book Georges-Henri had given her. "But he'll never learn about it since I don't plan to tell him." She thumbed through the pages. "Georges-Henri says Sartre insists that we, and not the world, give meaning to our lives. Well, that's what I'm doing here in Paris. If I want to ride a horse, I'm going to ride a horse."

Claudine cackled. "What happens if the horse doesn't want to be ridden?"

Chapter Six

Claudine rushed into their room the next morning munching on a croissant. "Guess what?" she said with her mouth full. "We, you and I, are all alone in the apartment." She swallowed. "Hélène has taken the children to the Luxembourg Gardens. Théo said they were going to sail boats in the pond."

Jacquie rolled over and yawned. "What time is it, anyway?"

"Nine." Claudine sat down on the edge of Jacquie's bed, chewing her croissant. "Want to go exploring?"

Jacquie propped herself up on her elbow. "Give me a bite of that."

Claudine ripped off a piece and handed it over.

"What do you mean? Exploring?" Jacquie asked as she stuffed the morsel into her mouth.

"As in having a peek into Paul's room."

"We wouldn't dare."

"Why not? If he's not here, as everyone insists, then what can it hurt? I'm curious about the view."

"Well, it's not right, Claudie. What if the person I saw in the window yesterday was him?"

"But..."

"But nothing. I'm not going along with it."

Claudine put her chin in the air. "I dare you."

Jacquie crossed her arms. "*Non*."

"Double dare you."

"*Non. Non. Et non. Absolument pas!*"

"Oh, come on, Jacquie," Claudine whined. "You know you're as curious as I am. Just a tiny peek. What do you say? We tiptoe down the hallway, open the door, and, if he's there, we'll know."

Jacquie hesitated. "Well...perhaps we could just sneak a quick look."

The door creaked open an inch. Just enough for Jacquie and Claudine to peer inside.

"Do you see anything?" Claudine whispered.

Jacquie put her finger to her lips and shook her head. Then she pushed the door open another inch. It made a loud creak. The two girls stood frozen, listening.

"I don't think anyone is inside," Jacquie whispered. She pushed the door open some more. By this time, Claudine's head was above hers, both of them trying to get a glimpse.

"I can't see the window," Claudine said.

Jacquie pointed to their left. "I think it faces northeast," she said, "so it would be on that wall."

"Then open the door some more," Claudine urged. "It's obvious no one's here."

The door creaked again as Jacquie pressed against it.

"Are you girls looking for something?"

Startled at the voice behind them, they spun around. Just down the hall, Georges-Henri stood a few feet away watching them.

Jacquie let the door shut. She felt her face reddening. "We were, ah, just exploring the apartment."

"We didn't think anyone would mind since everyone seemed to be gone," Claudine added.

Georges-Henri came forward. "My father's room is his private domain."

"We just wanted to see if there is a view of the Eiffel Tower. That's all," Claudine mumbled with a shrug.

"Oui," Jacquie nodded. "We were just curious."

He clenched his jaw. "The view of the tower, *Mesdemoiselles,* is much better from the cul-de-sac at avenue de Camoëns, I assure you." He cleared his throat. "If that is what you're looking for."

"We're so sorry," Jacquie said. "We didn't think it would do any harm."

He studied her for a moment. "Your curiosity is understandable. However," he put up his index finger, "we shall keep this our secret."

A door slammed and the sound of voices came from the salon. "Ah, my sister and the children have returned," he said. "That's my cue to depart." He turned to go.

"Will we see you at dinner?" Jacquie asked.

"Not tonight," he called over his shoulder.

"He's upset with us," Jacquie said as she and Claudine scurried down the hall and hustled into the kitchen. They had just enough time to sit down before Théo pushed the door open and entered. The little boy's face was flushed from running.

"What are you doing in here?" he asked.

Jacquie's heart beat in her chest. "Talking," she said as casually as she could manage. "Did you have fun in the park?"

"My boat sank," Théo said with a frown, "and Maman wouldn't let me wade into the pond to get it."

Hélène came through the door with a string shopping bag; Christine was behind her carrying a parcel wrapped in brown paper. "I didn't want you to catch cold," the countess said as she plucked two apples and a bunch of small bananas from the bag. "Such a treat to find fruit at the market today. Christine, can you put them in a bowl for me?"

The sound of church bells filled the quarter. Hélène cocked an ear. "Ah," she said, "a wedding, I think. Love is back now that the war is over. There have been a lot of ceremonies recently." She looked over at Jacquie. "I thought you might like to accompany me to the porcelain museum at Sèvres this afternoon. Would you like that?"

"Oh, yes," Jacquie said. "That would be wonderful."

Claudine looked from Hélène to Jacquie and back to Hélène again. Appearing to be on the brink of tears, she turned to leave.

Jacquie caught her arm. "You'll go, too, won't you Claudie?"

In a breach of the rules, Claudine answered her in English. "I know when I'm not invited," she hissed. "She invited you, not me."

Hélène furrowed her brow. "Ay-yi-yi, *les filles. N'oubliez-pas. En français!*"

Claudine's face flushed. She gave Jacquie an I-told-you-so look and stomped out of the room.

"May I go, too?" Christine asked. "I so want to." She put her palms together. "*S'il te plaît*, Maman."

"Not today, *ma chère*. I've arranged for you children to spend the afternoon with Sophie."

"Oh, Maman," the children moaned in unison.

Hélène shushed them. "You know Sophie always has something fun for you to do."

"Last time it was a trip to the library," Théo mumbled. "That wasn't fun."

"And what's wrong with reading books?" his mother asked, putting her hands on her hips.

"Nothing, Maman," he said with a pout.

Hélène shooed the children from the room and turned to Jacquie. "We'll leave for Sèvres as soon as Sophie arrives."

"Madame," Jacquie said, "can't we invite Claudine to go with us? I'm sure she would enjoy it."

She felt Hélène's amber eyes boring through her like a drill. "Claudine," she said, "needs to learn to follow the rules."

That night, Jacquie couldn't get to sleep. The look on Georges-Henri's face when he'd caught them earlier trying to peer into Paul's room haunted her. She should have known better than to let Claudine talk her into peeking into it. What had she been thinking? Where were her manners? She hoped Georges-Henri hadn't changed his mind about taking her riding in the Bois the next day.

She rose from her bed, put on her robe, and tiptoed to the door in her bare feet. Claudine was a sound sleeper, but she didn't want to take any chances awakening her. Opening the door quickly, she slipped into the hall.

Downstairs, the salon was darkened and the curtains drawn. All was quiet. She tried the French door that led to the inner courtyard. To her surprise, it was unlocked. She opened the door and stepped outside.

The moon was full. A delicate, shadowy light illuminated the garden, and the crisp fall air carried an earthy odor. She followed the stone path, smooth and cool on her bare feet, to the back wall where the flowering rose bushes existed in great profusion, and the scent was strong.

In this small private garden, the world was beautiful and secluded. She took a few more steps, rounded a bend, and found herself in a little open terrace. The sound of water bubbling in a fountain came from a darkened corner. In the center of this quiet space, there was a small, round table and two chairs. Jacquie stopped suddenly and held her breath. A figure in the shadows, a man, was sitting at the table with his back to her. He was rigid as the bronze sculptures she'd seen at the Rodin Museum. Perhaps it was a Rodin. Curious, she inched closer.

All at once, the statue moved ever so slightly and a puff of white smoke rose into the air. The distinctive smell of a cigar hit her nostrils. She gasped, but when she swirled around to escape being seen, her foot stepped on a twig. The snap resonated in the darkness. She winced and froze.

The man turned at the sound, the tip of his cigar casting an eerie glow over his face.

She held her breath. It was Georges-Henri.

For a moment, he contemplated her. Then he extinguished the cigar in an ashtray on the table and rose from his chair. He seemed stiff and stood straight after a moment, but not without some difficulty. "*Bonsoir,*" he said.

"I'm sorry. I...I didn't realize you were out here," she stammered. "I was just...I couldn't sleep...I needed some fresh air. *Bonne nuit*." She turned to leave.

He took a step forward. "Don't go."

Her bare feet wouldn't move if she'd tried. She did not answer him. She shivered.

"You're cold," he said, coming toward her.

"I don't know what I was thinking," she said, glancing at her feet. "I seem to have forgotten my slippers."

Face to face, they stared at each other for a long time. A lone bird uttered a short, sharp, chirp in the olive tree by the wall.

Finally, she said, "I owe you an apology. Claudine and I, we didn't mean to be snooping earlier. I don't know what got into us."

"It's already forgotten."

"You're not angry with me, then?"

"Don't be ridiculous," he whispered. He stepped forward and enfolded her in his arms.

She gasped. His embrace was so unexpected. She couldn't move, let alone speak.

"We should go inside," he said. Taking her hand, he led her back through the courtyard.

She followed in silence.

When they reached the door to the salon, he turned to her again and touched her face ever so lightly. "Are you still cold?"

She lifted her chin and shook her head. "Not anymore."

He leaned into her. She closed her eyes and let him kiss her. His lips were soft and smooth and she was drawn into the kiss. Never had she been kissed like that before.

A window on the floor above them swung open with a thud. "Jacquie? Are you out there in the courtyard?"

Jacquie opened her eyes. "*C'est* Claudine," she whispered.

Georges-Henri put his index finger to his lips. Speaking softly next to her ear, he said, "See you in the morning. Be ready by nine."Then, with a quick wink, he opened the door and slipped inside.

"Jacquie?" Claudine called again.

"Just getting some fresh air, Claudie," she said in a low voice. "I'll be up in a minute." She cupped her hot cheeks in the palms of her hands and murmured to herself, "After I gather my wits about me."

The memory of his soft lips came rushing back to her. *Mon Dieu*, he was a good kisser.

Chapter Seven

H oping Claudine had gone back to bed, Jacquie tiptoed up the stairs and down the hallway. She held her breath, turned the knob, and opened the door to their room as quietly as she could.

Inside, it was dark. The only light came from the moon shining in through the lace-curtained window. She breathed a sigh of relief. With any luck, Claudine was asleep. Jacquie slipped off her robe and slid quickly under the down duvet.

In the darkness, Claudine's voice came from the other bed. "What were you doing out there in the courtyard this time of night?"

"Just getting some fresh air. *Bonne nuit.*"

"You weren't alone, were you?"

"Why on earth would you say that? Of course, I was. Silly. Who else would be in the courtyard in the middle of the night? Go to sleep, Claudie."

Her roommate sat up and switched on the lamp between their two beds. "Was Georges-Henri out there too, by any chance?"

There was no stopping this conversation. Jacquie sat up, propped herself against the pillows, and pulled her knees to her chest. "It was such a beautiful, moonlit night. I simply slipped into the garden to get a breath of fresh air. That's all."

"And then?"

"At first, I thought there was a bronze sculpture near the back wall. I was curious whether it was a Rodin."

Claudine rolled her eyes. "A Rodin. Really?"

"Yes. Well, it wasn't, of course. It was…"

"Let me guess. A man? Georges-Henri perhaps? How convenient."

"Claudie," Jacquie said, "it wasn't planned. We both just happened to be out there. He was having a cigar. Our meeting was purely by accident."

"Oh. Come on. What do you take me for? You two planned a rendezvous, didn't you? Admit it, Jacquie."

Jacquie was quiet for a moment. Finally, she said, "I don't like your accusatory tone, Claudie. Nothing happened. We talked. I apologized for our attempt to break into Paul's room today. Then I got cold, and we returned to the house. That's it."

"Uh-huh."

"Why won't you believe me?"

"Jacquie, you've talked about little else but him for the past few days."

Jacquie pulled her duvet up to her nose. "So what if I have?"

"You're playing with fire."

Jacquie ignored the remark, but Claudine wasn't letting it go. "You kissed, didn't you?"

"M…maybe. But it's none of your business."

"Don't you think he's going to talk? He'll brag about it to all his friends, you know."

"I don't think he would do that."

"Huh. I know the type. They seldom keep their exploits to themselves. Besides, he's French."

Jacquie winced. "What's that got to do with anything?"

"Don't be naïve. They've all got their fiancées, or maybe even a wife, in one bed, and a mistress on the side. It's well known that French men are philanderers."

"You've been reading too much Flaubert. They're not all that way. Georges-Henri isn't like that."

Claudine yawned. "Think about it. French men like to date American girls, but they don't marry them." She leaned over to switch off the lamp. "Good night."

Jacquie stared at the shadows on the ceiling. Was Claudine right? Georges-Henri wasn't a philanderer. He just wasn't. She touched her lips with her fingers, the memory of his kiss still vivid. She wouldn't judge him on the basis of what Claudine had said. After all, hadn't Claudine admitted she was envious of Jacquie's relationship with him? Claudine was just plain wrong.

She lay back against her pillow and sighed. She'd thought she and Claudine were becoming good friends, but something had happened that was driving a wedge between them. Come to think of it, Claudine hadn't muttered a single word during dinner. Perhaps she was still angry that Hélène hadn't invited her to go along with them to the porcelain factory that afternoon. What rules had Hélène been referring to that Claudine had broken, anyhow? Speaking English just once wasn't a serious infraction. Something else had happened.

"Claudie," she said, "wake up, we need to talk."

"She told me she's going to send me home," Claudine mumbled.

Jacquie sat up. "What? Who?"

A muffled sob.

"Claudie? Are you all right?" Jacquie pulled back the duvet and got up to stand over her roommate's bed. "Who's going to send you home?"

Claudine rolled over. A ray of moonlight illuminated her face. "Hélène."

"*Mais pourquoi?* Speaking a sentence of English certainly..."

"It wasn't that. I don't want to discuss it, Jacquie. Go back to sleep."

Jacquie sat on the side of Claudine's bed. "Tell me what's going on, Claudie."

Claudine didn't answer her.

Jacquie placed her hand on Claudine's shoulder. "Don't be so secretive. Tell me."

Claudine sat up. "Can we speak in English for once?" Her voice cracked.

"Well," Jacquie said, switching to English, "all right. After all, it is the middle of the night. No one is going to hear us." She reached over and turned on the lamp. "I can tell you're really upset."

"I received a wire from home," Claudine said. "My father is very ill. He's in the hospital."

"Oh no. How terrible. Will he be okay?"

"I don't know. He's paralyzed and unable to speak. My mother is sending a letter to explain everything." Claudine paused and took a deep breath. "It could take weeks to get here, though. You know how slow the mail is."

"I know. Just this week I received a letter from my aunt. She posted it over a month ago."

"He's always been so healthy," Claudine went on. "So energetic and full of life." She put her face in her hands. "I feel so helpless."

"Maybe he'll recover even before you get the letter," Jacquie said, trying to be optimistic. "Did your mother say anything about your returning home immediately?"

"No. She wouldn't even suggest such a thing. She knows how important this year of study is to me. How hard I worked to get here."

The two sat in silence. Finally, Jacquie spoke. "I don't understand. Then why would Hélène say she was going to send you home?"

"The wire came the other evening when you were at the theater with Georges-Henri. She knew I was upset, so I had to show it to her. She asked whether it might affect my ability to pay her the rent for the rest of my year here. Can you imagine that? I was crying, and she had the absolute gall to quiz me about money."

"What did you do?"

"I couldn't help myself. I was so angry. I'm afraid I said some pretty harsh things to her."

Jacquie hesitated. "I don't know if I should say this, Claudie, but she had a good reason to ask. Her finances are tight. I can tell by how little she eats. Sometimes, she has less on her plate than we do, and she never eats when Georges-Henri joins us for dinner. She's probably worried she can't make ends meet."

Claudine stared at her. "Look. I'm not rich. I didn't have a fancy coming-out party at the country club like you told me you did. And I certainly don't have a name with baggage like *de* Montmorency. I'm used to working hard to get where I am. It's the way I was brought up. Most of the money for this trip I earned working in the local café after school, evenings, and weekends. If I hadn't won a scholarship to pay for my tuition at the Polytechnique, I wouldn't be here still."

"Does Hélène realize all that?"

"She knows only about the scholarship."

"Then you should confide in her, Claudie. Tell her the rest. She'll understand, I'm sure."

"Not after…"

"After what?"

Claudine buried her head in her hands. "She accused me of something… something awful."

Jacquie waited, speechless. Outside, the sound of a siren echoed through the quiet streets of the arrondissement. Somewhere a dog barked. A trash can crashed over in a dark alleyway.

Still, Claudine remained silent.

Jacquie got up and went over to stand at the window. Looking down on the courtyard where Georges-Henri had kissed her, she wondered if it had all been just a lovely dream. But she wouldn't allow herself to dwell on that now. She needed to find a way to help Claudine.

"What was it, Claudie? What did Hélène accuse you of?"

"She thinks I stole something of hers…"

Jacquie swung around. "What did you say?"

"When she asked if I was going to be able to pay the rent for the rest of the year, I told her I couldn't bear to ask my parents for more money. I said she might have to wait a bit to be paid, but that I'd get the money for her somehow. That's when she said one of her strands of pearls had gone missing, and she was certain I'd taken it."

"Did you?"

"No!" Claudine snapped. "Of course, I didn't. How could you even ask such a question? I'm not a thief."

Jacquie furrowed her brow. "Then why would Hélène make such an accusation?"

"Shortly after we arrived here, she caught me in her room one day looking through her jewelry armoire. I was just curious. I was admiring one of her pearl necklaces, trying to figure out if the pearls were real or fake, when she walked in." Claudine's voice was barely audible. "She got very angry and made it clear to me I wasn't to go in there ever again. I apologized and said I wouldn't."

"And you didn't, right?"

Claudine didn't answer for several seconds. "I'm just so curious about…things."

"What things?"

"How people live. Especially people who are, you know, high society in Paris. I like to imagine what it would be like."

"You've been snooping around the apartment."

Claudine nodded her head slowly.

"That's why you wanted to go into Paul's room?"

Again, a slow nod.

"What else have you seen?"

"You don't want me to tell you."

Jacquie stared at her. "Have you been in Georges-Henri's room?"

"Uh-huh."

"You went down there? Why?"

"I was intrigued. He said it had been the maid's room. I wanted to see what it looked like."

"You shouldn't have."

"Don't you want to hear what it was like?"

Jacquie crossed her arms in front of her chest. "No. And don't tell me. I don't want to know."

"Surely you're curious."

Jacquie stood in her place. Of course, she was. Who wouldn't be?

"It's small, spare, except for the books. There were piles of them— on the bookshelf, floor, and a small desk in the corner. The bed was neatly made, though. I was impressed by that."

Jacquie cupped her hands against her ears. "Oh, pull-ease. Just stop, Claudie. I don't want to hear anymore."

Claudine ignored her and went on. "I didn't open the chest of drawers to see what his underwear looks like, if you must know."

It was no use. Jacquie glared at her. "That's enough. I don't want to hear this." She threw herself on her bed and drew the duvet up over her head. "Go to sleep. We'll figure out what to do about the dilemma you've created for yourself with Hélène tomorrow."

Claudine lay back against her pillow. "I guess you don't want to hear about the photograph on his bed stand then."

Jacquie peeked from the duvet and sat up. "What photograph?"

"It's why I warned you earlier about him. He's got a girl, Jacquie. A pretty girl. There's a photo of the two of them in a silver frame on the table next to his bed. They're looking into each other's eyes and their arms are…"

"Stop!" Jacquie hissed.

Claudine switched off the lamp, scooted under her duvet and went silent.

Jacquie didn't sleep for the rest of the night.

Chapter Eight

Jacquie felt strangely awkward getting ready to spend the day riding with Georges-Henri. All she could think of was what Claudine had told her the night before. Was he really two-timing his girlfriend?

He was in the sitting room waiting for her when she descended the stairs just before nine. He rose and smiled at her.

She had decided on simply-belted, full-length riding breeches tucked into knee-high boots and a short-sleeved, fitted blouse. "Do I look okay?" She felt herself blush. "I mean, is my outfit appropriate? I...I didn't know...I always wear jodhpurs when I'm going out to ride Danseuse at home."

Georges-Henri studied her from head to toe, then said, "You look perfect." He held out his arm. "Shall we go?"

An hour later they were clopping along on their rented horses. The riding path led them through a thick wood, across a stone bridge, and alongside a peaceful pond with a population of ducks. It was a warm, sunny day. Tall trees, their leaves just beginning to turn, formed a golden autumn canopy over their heads and cast lacy shadows everywhere.

Jacquie was still thinking about that girl in the photograph.

Georges-Henri shifted in his saddle. "Are you comfortable?" he asked.

She nodded.

A minute later, he spoke again. "You are quiet. Is something bothering you?"

She shook her head.

"Is it the..." he cleared his throat "what happened last night in the courtyard?"

She looked over at him. "I don't know what got into me," she said. "It shouldn't have happened."

He smiled a crooked smile and scratched his temple. "It was quite nice, *quand même.*"

Nice? Compared to his girlfriend's kisses? She clucked her tongue and urged her horse forward, leaving him behind as she picked up speed.

He caught up a few seconds later and came to an abrupt halt next to her. "*Attention!*" he warned. "We can't have you falling and breaking something again."

She held on to the horse's reins. "I'm a good rider," she said defensively. "That was a chance occurrence. Bad luck. I wouldn't have fallen off if Danseuse hadn't been spooked by a rabbit."

"There are rabbits here in the Bois also. This used to be the hunting ground for the kings of France."

"I'll race you back to the Centre Hippique," she said, and, before he could answer, she snapped the reins and the horse galloped on ahead.

"Why did you say what you did earlier?" he asked.

The two of them were seated on the terrace. Georges-Henri had ordered lemonades after their ride.

She peered at him from beneath her dark lashes. "What did I say? I don't recall."

"About last night." He seemed puzzled that she didn't seem to understand. "*Le bisou.*" When she hesitated, he switched to English. "You don't know the French word for kiss?"

"Oh that. Of course, I do. It shouldn't have happened, that's all."

"Oui, that's what you said. Do you regret it?"

Their gaze held a fraction of a second longer than she'd intended. She took a sip of her lemonade. "I've been wanting to ask you something."

"Anything," he said, leaning back in his chair.

She took a deep breath. "Can you talk about it? How you got your limp, I mean? Was it during the war?"

He looked away as if deep in thought.

"If you don't want to tell me..."

His eyes fixed on hers. "It's not that I don't want to tell you," he said finally. "It's just that the story will not be so pretty to hear."

"Tell me anyway," she said.

He sucked in a deep breath. "It was in 1944. Six months before Paris was liberated." He lifted his glass and studied it. "I was active in the Résistance. I had just completed my part of a job when I ran into a trap."

"By the Germans?"

"*Non.* French. The Milice. Do you know that word?"

"Wasn't that the name for the French police who joined forces with the Nazis?"

He nodded. "Many were executed after the Liberation." His face grew red. "Some are still at large, but they will be hunted down eventually. There was no punishment too harsh for those…"

He stopped short, instead took a sip of his drink.

"So, you were captured by the Milice?"

"Yes, and handed over to the Gestapo. They took me to their headquarters. It was very unpleasant." He went silent for several seconds.

Jacquie saw the dazed, empty look in his eyes. "What did they do to you?" she asked.

He shook his head as if coming out of a trance. For a moment, she wondered if he knew where he was. "Are you all right?"

He cleared his throat. "Let's just say I am lucky to be alive. They deported me on a convoy out of Paris to a labor camp in Germany." He shifted his bad leg and rubbed his thigh. "That's where I got this little souvenir. I remained there until the end of the war."

He tilted his head and checked his watch. "Enough questions for today. Now, I think it's time to consider where we will have lunch."

"Will you tell me some day? The rest of the story, I mean. How was your leg injured?"

He didn't answer. Instead, he stood and extended his arm. "Do you want to return to Paris or shall we find a little café nearby?"

Telling herself it was time to drop her own interrogation, she took his arm and smiled at him. "Wherever we go, I want to try escargots. I've never had them."

He laughed and said the word in English. "Snails? Are you sure?"

"Aren't they supposed to be French?"

"You don't eat *escargots* in America?"

"Only those found in little cans in the specialty stores…imported from France."

A two-page letter from Claudine's mother arrived the following week. It was sitting on the table in the foyer when Jacquie and Claudine returned from a Saturday afternoon browsing the bookstalls along the Seine.

"It's worse than I imagined," Claudine said. "My father had a massive stroke. The doctors say he will live, but he'll be in the hospital for a very long time." She swiped a tear from her cheek and continued reading. "He'll never walk again. Mother says, with help, he might regain his speech."

"That's so sad," Jacquie said.

Claudine sighed. "She says the worse part for them is…" she choked back a sob, "that he may never be able to return to running his business." She rubbed her forehead. "It's a disaster. He could lose everything he's worked for. He's put his entire life into that bakery. Everyone says he makes the best hand-braided challah in the neighborhood. He even drives the truck himself to deliver rugelach on holidays."

"Doesn't he have someone who can handle all that for him? Perhaps a partner?"

Claudine got up and looked out the open window. "My uncle helps out in the shop from time to time, but he's unreliable. He drinks too much, especially now that his daughter came down with polio and is in an iron lung."

"Oh dear," Jacquie sympathized. "How unfortunate."

"Mother says she might be able to take over eventually, but she will have her hands full in the meantime." Claudine leaned her elbows on the windowsill. "She's so worried about how they will be able to pay for the medical expenses."

"They don't have insurance?"

Claudine shook her head. "My father never believed in it. He said he wasn't planning to get sick. He's old world. Polish. His parents immigrated to the United States when he was a teenager." She swung around. "I guess your next question is how am I going to pay Hélène."

"Actually..." Jacquie cleared her throat. "No." She got up and went over to stand by Claudine. "How about if we go down to the courtyard? There's something I want to tell you."

Claudine grabbed her sweater. "Okay, but are you going to give me a hint what it is?"

"Only that I have some news."

Claudine's eyes grew large. "You didn't ask Georges-Henri about the picture!"

"No, silly," Jacquie said. She led Claudine to the back of the garden where she'd come across Georges-Henri that night seated at the table next to the fountain. She'd been there a couple of times since to read the Sartre book he'd given her.

Claudine sat at the table. She shivered and pulled her heavy cardigan around her. "It smells like rain is coming."

Jacquie looked up into the pewter-gray sky. "It's already snowing at home. My mother said so when she and I talked."

"You had a phone call with your mother?"

Jacquie sat down at the table across from Claudine. "Yes. I could barely hear her, but..." she hesitated, "that's what I wanted to tell you. After you received that wire about your father and told me your concerns about paying Hélène, and that she had accused you of theft, well, I sent a wire to my mother. In it, I asked if we could loan you the money."

"You didn't! How could you! I never would ask you to do that."

Jacquie held up her hand. "Stop, Claudie. I know that. When I explained it all to my mother, she agreed we should help out."

"But…"

Jacquie interrupted her. "It will only be a loan until you can pay us back."

Claudine burst into tears. "I don't want your charity, Jacquie. Just because I'm a poor kid doesn't mean I'm second-class. I'm going to show the world I'm not inferior, not intellectually anyway."

Jacquie leaned forward. "Listen to me, Claudie. You are not inferior. Your family has just run into some bad luck. I admire you in so many ways. You're smart. You told me you won that scholarship because you were at the top of your class in science and math. Mark my word, Claudie. You have the courage and determination to go after whatever you want in life."

"Where's it going to get me when…" Claudine suppressed a sob. She got up to peek over the wall.

Jacquie rose to stand by her. Muted sounds came from the street—snatches of conversation, the clanging of security shutters, the honk of a car horn. "My mother has wired Hélène the money to pay for the rest of your year here. When you get home and have a superior job to anything I'll ever be able to get, you can pay us back."

"I don't know what to say. That's so generous."

Jacquie put her arms around Claudine's shoulders and gave her a hug. "I think of you as a sister, Claudie."

The babble of children's voices startled them. Jacquie peered around the fountain, put her finger to her lips and whispered, "Christine and Théo are in the garden."

They could only catch snippets of the conversation, but the children seemed to be discussing something in hushed tones. It was as if they were sharing a secret. One word stood out. It sounded to Jacquie like *mannequin*. It was the same in French as in English. At least that's what she thought. Maybe there was a secondary meaning. She'd have to look it up in her dictionary. All she could catch from the conversation was that there was something forbidden regarding a *mannequin* and *la chambre*. And Théo was to blame.

Suddenly the door to the courtyard opened and Hélène yelled, "*C'est trop froid, petits. Allez! Rentrez toute de suite!*" Come back in this minute.

"*Oui, Maman,*" the children said in unison. The patter of their footsteps followed, and then the French doors slammed shut.

"I wonder what that was all about," Claudine said.

Jacquie chuckled. "I'd love to know what secret they were sharing. Maybe we'll find out at Sunday dinner tomorrow. Théo told me it's going to be special since Paul will be home."

It rained on Sunday. A cold rain that sent fat raindrops pounding against the windowpanes. The apartment had a gas heater, but it had quit working during the night leaving the inside air nearly as chilly as that outside.

Jacquie and Claudine, bundled in shawls and sweaters, huddled in front of the fire in the salon all day reading the books they'd found in the bouquinist's stall by the Seine the day before.

Promising a special feast for her father's return, Hélène had spent the morning in the kitchen. The mouth-watering smell of roasting chicken and garlic filled the air.

Sometime around five in the afternoon, the front door opened and the foyer was filled with commotion. Shaking off wet umbrellas, Hélène and the excited children entered, all chattering at once. They had just met Paul at the train station.

"He's here," Théo called, pulling his grandfather into the room. "Papy is here."

Jacquie and Claudine got up to greet the old man, who immediately announced that he was going to his room for a nap and he'd see them later at dinner.

Hélène disappeared into the kitchen while the children brought out a puzzle, set it on the oval marble-top coffee table, and went to work putting it together.

Jacquie was just wondering if Georges-Henri would show up when she heard the door open, an umbrella being shaken, and then heavy footsteps clomping up the stairs.

"I'll be right back," she said to Claudine. She left the salon, and climbed the stairs.

From the landing, she could see George-Henri standing halfway down the hallway next to her door. He hesitated, then tapped lightly, twice in succession, with the back of his hand.

Her slippers made little sound as she quietly came up behind him. "Are you looking for someone?"

His hair was wet from the rain. "Oh! *Tu es là*," he muttered, as if taken by surprise. "I…I just wanted to…" He smiled and, seemingly on impulse, wrapped his arms around her.

"Brr. You're cold," she whispered.

He bussed her on each cheek, then let her go. "I just wanted to warm up," he said with a wink. "I'll see you at dinner."

She caught her breath as she watched him limp slowly down the hallway and descend to his room.

To heck with that girl in the photograph, whoever she was.

The table was set with candles and crystal. While rain pounded against the windows, the family took their seats—Hélène and Paul at either end, the three children on one side of the table, and Jacquie and Claudine opposite. A third chair next to Jacquie's remained vacant.

"Where is Georges-Henri?" Paul asked. "I thought he was coming."

Jacquie didn't know whether she should admit she knew he'd shown up.

Hélène smiled. "He might have fallen asleep. Théo, why don't you go and knock on your uncle's door?"

"No need." Georges-Henri's voice came from the doorway. "Sorry I'm a bit late. I was absorbed in a book."

Jacquie pictured him reading in his bed, the photo of the girl next to him on the nightstand.

He entered, patted his father's shoulder, and slid into the empty seat next to her.

Paul poured glasses of wine for the adults and a half glass to which he added water from a pitcher for Christine.

Théo said grace, which he was in the process of embellishing with a lengthy plea for a puppy for Christmas, when a flash of lightning followed by a loud rumble of thunder outside cut him short.

"That will do, Théo," Hélène said. "I'm sure *le bon Dieu* is well aware of what you want from Père Noël." She began to serve bowls of potage Crécy from the ornate Sèvres soup tureen sitting in front of her.

Paul cleared his throat and raised his glass of wine. "To family, friends, and food," he said. After taking a swallow, he shot Théo a sideways glance. "Since we are all together for this happy celebration, I wish to ask a question."

They all raised their heads in anticipation.

"Has someone been playing with the Signalé?"

Jacquie gave Georges-Henri a questioning look. He shook his head slightly, as if cautioning her to wait for what came next.

Meanwhile, Hélène tore off pieces of a baguette for the children then passed the rest of the loaf down the table.

Christine looked over at her little brother and smirked.

Charlotte, the youngest, spoke up. "I haven't been in your room, Papy. You said I shouldn't go in there when you are gone. Remember?"

Paul nodded his head. "Oui, Charlotte, that is what I said, and I believe you, *chérie*."

Charlotte gave her siblings a self-righteous smile.

Jacquie answered. "What is Signalé? I don't know that word."

Paul tore off a piece of the baguette. "*Eh bien*," he began, "it's from Old French. Fourteenth century. During the war, we in the Résistance had our special ways to send and receive signs or messages." He tapped his temple. "Calling it the Signalé was my idea."

Théo was listening intently to the conversation. Finally, not able to help himself, he blurted, "It's a mannequin."

"A mannequin?" Jacquie asked.

"One that was dressed up to look like my father," Georges-Henri added.

"It came from a dress shop that belonged to a Jewish friend who was deported," Hélène contributed.

"But it's not a boy mannequin or a girl mannequin,"Théo said.

"Please," Paul said with a chuckle, "allow me to explain. I called the mannequin Signalé because I used it to alert the network when a downed flyer we were hiding needed to be picked up. I would place it in the open window of my room so the courier could see it from the street."

Jacquie looked at Claudine. So that's what she'd seen in Paul's window that day—a store mannequin.

"I don't understand," Hélène said. "Why on earth did you ask if someone had been in your room playing with it?"

"Because, *ma chérie*," Paul went on, "I found evidence." He looked around the table, withdrew a strand of pearls from his pocket, and held them up. "The unknown someone apparently dressed the mannequin as a woman and left this behind."

Claudine gasped.

Hélène put down her soup spoon. "Let me see those," she said, wide-eyed.

Paul passed the pearls to Georges-Henri who passed them to Jacquie. "I assume these are yours?" she said as she handed them over to Hélène, bypassing Claudine who appeared to be near tears.

Hélène examined the strand. "Théo," she said, "did you take my pearls?"

Slowly, the boy nodded and looked down at his plate. "*Oui, Maman.* I'm sorry. I didn't think you would mind."

Without asking to be excused, Claudine rose from the table and hurried from the room.

Hélène stared after her. "Oh dear," she said. Standing, she grabbed Théo's ear. "Come with me, *jeune homme*. Tonight, you are going without dinner, and that puppy you want so badly is in serious jeopardy."

"*Mais, Maman*," he protested as his mother pulled him toward the door. Then, to everyone's surprise, he turned, cupped his hands, and shouted, "The Signalé is hiding a secret, and I know what it is."

"Théo!" his mother hollered as she yanked him from the room.

Paul looked stunned. Georges-Henri glanced at his father. The two remaining children sat in awkward silence.

Jacquie couldn't help wondering about what Théo had said. What secret was that mannequin hiding?

"Why was Claudine so upset?" Georges-Henri asked finally.

"I believe that is between her and Hélène," Jacquie said, trying to put it delicately.

A few minutes later, Hélène and Claudine came back into the dining room together. Claudine's eyes were red, and she was sniffling. They quickly slid into their places at the table.

"Before I serve the main course, I have an announcement," Hélène said. "There has been a serious injustice done." She put her hand over Claudine's. "I owe our American guest an apology. I hope she can forgive me."

Jacquie reached over and gave Claudine a reassuring hug. There was justice in the world after all.

Normandy
November 1945

Chapter Nine

G eorges-Henri sat at the kitchen table helping Mathilde peel apples. Outside, the sky was dark, and a howling wind battered the newly-repaired windows of the Château.

In the four months since they'd returned, Paul and Georges-Henri had accomplished a lot. Potatoes and root vegetables from the garden, sufficient to get them through the winter, were stored away in the cellar. Jacques and his crew from the village had cut firewood, and repaired furniture deemed useable. The living quarters of the drafty old castle were reduced to the kitchen and dining room downstairs, an upstairs salon, and a bedroom each for Paul and Georges-Henri. They would be warm and comfortable for the winter. Then, come spring, the renovation would resume.

Jacques and Mathilde were now permanently installed close by in the caretaker's cottage. Mathilde prepared the meals, and they all ate together at the same table. Paul and Georges-Henri considered them part of the family.

Paul entered the room and plucked a slice of apple from the pile just as lightning flashed and a subsequent clap of thunder shook the thick walls.

Mathilde's face went pale, and she stopped what she was doing. "That sounded like guns," she said, shaking her head.

"The war is over, Mathilde," Paul said.

She sighed. "I know, but I'll never get used to not being afraid."

Georges-Henri rose from his chair and looked out the window. "The storm is coming in from the coast," he said. Another thunderclap rumbled overhead. "Good that Jacques was able to guide the animals into the barn earlier."

Mathilde chuckled. "That old donkey didn't want to cooperate, though. It had the nerve to bite Jacques on the arm."

Paul laughed and took a seat at the table. "I'm beginning to think he is our Rue after all." He tapped his temple. "*Têtu.* Headstrong."

Jacques entered from the side door. "There's a stranger walking up the driveway," he said.

Georges-Henri peered out the window again. "I see him."

"Probably looking for work," Mathilde said.

"Or a hand-out," Paul added. "Anyone with him?"

Georges-Henri shook his head. "*Non.* He's alone." He pulled his pistol from his pocket and checked to see that it was loaded. "It's best to be prepared…"

Mathilde nodded knowingly. "It could be a Boche trick."

"Mathilde, the Boches are gone," Jacques reassured her. He plucked an unpeeled apple from the basket and took a bite. "If you need me, I'll be in the barn milking the cow." With that he opened the side door again, and headed back out into the storm.

Seconds later, there was a loud pounding on the front door.

Paul rose from his chair and went into the foyer. Georges-Henri followed. "What if this is a trick?" he asked his father.

"It's heartless to turn a *mec* away in this weather," Paul said as he opened the heavy wooden door. A strong gust of wind whooshed inside.

The man standing on the doorstep was tall and thin with a long, narrow face and bead-like eyes. His coat was drenched, and he was shaking. "*Bonjour, Messieurs*," he said, removing his beret. "I'm looking for Marielle Rosen."

Georges-Henri's face drained of color at the mention of Marielle. He had had no word from her.

"My name is Joachim Herz," he said. "Marielle told me…"

Paul stepped forward. "Please come inside, Monsieur."

The man nodded his thanks and shuffled into the foyer.

Paul closed the door behind him.

"What is your business here, Monsieur Herz?" Georges-Henri asked. "Why are you looking for Marielle?"

"I escaped Paris to Buenos Aires, Argentina, in forty-four. Now that the war is over, I have returned hoping to find if there are any surviving members of my family. We are Jewish, you see."

Georges-Henri stared at him; Paul held his breath.

Joachim wiped his nose with the back of his hand. "Marielle told me that the family of her fiancé owned Château Delacroix in Manche Normandy. That was all I had to go on. I wasn't sure if I'd found the right place. I was hoping to find her here."

Paul held out his hand. "Paul Delacroix. This is my son Georges-Henri. Indeed, you have found the Château Delacroix."

The stranger shook Paul's hand. "I am pleased to meet you." He looked at Georges-Henri. "Are you Marielle's fiancé?"

Georges-Henri nodded and reluctantly took the man's hand.

"Is she here?" Joachim asked hopefully.

Georges-Henri shook his head.

"Will you have something to drink and warm yourself?" Paul asked.

Joachim smiled for the first time. "*Oui, merci beaucoup*, Monsieur. You are very kind."

They led him to the kitchen and invited him to sit at the table. Paul poured a generous glass of Calvados. The stranger downed it in one gulp.

Mathilde took his coat and hung it on the rack. Then she placed a biscuit and a little earthenware ramequin of marmalade on the table in front of him.

"Have you found any of your family members?" Paul asked.

Joachim shook his head. "I fear the worst. There is only one hope remaining. One or two may have survived and returned to the village where I grew up."

"Where is that?"

"In Brittany. Near Saint-Malo. I'm headed there now."

Georges-Henri stared at him from across the table. "How do you know Marielle? Her parents are Jewish also. They, too, escaped to Argentina. Did you meet her there?"

Joachim picked up the biscuit, dipped a corner of it into the marmalade, and took a bite. "I met her only once. It was in March 1944. In Paris."

"That was a month after I was captured," Georges-Henri said.

"How did you meet her?" Paul asked, his mind filled with growing dread.

Joachim wiped an eye. "When my parents and I realized it was time for us to leave France, we were referred to a doctor—Docteur Yves, he said his name was. We were told he was helping Jews get passage to Argentina." He hesitated. "For a price."

Paul froze. His hand shook as he picked up the bottle of Calvados and poured the man another glass. This time, he poured one for himself and for Georges-Henri, too.

"My father gave Docteur Yves everything he had in exchange for our passage," Joachim went on. "Gold coins, silver, artwork. We were told to arrive on a certain date at the doctor's office. The tenth of March, to be exact. His office was in a townhouse on rue Le Sueur in the sixteenth. We were to receive final instructions and our injections for the voyage, and then be led to the escape route."

Paul felt his heart beating faster.

Joachim finished the biscuit, scooped the rest of the marmalade up with his finger, savored it, and looked over at Georges-Henri. "A young woman named Marielle Rosen was also there that night with her parents. There were about twenty people in the waiting room. The Rosens were excited about the trip, as were my own parents. I remember being very nervous.

"We sat there awaiting our turn. One by one, each family was summoned from the room by the doctor. My family and the Rosens were the last to be called."

Mathilde put another biscuit in front of him.

Joachim nodded in appreciation and continued. "When our turn came, we were led down a dark stairway to the basement. I became suspicious immediately. There was a strange smell. While my parents were being injected, I scrutinized the walls. We were told that there would be an underground tunnel through which we would go to find the people waiting to guide us to the coast. Seeing no tunnel, I asked the doctor where the exit to the escape route might be. He held up a syringe, smiled and said, 'You will soon arrive at your destination.'"

Shaking, Joachim picked up his glass and stared into it for several seconds, turning the small, short-stemmed snifter around as if it were an orb providing him a glimpse into the past.

Paul and Georges-Henri remained silent.

Finally, Joachim shook himself out of his daze, quickly gulped down the rest of the brandy, and continued. "Just as the doctor started to put the needle in my arm, I looked over at my father and noticed he was having trouble breathing. I pulled my arm away and rushed over to him. Then I saw my mother had lost consciousness. Panicked, I ran through the basement feeling the walls until I found a door and opened it. I thought it was the exit to the tunnel, but it was another room with an operating table in the center. Next to it, piles of bodies covered with quicklime lay in a pit.

"Suddenly, I felt a pain in my shoulder. I realized with horror that the doctor had stabbed me with the needle and was struggling to inject whatever it was into me. I pulled away and ran up the stairs. I could hear the doctor behind me on the steps."

"Where was Marielle in all this?" Georges-Henri asked wide-eyed.

"She and her parents were still in the waiting room. The Rosens were the last family to be called, you see. I yelled to them that it was a trap. Marielle said she didn't believe me. Then the doctor appeared. He was wild-eyed, and he had a pistol which he pointed at us. I was in such a panic. I don't recall if he said anything.

"Monsieur Rosen, Marielle's father, was a large man. He stood in the doctor's way and shouted for us to run. Marielle tried to pull her mother with her, but the woman refused to leave her husband. I grabbed Marielle's hand. As we fled, we heard her parents pleading for their lives. Then shots rang out." He shook his head. "The Rosens saved their daughter's life, and mine, that night."

"What did you do next?" Georges-Henri asked. "Where did you go?"

"Once we were well away from the sixteenth, we hid in a dark alley until daybreak. It was then that Marielle told me a little about herself, that she was engaged, that the young man had been captured, and she feared for his life. She also mentioned that his family owned a château in Manche Normandy, but it had been requisitioned by the Boches."

Joachim rubbed his temples. "We parted the next day. I never saw her again."

Georges-Henri gulped down the last of his glass of Calvados and looked over at his father. "I don't understand. Did you know about this?"

Paul shook his head. That much was true. He had no way to know what the doctor had been doing or that Marielle had escaped.

"Why wouldn't she have gone immediately to you or Hélène? Surely, she knew you would have helped her."

Paul shrugged.

"There is more to the story. She had a reason," Joachim said.

Georges-Henri leaned forward in his chair. "What reason?"

Joachim seemed surprised by the tone of his voice. "Be patient, Monsieur," he said, "I shall tell you." He pulled a handkerchief from his pocket and blew his nose. "We were both grief-stricken. She was sobbing over the loss of her parents. I tried my best to be a comfort to her, but I, too, was hurting for my own father and mother." He looked at Paul. "It was then that she confided her secret…" he hesitated and turned his eyes back to Georges-Henri. "I don't know why. She no doubt assumed she would never see me again. She said…" he paused, "she said she was with child."

Georges-Henri's eyes grew wide. "What? What are you saying?"

"Three months along. It was her fiancé's child. Your child, Monsieur."
He wiped his nose again. "She said you were captured before she could tell
you. I asked her where she would go to have the baby. She wouldn't tell me.
Her own words were, 'somewhere where no one will be able to find me'."

Georges-Henri leaned his elbows on the table, closed his eyes, and
cupped his hand over his mouth. Tears welling in his eyes, he rose and
picked up his crutch. "I didn't know," he said, shaking his head as he limped
from the room. *"Mon Dieu.* If only I'd known."

Once Paul had bid Joachim Herz adieu and sent him on his way with a sack
lunch put together by Mathilde, he went to find Georges-Henri.

Upstairs in the sitting room, a log crackled on the fire. Georges-
Henri sat slumped over in a chair in front of the fireplace, his back to
the door.

Paul pulled up a chair and sat down next to him. "Are you all right?"
he asked, putting a hand on Georges-Henri's shoulder.

Georges-Henri flinched and pulled away, not answering the question.

Paul stared into the fire. Words failed him.

Finally, Georges-Henri broke the silence. "The doctor, Yves, that
man said his name was. It can't be coincidental. Wasn't he the cell leader?
The one who coordinated our Résistance efforts in the sixteenth? I never
met him."

Paul hesitated. "Oui. The same."

"Did you know him? You and Hélène?"

"I met him only once. He mostly communicated through written
notes that were delivered via couriers. Marielle, as you know, was one
of them."

Georges-Henri looked over at him. "Marielle must have assumed we were in on it." He pinched the bridge of his nose. "Killing Jews and taking all their valuables. That had to be why she didn't come to you for help. She couldn't trust anyone. Not even me."

"Remember that she did tell Joachim the name of our château."

"You must have thought something happened to her when she stopped running courier."

Paul leaned forward. "Yes. I assumed she and her parents had escaped." He stared into the fire. "When the truth about the doctor was discovered, there was only one conclusion. They must have been among his victims."

Georges-Henri clenched his jaw, and his voice rose in anger. "Why didn't you tell me this earlier, Papa? Why?"

Paul hung his head. "I planned to," he muttered, "but when you came home, I...I just couldn't find the words. I knew it would break you if you learned what had happened to her."

"You let me believe she was in Argentina all this time? How long did you plan to carry on this charade? Years?"

Paul shook his head. "*Non*. Just a little while longer...until you grew stronger."

Georges-Henri stood from his chair. "The child would be over a year old by now. I must find out what happened after she and Joachim parted ways." With that, he left the room, went into his bedroom, and slammed the door behind him.

Southern France
Six Months Later

Chapter Ten

Georges-Henri arrived mid-morning. The convent wasn't difficult to find, perched as it was high up on a hill overlooking the village of Les Moulins.

He crossed a stone walking bridge and slowly made his way up the steep pathway. Halfway, he paused, took a deep breath, and sat down on a wooden bench to rest his leg. The long journey combined with the climb from the village had made it ache.

Ahead of him, two sandstone pillars crowned by ornate wrought-iron crosses framed the entrance to the convent grounds. It was an imposing complex of large pink stucco buildings with tile roofs, all surrounded by tall Italian cypress trees swaying in the wind. A slim, two-story-high carillon tower with arched openings and a cross on top rose above it all.

He shifted his weight and stretched his stiff leg as he thought about Marielle.

She was tall and slim with pretty dark brown eyes, thick eyebrows, and soft, curly hair that matched the color of her eyes. She smiled easily and spoke with a slight, yet unidentifiable, accent. He thought she was beautiful.

An active courier for the network, she delivered the cell leader's notes and awaited responses. That was how they met. One rainy day, he barged into the foyer of his sister's apartment in the sixteenth and discovered her standing there. He was immediately smitten.

Their love affair began with stolen kisses at the top of the staircase on avenue de Camoëns. With the Eiffel Tower in the distance, they would kiss for a precious few minutes after she had picked up a message from the cell leader on rue Le Sueur. Then, reluctantly parting, they would go their separate ways to avoid being detained.

One night, they were both assigned to help with a sabotage on the outskirts of Paris. A Nazi troop train was en route to the coast. The two of them were to spot the engine just as it rounded the corner and send a signal to members of the Résistance waiting farther up the line. They hid in a dark tunnel beneath the tracks for more than three hours. Because it was cold, he put his arms around her to keep her from shivering. When it was evident the train was going to be later than anticipated, he spread his coat on the ground and the two of them laid down on it together. Inevitably, the closeness led to more than kissing.

It wasn't until they'd known each other for a few months that she admitted to him that she wasn't Jewish. The Rosens, her adoptive parents, had brought her to Paris when she was very young, given her their name, and raised her as their own. He asked her where she'd spent the first few years of her life, but she was strangely reluctant to tell him.

A miracle had led him to this village. A month after Joachim Herz visited them in Normandy, a letter arrived. Joachim wrote that he had found a lone survivor of his family in Saint-Malo, an aunt who had been in one of the camps and was very ill. He planned to stay in France to care for her.

He had added a postscript.

I don't know if this piece of information will be of interest to you, but I remembered something after I left you that night. It was about Marielle's accent. You may recall that she had a rather sing-song way of ending her words. It was very subtle, but I recognized it. A friend of mine in Paris before the war was from the south of France, Provence specifically, and he spoke with the very same accent. It may be a clue as to her whereabouts.

Joachim's letter had jogged Georges-Henri's memory. He recalled a comment Marielle had made one cold, snowy day in Paris when they were huddled together on a bench in Luxembourg Gardens. "Sometimes I miss the warmth of Provence," she said. When he pressed her, she dismissed the subject with a wave of the hand, but later, she told him her parents had adopted her from a Cistercian convent. There weren't very many such convents in Provence.

All that winter, it had gnawed at him. Maybe that's where she had gone to have the baby. By spring, he made up his mind to travel south.

Though it was very difficult to find birth records in a country where many of the village churches had been nearly bombed into oblivion, he found something to go on in the final village he visited—a name. Not Marielle Rosen, as he had hoped, but listed in the church's baptismal register was Marielle X, a foundling left on the doorstep of the local Cistercian convent in 1925.

He rose from the bench, picked up his back-sack and his cane, inhaled a deep breath, and went up to ring the bell at the huge entrance door of the convent.

The portal opened slowly. A diminutive woman, her face framed in a black veil, peered cautiously at him through tiny wire-rimmed glasses.

"*Bonjour, ma Sœur,*" he said.

"Your name and reason for coming?" she asked cautiously.

"Georges-Henri Delacroix. I am in search of information about a girl who may have lived in this convent as a child."

The nun nodded. "Since the war, many people have arrived hoping to find the missing." She opened the door wider and stepped aside to let him enter. A wide, black belt fixed the black-and-white fabric pieces of her penguin-like habit at the waist, and a small silver cross hung on a long cord at her neck.

"I am Sœur Thérèse," she said. "Please come in. The Reverend Mother may be able to help you. I shall take you to her."

She led him across a cobblestone courtyard and into the largest of the buildings. The only sound was the slight rustling of her habit as they walked down a long hallway. Her sandals made no sound at all on the tile floor. At the end, she halted and rapped lightly at a double door.

"*Oui?*" a woman's voice called.

"You have a visitor, Mother Marguerite."

Seconds later, the door opened and Georges-Henri saw a tall woman dressed in the same penguin-like habit as Sister Thérèse but with the addition of a snowy-white wimple. A large, ornate filigree cross hung on a long, silver chain at her front.

He bowed. "Mère Abesse."

She removed her spectacles. "How can I help you, *jeune homme?*"

"I am looking for someone who disappeared during the war," he said. "She may have come here."

She studied his face for a moment, then nodded her head and said, "Please, come in."

Sister Thérèse remained in the hallway. "You may be excused now, Sister," the Reverend Mother said. "I shall escort him out when we have finished."

The younger nun bowed slightly and turned to walk back down the hall.

Georges-Henri studied the room. A large desk with books and papers neatly arranged on top sat in the center next to a file cabinet. Shelves overflowing with books climbed to the ceiling. Two Louis XVI chairs, a floor lamp and a small round table in between, sat near open French doors leading to the garden.

Indicating he should take one of the chairs, Mother Marguerite pulled her habit around her knees and settled into the other. "Now, tell me, for whom are you searching?"

Georges-Henri sat down. "My fiancée's name is Marielle," he began. "Marielle Rosen."

The Abesse listened patiently, occasionally nodding, as he went on to explain how he had fallen in love during the war, and what he had learned the past November when Joachim Herz had shown up in Normandy.

After he finished, Mother Marguerite rose from her chair and went over to the file cabinet next to her desk. "Born 1925, you say," she said, putting on her glasses. She pulled open one drawer, thumbed through some files, closed it, and then opened another. "Our community was still in Reillanne then."

After a few more minutes of searching and muttering to herself, she lifted a file and studied its contents for a moment. A glimmer of recollection crossed her face as she pulled out a photo. Closing the drawer, she sat down at her desk to read more.

Georges-Henri watched her, not knowing what to say or do, so he said nothing, and didn't move from his chair. Outside, the sun shone brightly, birds twittered in the trees, and the raspy drone of the cicadas became impossible to ignore.

It was some time before the Reverend Mother removed her glasses and rubbed the bridge of her nose. Closing the file, she got up and went over to stand next to the French doors. "Come take a walk in the garden with me, Monsieur," she said.

Outside, the air was filled with an intoxicating perfume—a combination of roses, orange blossoms and jasmine. The Abesse led Georges-Henri along a path, passing garden rooms partitioned off by low stone walls and manicured boxwood hedges. Meticulously-sculpted topiary trees in the shape of round lollipops lined the way. In one corner, a statue of the Virgin Mary and child was flanked by lemon trees in terra-cotta pots. In another sat a small, ivy-covered archway with the chiseled granite figure of a monk set into the recess. She informed him the Cistercian monk was Saint Bernard, the monastery's patron.

"The garden is magnificent," Georges-Henri said as they lingered under a pergola covered with masses of climbing roses.

"We take care of it all ourselves," the Reverend Mother said. "Planting and pruning provide the opportunity for prayer and meditation." She smiled. "And the beauty is our reward."

Georges-Henri winced as he shifted his weight to his good leg. He pointed his cane toward a wrought iron bench sitting in the dappled light of a flowering myrtle tree. "Do you mind if we sit for a bit?"

"Please, by all means, have a seat," she said. "Were you injured during the war?"

He nodded. "I was sent to a German labor camp." He sat down and stretched the leg out in front of him.

She sat next to him. "Now then," she began after a few minutes. "I shall tell you about your Marielle."

Georges-Henri felt a surge of elation. "She was here, after all?"

She nodded. "When I came to the convent, there was a child, a girl who had been found just inside the gate as a baby. I wasn't clear whether the parentage was known, or whether someone would come back for her. All I knew was, as a young novitiate, I was to look after her. It was one of my duties. I didn't quite understand what that meant. I was just a youngster myself, you see." From an inside pocket of her habit, she pulled a worn, sepia-toned photo, looked at it, then handed it over to him. "This was in the file. I don't recall when it was taken."

Georges-Henri fingered the photo. It showed a dark-haired little girl of about four or five seated on a bench next to a younger version of the Reverend Mother. The picture had been taken in this same garden. Though the eyes looked similar, it was hard to tell if it was the young woman he had known.

"Marielle was a curious child," the Abesse continued, "always asking questions." She paused to listen to a bird singing in the tree above them.

Georges-Henri waited impatiently for her to tell him more.

"I had made a vow of silence," she continued, her soft voice mingling with the birdsong, "and so I became frustrated with so much chatter. To quiet her, I chose books for her. Though very young, she would devour the pictures, and then ask more questions.

"One day, I told the Mother Superior I couldn't take care of the child any longer if she expected me to fulfill my vows." She peered at Georges-Henri over the top of her wire-rimmed glasses. "And do you know what she said?"

He shook his head.

"She told me I would need to learn patience if I wanted to remain a nun. And, if I ever wanted to become Mère Abesse, I would have to embrace a great many more virtues." She smiled. "Of course, she was correct."

"How long was Marielle here?" he asked, impatient to keep the conversation on track. "Do you recollect when she was adopted?"

She nodded. "I do. She had just passed her fifth birthday. I remember because I gave her a small gold cross on a gold chain to wear."

Georges-Henri recalled that necklace. It had seemed odd for her, a Jewish girl, to be wearing a Christian symbol. He had asked her about it once. After that, she always tied a scarf at her neck to cover it.

"One day," the Reverend Mother went on, "a couple from Paris came to visit the convent. They took Marielle away with them." She fingered the ornate cross that hung from her own neck. "It was on one of my days of silent meditation. I didn't have an opportunity to say good-bye to her."

Georges-Henri handed back the photo. "Did you ever see her again?"

She rose from the bench. "No, but she did return once."

"When was that?"

"Two years ago. That's why I had to search in the files just now. I was away, in a field hospital near the German border." She shook her head. "Such difficult work. Such suffering, especially after the invasion. Upon my return after the war ended, I became the new Mère Abesse as the previous one had passed away of old age during my absence."

"Were there any notes left in the file? About when Marielle returned, I mean? How long did she stay? Did she tell anyone about being with child?"

"She apparently stayed in our guest house for a time. In the file, there is a reference to a woman who owns the chocolaterie in the village. That's all. There was no explanation."

"No mention of a baby?"

She shook her head. "I'm afraid *non*."

Their conversation was finished. The Reverend Mother escorted Georges-Henri back to the convent's main entrance.

As she took his hand in hers, he had a thought.

"The woman at the chocolaterie—is she still there?"

"I believe so. She is very old."

He thanked her and turned to go.

"You will find Marielle," she said. "*Le bon Dieu* will guide you."

Georges-Henri walked down the hill from the convent. The bells in the carillon tower behind him chimed noon.

After wandering the narrow streets of the village, he stopped to watch a group of men playing a game of *pétanque* in the park. Life, he thought, goes on. For some. He held out little hope of ever finding Marielle, despite the encouragement he'd received from the Reverend Mother.

A gurgling fountain crowned by a stone artichoke and surrounded by flowers sat in the center of the village square. At one end of the square was the *mairie*, the eighteenth-century town hall, with the French tricolor flying over the front entrance. He paused to consider the flag. Not that many months ago, the building would have been draped in the sinister swastikas of Nazi Germany.

Few people were in the square that time of day. A couple strolling by paused to inspect the display in the hardware store window; two elderly women seemed to be absorbed in a discussion. No one entered the shops, though. All were closed for the mid-day *sieste* and wouldn't reopen until late afternoon. It was the way in Provence.

Realizing he would have to wait for the chocolaterie to open, Georges-Henri sat at a table on the terrace of a small outdoor café across from the fountain. A young couple at the next table whispered to each other. Inside the bar, a group of locals played a game of cards at the back, and an old man sat at the zinc counter drinking a glass of Pernod.

After ordering a *sandwich jambon* and *un demi* of the local rosé, Georges-Henri studied the shops facing the square. There was a hardware store, a *boulangerie-pâtisserie*, and a *boucherie* with a life-sized statue of a butcher in a bloodied apron beside the entrance. The village's only hotel was just off the square.

He sipped his wine and focused his attention on the chocolate shop. It reminded him of the small shops in Paris. The door and windows were framed in green-painted wood, and a green-and-white striped awning hung overhead. In large gold letters, the sign on the storefront read Miniet Chocolatier. Underneath in smaller letters was the year the business was established—1888. Above the shop, white lace curtains billowed out from the open windows of an apartment.

As he watched, an older woman with a colorful kerchief tied at her chin and a small boy in short pants stopped to peer into the chocolaterie's window. After some pointing and discussion, the woman grabbed the boy's hand, opened the door, and entered. Georges-Henri heard the sound of a tiny bell jangling. The shop was open.

When the two exited a few minutes later, the child was licking a lollipop, and the woman, he guessed she was the child's grandmother, carried a small green box tied with a white ribbon. The two continued down the street with the boy skipping happily ahead.

Next, a slim young woman in a yellow dress caught Georges-Henri's attention. In one hand, she carried a string shopping bag bulging with lemons and a baguette. In the other, a bouquet of pink tulips. Glancing briefly over her shoulder, she pulled open the door of the chocolaterie and disappeared inside.

Georges-Henri's heart skipped a beat. Marielle? He couldn't be certain. The woman's hair was longer, but it was the same dark brown. He hadn't been able to get a glimpse of her face. He downed the rest of his wine and paid the waiter. Then he rose from the table and crossed the square.

The window display consisted of the traditional chocolate bunnies, flying bells, and assorted Easter confections. Though he had just eaten his lunch, his mouth watered. He pulled the door open. The bell jangled, and he entered. The aroma of cacao hit him immediately.

An elderly woman with frizzy salt-and-pepper hair was working behind the counter.

"*Bonjour*, Madame," he said, looking around. Where, he wondered, had the young woman with the shopping bag gone?

A world-weary face looked up at him. "*Que voudriez-vous,* Monsieur?"

Georges-Henri studied the display and pointed to a small, dark chocolate disk topped with pieces of candied fruit and nuts. "*Je veux çelui-là, s'il vous plaît,* Madame.*"

"Ah. *Un mendiant. La spécialité de mon fils,*" she declared. Her son's specialty. She picked up a pair of tongs, lifted one of the chocolates, and placed it on a square of parchment paper. "*Voilà.*"

She began to fold the corners toward the center. "No need to wrap it," he said. "How much do I owe you?"

"It's for you to taste, Monsieur. *Un goûter.*"

He thanked her and popped the confection into his mouth.

"You want only one, Monsieur?" She raised her eyebrows and held the tongs in the air. "Perhaps another one or two to take with you for later?"

What could he say? *"Eh bien,"* he hesitated, looking at the variety of choices before deciding. "One each of the dark chocolates," he said finally.

Her black eyes studied him. *"Ah bon!"* She plucked six pieces from the case and carefully placed them in a small green box printed with the name Chocolaterie Miniet. "Are you visiting Les Moulins, Monsieur?" she asked.

Just the opening he was hoping for. *"Eh bien, oui,"* he said. "Actually, I'm looking for a young woman I knew during the war. She may have…" No, that was coming out all wrong. He cleared his throat and began again. "Actually, the Reverend Mother at the convent told me you might have information about someone. Her name is Marielle. Marielle Rosen."

The woman stopped what she was doing. Her eyes grew wide, her deeply-wrinkled face drained of color, and her hands trembled. She finished tying the box with a white ribbon and slid it abruptly across the counter. *"Soixante centimes,* Monsieur," she said.

He put the coins on the plate in front of her, picked up the box, and asked again, "Do you know her? Marielle? She lived in the convent as a little girl and may have returned here to Les Moulins in 1944."

The woman shook her head. Her face had become as white as the ribbon she had used to tie the box. *"Connais pas. Au revoir,* Monsieur." Herding him to the door, she closed it once he was outside, and immediately lowered the shade.

As he stood in the street considering what had just taken place, he saw the sign in the window turn to *FERMÉ.*

Seconds later, women's voices floated down from the open windows of the apartment above the shop. A younger woman's voice asked, "What do you mean? Who was it?"

"He said he was at the convent…" Georges-Henri recognized the second woman's voice as Madame Miniet's. At that point, the older woman appeared in the window, saw him standing there, and slammed the shutters closed. He wasn't able to hear what came next.

Slowly, he walked across the square to the lone hotel where he planned to stay the night while he decided what to do next. One thing was certain. If it was Marielle whose voice he had just heard, he wasn't leaving the village without seeing her.

Halfway across the square, he stopped and turned around. "*Non*," he whispered to himself. Returning to the chocolaterie, he pounded loudly on the door.

Paris
November 1950

Chapter Eleven

At the end of the evening, Georges-Henri accompanied Jacquie and Claudine up the stairs. The rain was still coming down outside, but the apartment was beginning to warm up.

"The heat feels good," Jacquie said. "What did your father do to get it working again?"

Georges-Henri chuckled. "No one knows his secret," he said. "It's a mystery."

"Well, I for one, am grateful."

"Me, too," Claudine said. She paused before opening the door to their room and added, "*Bonne nuit*, Georges-Henri." Then, discreetly leaving the door ajar for Jacquie, she disappeared inside.

"So, Monsieur Delacroix," Jacquie said as she quietly pulled the door closed and turned to face him. "Lunch tomorrow at Brasserie Balzar, as usual?"

He wrapped his arms around her. Their noses were nearly touching. "I can't, unfortunately. I have some business that will take me most of the day."

"*Dommage.*" She faked a pout. "I was going to tell you I have begun dreaming in French."

He brushed her cheek with his lips. "Why don't you tell me about it now."

"Well, I was walking through a museum. And, all of a sudden, I heard a conversation going on. In French, of course. I realized I was inside a painting! You might know the one. Renoir's *Luncheon of the Boating Party*. I saw it in a museum in Washington once. It's so large, it's almost life-size."

He smiled. "And what was the conversation about? Inside the painting, I mean."

"That's the funny part. I was seated next to the girl in the hat, the one with red flowers. She was holding a puppy. I asked her what the puppy's name was. In French, of course."

"And what did she tell you?"

"She didn't. She was staring at this young man standing across from us flirting with a girl seated at the table." She hesitated. "Come to think of it, he looked just like you."

Georges-Henri put his hand behind her neck and pulled her in to him.

"I know it was in French, but I can't quite remember what was said after..." She didn't get to finish the sentence because his lips were on hers.

They heard tittering coming from the top of the landing. Separating quickly, they turned their heads just in time to see Théo and Christine scampering back down the stairs giggling.

"*Merde,*" Georges-Henri said.

Jacquie laughed. "I thought Théo was confined to his room for the rest of the evening."

"Christine must have let him out."

"What was he talking about earlier? A secret the mannequin holds?"

Georges-Henri cast a glance toward the landing. "Just something he made up, I suspect. He has a good imagination."

"But…"

He cut her off abruptly. "I'd better go to my room now. *Bonne nuit.*" He kissed her forehead and turned to walk down the hall.

She stood in the deserted hallway for a few minutes, briefly wondered if the children's sudden appearance had upset him, then, dismissing the thought, opened the door to her room.

Claudine was sitting up in bed reading. "Well, finally. Did you two enjoy the lip sucking?"

"Oh, Claudie…" Jacquie fell onto her bed. "Okay, you know we kissed. So what? He apparently isn't seeing that girl of his anymore."

Claudine nodded. "I think he really likes you, Jacquie. I really do. It's obvious."

Jacquie looked over at her friend. "Hélène apologized to you tonight. That was good."

"Yes, and what's more, she told me she's going to pay for me to travel back to the states to see my family for Christmas."

Jacquie sat up. "Really? That's wonderful!"

"I guess that changes the plans we made over the school break to see the Côte d'Azur."

Jacquie got up and stared at herself in the mirror. "Not really," she said. "I'm still determined to travel. As a matter of fact, a couple of girls

from my art history class asked me recently if I would like to join them."
She swirled sideways to study her figure. "Maybe it's a good thing I'll not
be wearing a bathing costume. I think I've gained a few pounds from all
those croissants."

"You look fine," Claudine said.

Jacquie harrumphed. "My mother, the fat critic, would
judge otherwise."

"Where are your classmates planning to go? Have they already
decided on a destination then?"

Jacquie swung around. "Yes. Germany. To visit a concentration
camp. Dachau."

Claudine glared at her. "Oh, a much-preferred alternative, I'm
sure, to Saint-Tropez," she scoffed. "Why on earth would you consider
going there?"

"Why not? I'm curious about it. It was the first camp. The Nazis
used it in 1933 for political prisoners. Over forty thousand prisoners died
there of malnutrition and typhus. Some were gassed or just plain worked
to death; others were subjected to medical experiments."

"How do you know so much about it?"

"Hélène told me she has a friend who was there and managed to
survive until the end of the war. She said she's going to introduce me to
her." Jacquie returned to her bed and ran her hands over the duvet. "It's so
sad. She slept on the floor when she first came home because she wasn't
used to comfort."

"Sounds terrible to me," Claudine said, shaking her head. "I can't
imagine surviving something like that."

"Nor I," Jacquie said.

Two days later, Jacquie was putting on her makeup when Claudine came flying into the room. "Are you still going to that jazz club in Montmartre? What was its name?"

"The Eléphant Blanc. And yes. Get dressed. You're going, too. Georges-Henri is taking us both, and he's invited a friend."

Claudine's eyebrows shot up. "Male or female?"

"A gentleman, of course," Jacquie clucked as she fastened a pearl choker at her neck. "He also teaches at the Sorbonne."

"O…kay." Claudine peeked into the armoire. "I'm not sure I have anything left to wear. Most everything is already packed for my trip home."

"You must be so excited. In three days, you'll be on the ship."

Claudine pulled out a green plaid skirt and studied it. "It hasn't really sunk in yet. It will, I'm sure, when I'm on the train to Le Havre."

Jacquie got up from the dressing table. "You can't wear that," she said taking the skirt and hanging it back in the armoire. "We've been invited to a fancy house party first, and then we'll go to the jazz club afterwards." She looked into the armoire. "Where is that vintage red dress?"

"Already packed. I got such a deal on it at the flea market I couldn't resist taking it with me to show my friends at home."

"Here." Jacquie pulled out a yellow chiffon and lace evening gown from her side of the wardrobe. "Try this. It should look good with your new bob."

"It's a bit fancy," Claudine said. "You're wearing black satin with straps. Do you have anything…ah…a little less bright?"

"I thought you didn't like to wear black," Jacquie said.

"Okay, I think you're weird because that's all you ever wear when you go out, but you always look so elegant. I admire that."

Jacquie shoved the yellow dress back into the armoire and pulled out a chic black wool sheath with a black satin rose at the high neck. "This better? We'll be the only two girls at the party wearing black."

Claudine took it and smiled. "Perfect."

Everyone at the party was between eighteen and twenty-five. The men wore tuxedos; the women were in evening gowns. They danced to Claude Luter records and drank cheap champagne.

Jacquie watched Claudine as she danced with the young man Georges-Henri had introduced her to. Duff, his name was. An American from Texas. She couldn't imagine a more perfect send-off for Claudine.

Georges-Henri was standing beside her. "You chose Duff well," she said to him. "Claudine seems happy tonight."

He looked sullen. "If you want to dance, go ahead," he said turning to her. "Don't feel as if you have to hang out with me all evening."

She smiled at him. "Oh, but I want to." She put her hand on his shoulder. "You look good in a tux."

He stiffened. "You should be out there on the dance floor, Jacquie, not standing on the sidelines with a…" He didn't finish the sentence.

She frowned. "I'm having a perfectly lovely time, Georges-Henri, aren't you?"

He turned and walked away from her.

She followed him out onto the terrace. "Wait," she said. "Is something the matter?"

He swung around. "I…I…We…" He looked at her. "We'll discuss it tomorrow."

"Aren't you going to the jazz club with us?"

He shook his head. "*Non*. You go on. Duff will escort you both. Have fun." With that he turned and limped down the flagstone path to the street.

She stood watching him. He was brooding about something. Had she made a comment he didn't like? She didn't think so. She wanted to run after him, get to the bottom of it, but she didn't know him well enough. It would just have to wait. She rejoined the party and grabbed the first available partner to dance. Whatever was going on with Georges-Henri, she wasn't going to let him ruin her evening.

The next morning, Jacquie and Hélène saw Claudine off at the train station. She would go by rail to the Port of Le Havre where she would board the SS *De Grasse*, the same ship on which Jacquie had crossed the ocean just six months before. It was a liberty ship that had been refurbished for tourists after the war. The voyage to New York Harbor would take a week.

As they hugged good-bye, Jacquie handed Claudine a hat pin. "Take this. You'll need it," she said.

"What? I don't understand."

"It's for self-defense. In case a man tries to grope you."

Claudine laughed. "You're just joking, of course."

Jacquie shook her head. "I'm dead serious. You're traveling alone. Watch yourself." She hugged her friend. "I'll miss you."

"No, you won't. You'll be too occupied with Georges-Henri to even think of me," Claudine retorted. "See you in a month."

A whistle blew, and the train groaned to life. Claudine embraced Hélène, and, giving them a quick wave, scrambled aboard.

After watching the steam-spewing monster chug slowly out of the station, Hélène took Jacquie's arm and they descended into the nearest Métro. "I've arranged for us to meet Francine at a little *salon de thé* in Passy. It's not far from where she lives."

Francine Fournier was the woman Hélène had told Jacquie about. The survivor of Dachau. "Are you certain she will want to meet me?" Jacquie asked as they negotiated the crowd in the Métro. "I feel like it will make her feel uncomfortable to talk about her experience."

"She knows you are American," Hélène said. "She likes Americans. You will understand why. I'm more worried about tiring her out. She seems so fragile. We'll just have to see how it goes."

"Ah," Hélène said as they emerged from the Métro and approached the tea room a few minutes later. "There she is now."

Francine was about Hélène's age. A tall, thin woman with a mop of black, curly hair, she wore a hat with a dark green band, a matching two-piece suit, and a small pearl choker. She greeted them with a shy, slightly nervous smile.

Hélène embraced her friend and introduced Jacquie.

The Salon de la Tour was an elegant tea room decorated in the Belle Époque style of the nineteenth century. The walls were covered with mirrors framed in gold-leaf that reflected the light of wall sconces, and a huge crystal chandelier hung in the center of the high ceiling. Brown leather chairs invited patrons to sit at white-linen-draped tables.

Jacquie noticed Francine's eyes darting around the room, her forehead lowered. She seemed afraid.

The three women were shown to a table in the corner. Hélène ordered the day's special menu—croque madame sandwiches with choice of tea and a selection of pastries and tea cakes.

"How is your family?" Francine asked Hélène.

Jacquie struggled to follow their conversation. It was obvious they were catching up. She caught a mention of Hélène's children, but they were speaking so fast. Bored, she found herself intrigued by a woman seated alone at a table a few feet away. She wore a huge pink hat with a feather, and she was feeding small bits of a biscuit to a little white poodle at her feet.

Jacquie was imagining what that woman's life was like and what the little dog's name might be, when her ears perked up at the mention of Georges-Henri. Francine seemed to be lamenting about something *malheureux*. Unfortunate? Was that about his leg? No. It was something else. A name Jacquie didn't recognize. Then a place she'd never heard of. Somewhere in Provence. She wished she had been paying better attention. "*Excusez-moi,*" she said. "I don't understand…"

Hélène glanced uncomfortably at Jacquie and leaned over to whisper in Francine's ear. Patting her friend's hand, she said, "We can chat about that later, *ma chère.*"

Jacquie wanted to ask what all that was about Georges-Henri, but before she could say anything, the waiter arrived. Wishing them *bon appétit*, he placed their plates in front of them and a three-tiered tray of assorted *mignardises* in the center of the table.

"I'll warn you both," Hélène said, conveniently changing the subject. "Those pastries are small, but they're absolutely irresistible." She turned to Francine. "I believe I told you our American guest is planning to visit Dachau over her break from studies at the Sorbonne?"

"Yes," Francine replied softly. "You did tell me." She pursed her lips.

"Tell her the story about the Americans...the one you told me," Hélène encouraged.

Francine nodded. "It was late in the war. One morning, at the camp, everything was quiet when I awoke. All night, planes roared overhead, artillery shook our beds, and dust and dirt rained down from the roof. There had been a frightful amount of shouting and gunshots, and I was certain we were all going to be shot." She paused. "We didn't realize until later what happened. We staggered out of the barracks to find everyone gone. The camp was totally empty." She paused. "Have I been speaking too fast for you, Jacquie?"

Jacquie shook her head. "I understand you, Madame," she said. "Go on, please."

Francine nodded. "Someone warned us that soldiers were coming. I remember being so weak I knew I wouldn't be able to run even if I'd wanted to. It was then that tanks entered the camp. I thought that was it. I was done. But they were flying American flags." A tear rolled down her cheek, but she put her hand up and quickly wiped it away. "I liked the Americans. Very much."

"Francine is writing a book about her experience," Hélène said to Jacquie. "Before the war, she wrote a novel while also practicing law." She looked at Francine. "I believe it was a romance, *non?*"

"Did you publish it?" Jacquie asked.

Francine shook her head. "I planned to." She sighed. "But I was arrested, and I don't know what happened to the manuscript." She pulled up her sleeve to expose the number tattooed on her arm. "This is how I was known after that."

Jacquie stared at it.

Francine quickly covered it with her sleeve. "There were fifteen hundred prisoners crammed into barracks built to house a sixth that number," she continued. "Explosions shook the camp every night. I would cover my head. There was no place to go or hide. Sometimes I wished for a bomb to fall on me to end it all." She stopped talking and stared at her food.

Hélène said, "Don't continue if you can't, Francine."

Francine put up her hand. "*Non non.* It's not that. I was just remembering something." She drained her cup of tea.

Jacquie couldn't help thinking about that tattoo. The woman would have to go through the rest of her life with it as a reminder of the horrors she'd experienced.

"It was the smell," Francine said, suddenly breaking the silence. "Prisoners died by the hundreds. The chimneys burned day and night." She looked at Jacquie. "If they tell you when you go there that they didn't run the ovens, do not believe it." She pointed to herself. "I remember the smell."

Jacquie put down her fork and knife. She'd lost her appetite.

The quiet chatter from the other tables rose. The woman with the poodle got up and left. Jacquie was thankful when Francine stopped talking about Dachau. It was a lot to stomach. She almost feared visiting the place. Would it have the same effect on her?

Selecting a small fruit tart with a raspberry on top, Hélène said, "Help yourselves."

Jacquie eyed the miniature pastries. Should she, or shouldn't she? All day, she'd wondered if Georges-Henri had deserted her at the party the night before because she had gained weight. She selected a chocolate square and took a bite. Tomorrow, she made up her mind, she was definitely going on that diet.

"Thank you for listening to my story," Francine said to them as they left the tea room. "The worst for me is that people don't want to believe what I say." She heaved a sigh. "I guess they don't want to hear about what happened."

"Thank you," Jacquie said to her. "I won't forget. And I'm looking forward to…" She stopped. She couldn't say she was looking forward to visiting Dachau. Instead, she said, "…reading your book."

Later that afternoon, when Jacquie returned to the apartment, she found a sealed envelope had been slipped under her door.

She picked it up, kicked off her shoes and tossed her handbag on the chair in the corner. With a sigh she looked over at Claudine's neatly-made bed. Not only would it remain untouched for the next month, but the room wouldn't seem the same without her. She had looked forward to the solitude, not having to answer for her daily schedule, and the reprieve from the constant questions about her relationship with Georges-Henri. Now, Jacquie realized, she would miss Claudine.

She looked at the envelope in her hand. A large 'J' was printed on the front. She slit it open with her thumbnail and plopped down on her bed.

Inside was a one-page letter. To her surprise, it was from Georges-Henri. That was odd. Why was he writing her a letter? They were planning to see each other at dinner.

As soon as she read the first sentence, a lump formed in her throat.

Though I am very fond of you, Jacquie, I fear we are moving too fast. I have decided it best if I go away from Paris for a time. My duties at the university have been suspended until the Spring semester so that I can pursue my research or travel as I deem necessary. I have chosen to do both. Therefore, we won't be seeing each other for a while. This is a good thing, Jacquie. You need to get out and meet other young men more suited to your age and interests. I have been monopolizing your time, and I apologize for that selfishness on my part. I do so enjoy your company.

Please do not feel that this is a rejection. By no means is it that. I truly adore you and will keep you in my thoughts when I am away.

You will likely wonder where I am going. There is only one destination for me. I haven't told you about it, regretfully. I own a simple maison de campagne in the south. In Provence, to be specific. It sits on a lovely sun-drenched hillside with a view of massive lavender fields in the valley below. I plan to read, swim in the nearby lake, drink the local rosé, and outline my course for the spring semester. I'm to teach a comprehensive comparison and critique of the existentialist works of Sartre versus those of Camus.

Jacquie turned the page. More boring details about the course he was going to teach, then something about preparations for Christmas. Her eyes skipped to the bottom of the page.

What I look forward to most every year is seeing ma petite Odile.

Wait. Odile? Who was he talking about?

Southern France
May 1946

Chapter Twelve

Georges-Henri waited in front of the chocolaterie. When no one came to the door, he pounded again.

"*Attendez! Attendez! J'arrive!*" a male voice shouted from within.

The *FERMÉ* sign, indicating the shop was closed, swung from side-to-side, the door opened abruptly, and the bell inside jangled.

A tall man in a chocolate-stained apron stood in the doorway. "It is not necessary to break down the door, Monsieur," he said, studying Georges-Henri as if sizing him up.

Handsome, with black hair, bushy eyebrows and a mustache, the chocolatier appeared to be in his early forties. "We are closed for the afternoon *sieste*," he said. "What do you want?"

Georges-Henri stared at him. Madame Miniet had mentioned the chocolate *mendiants* were her son's specialty. Was this the son? "Monsieur Miniet?" he asked.

"Miniet *fils*. My father died in the Great War."

Georges-Henri held out his hand and introduced himself. "I was here earlier. I spoke with your mother."

Miniet hesitated. "About?"

"I inquired about a young woman named Marielle."

A flicker of dread spread across the man's face. Almost as suddenly as it appeared, it disappeared. "*Entrez*," he said, glancing quickly up and down the street before standing aside to allow Georges-Henri to enter.

"You have a limp," he said as he closed the door. "Were you wounded in the war?"

Georges-Henri nodded. "I was working with the Résistance when I was arrested and sent to a labor camp."

Miniet turned the bolt in the door and offered his hand. "Bernard," he said. "I was also with the Maquis. For the liberation of Corsica."

The two men stared knowingly at each other. There was no need to say more.

Miniet went behind the counter. "I was just about to have a cup of hot chocolate. Would you care to join me?"

Georges-Henri nodded.

Miniet poured two cups and set them on a small round table in the corner. "Have a seat," he said.

Georges-Henri sat down and took a sip of the chocolate. It was smooth and thick. "*Merci*," he said. "*C'est bon.*"

Bernard sat across from him. "*Et alors?*" he said, inviting Georges-Henri to explain himself.

"La Mère Abesse…" Georges-Henri began.

"Mother Marguerite at the convent?" Miniet clarified.

"Oui. I have just been to see her."

Bernard looked confused. "*Mais pourquoi?*"

Georges-Henri took another sip of the hot chocolate. "I was searching for a young woman whom I knew during the war. Marielle Rosen. Mother Marguerite said she remembered her. Marielle lived in the convent when she was very young."

There was no reaction from Bernard.

Georges-Henri went on. "Marielle returned to the convent two years ago, then departed again. The Reverend Mother wasn't there at the time."

Seeming to grow impatient, the man stroked his jaw with the back of his fingers. "I don't understand, Monsieur. What led you to this chocolaterie?"

Georges-Henri remained calm. "There was a brief mention of this shop in the convent archives. Without explanation. I came here hoping to find something." He leaned back in his chair and stared at Miniet. "You see, Monsieur, Marielle was... that is... she and I were..." He stopped abruptly because Miniet's face had paled.

"Her name isn't Rosen anymore," Miniet said.

Georges-Henri felt a frisson of excitement run through him. "Then she's here?" he asked, thinking of the young woman with the net shopping bag he had seen enter the shop earlier. It wasn't surprising that she would have changed her name. "Can I see her?"

Miniet remained silent for a moment. Finally, he said, "Now I realize who you are." He reached over and put his hand on Georges-Henri's shoulder. "She told me about you."

"She did?"

"There is something you should know." Miniet's black eyes bored into Georges-Henri's. "Marielle is my wife."

Georges-Henri fixed his eyes on him. Marielle was married to this man? He swallowed hard, a lump forming in his throat. "And the child? What about the child?"

Miniet pulled his hand away from Georges-Henri's shoulder and stared at him. After what seemed like a long minute, he got up from the table, went behind the counter and called up a stairway at the rear of the shop. "Marielle?"

A sound of shuffling feet. Then a female voice. "Oui?"

"*Descends, chérie*," he said. "*Maman aussi.*"

The old woman Georges-Henri had spoken to earlier descended the stairs. When she saw Georges-Henri, she stopped. "*Mais,* Bernard, *non!*"

"*Viens, Maman. Tout est bien,*" Miniet said in a reassuring tone. Then, to Georges-Henri, he added, "My mother is very afraid since the war."

Georges-Henri rose from his chair. He wasn't looking at Miniet's mother. His eyes were focused on the young woman following her down the stairway.

Marielle.

Chapter Thirteen

Reaching the bottom of the stairs, she followed her husband's eyes. When she saw Georges-Henri, she let out a gasp and clasped her hand over her mouth.

Bernard put his arm around her waist and pulled her close to him. "*C'est lui, chérie?*" he whispered.

She nodded, gently patted his cheek, then pulled away from him and went over to Georges-Henri.

She was prettier than Georges-Henri had remembered. Her cheeks were rosy, and her brown eyes sparkled. "*Comment vas-tu?*" she asked warily.

"*Bien,*" he answered in a low voice.

Bernard came to stand next to her. "My wife believed you were dead, that you had been killed in the war."

Georges-Henri nodded. "I was dead…" he hesitated, "until today." How he wanted to take her in his arms and kiss her. A deep sadness came over him. She belonged to Miniet now.

"How did you find us?" she asked.

"A man came to the château. He said he had been with you the night you escaped from…" he stopped and looked at her husband.

"It's okay. He knows the story," she said, taking Bernard's hand. "My husband knows everything. What was the man's name?"

"Joachim. He told us how the two of you escaped and spent the night in a dark alley."

She nodded. "I remember him. Barely. He survived then?"

"Yes. He managed to get to Argentina." Georges-Henri hesitated. "Until he showed up, that's where I thought you had gone also."

Her eyes narrowed as if recalling something. "What else did he tell you?"

"You apparently mentioned our family château in Manche. It was how he knew to go there when he returned to France this past November." He looked at her. "He also told me about the baby."

Tears flooded her eyes. She let go of Bernard's hand. "I'm sorry," she said, and she ran back up the stairs.

Her mother-in-law scowled at Georges-Henri and followed her.

The two men stood in the center of the shop. "There was a baby, wasn't there?" Georges-Henri asked, uncertain now. He felt awkward. "Joachim may have been mistaken about her being with child. There was no way for me to know whether his story was true."

Bernard put up his hand. He removed his apron and tossed it on the counter. Then, snatching his beret from the wooden coat rack, he went over to the door, unbolted the lock, and opened it. "Let's take a walk," he said.

The chocolatier led the way to the park where, earlier, Georges-Henri had seen the old men playing a game of pétanque. They sat on green-slatted chairs under a canopy of plane trees.

"Marielle came into the chocolaterie looking for work one day in 1944," Bernard began. "I believe my mother said it was in early summer. I was still at the front. *Maman* was overwhelmed and in need of help, so she agreed to let Marielle stay in the apartment above in return for her assistance in the shop.

"Marielle was a hard worker. Despite her condition. She told my mother that her husband had been killed in the war and that she needed to support herself and her unborn baby." He removed his beret and leaned forward with his elbows on his knees. "It happened before I returned. One day at the beginning of September, Marielle found a pistol." He lowered his head and fumbled with the beret in his hands. "I don't know how she came across it. My mother had hidden it away…" he hesitated, "to protect herself in case the war came to Les Moulins."

Georges-Henri felt his muscles tense. "What happened?"

Bernard sighed. "Marielle left a letter thanking my mother for taking her in. Sadly, she wrote, she had reached the point where she could not continue to live." He paused. "Whether from guilt over what had happened to her parents, or hopelessness over her situation, she never said, but she…" He stopped talking. A pained look swept over his face.

Georges-Henri held his breath.

Bernard finished the sentence. "Shot herself." He pointed to his chest. "Here. But the bullet missed her heart." He blessed himself. "*Dieu merci*. She was a poor shot."

Anger rose in Georges-Henri. Such a selfish act, when she was with child, too. How could she even think of doing such a thing? "And the baby?" he asked, trying to calm himself. "What about the baby?"

"They both survived, but the birth was difficult. The nearest doctor was in a village several kilometers away. Marielle nearly bled to death before he arrived."

Georges-Henri's heart pounded. "A girl or a boy?"

"*Une petite fille.*" Bernard smiled. "Odile."

"Odile," Georges-Henri whispered, tears flooding his eyes.

Bernard went on. "A sweet baby, *mais*..." He stared at the sunlight filtering through the laced fingers of the trees above.

"But what?" Georges-Henri asked.

Bernard shook his head. "Early birth. A lack of oxygen. We'll never know for certain. The trauma of it all unfortunately left her without the ability to see."

Georges-Henri let out a sob. "No. Blind?"

Bernard rubbed his chin. "*Eh bien*, we can't be certain. The doctor says it could be temporary." He sighed. "We won't know until she is a little older. I returned to the village just days after the birth. Marielle was still very weak. I took charge of the chocolaterie. My mother cared for the baby. Marielle gradually regained her health, Odile thrived, the war finally ended, and we realized we were a family."

"Marielle looks well," Georges-Henri said, wiping tears from his cheek. "I am in your debt. You and your mother."

Bernard nodded.

They sat together in silence.

"I would like to see the child," Georges-Henri said finally.

Bernard bit his lip and finally agreed. "As you should. Are you planning to stay the night?"

"Yes. In the hotel off the square."

"*Bon.*" Bernard replaced his beret and rose from his chair. "I need to return to the shop. Come for dinner after we close for the evening. Meet Odile." He hesitated. "She has your eyes." Then he turned and walked away.

Chapter Fourteen

The hotel room was sparse, but clean. It smelled of lavender, and there was a view of the town square. Georges-Henri opened the French doors, moved the desk chair onto the small balcony, and sat down to breathe in the fresh air.

He checked his watch. From his perch, he could see that the chocolaterie had reopened. He had three hours, maybe four, to mentally prepare himself for meeting his daughter. She would be a little over a year-and-a-half old by now. Blind since birth.

And Marielle married to someone else. They were lost to him forever. At the thought, a wall of anguish burst over him, and tears ran down his cheeks. He covered his eyes with his hands and gave into the overwhelming sadness, great sobs shaking his whole frame.

After a while, his tears dried. His head throbbing, he stood and went inside to lay on the bed. His leg was sore and stiff from all the walking he'd done, and he was exhausted. Almost immediately he fell asleep.

Church bells woke him sometime later. He sat up in a panic. What time was it? A slight breeze entered through the open windows, and the late afternoon sunshine cast a golden light into the room.

He rose from the bed and went out to stand on the balcony. The chocolaterie's door was open and Bernard stood outside passing out chocolates to a crowd of villagers in the street. Next to the fountain, a small outdoor market had been set up, and the town band was warming up. Tricolor buntings decorated the stage.

A celebration of some sort. Georges-Henri tried to think. What was the date? May the seventh. Of course. How could he ever forget? The victory over the Boches, La Libération, had happened just one year ago. Tomorrow would be the anniversary.

He went over to the wash basin and looked at himself in the mirror. His eyes were sunken and he needed a shave. He opened his valise and pulled out his shave kit and a clean shirt.

Underneath his shave kit was the small pouch containing several gold coins his father had given him before he left the château.

"To pay for your trip," Papa had said as he took them one at a time from the leg of his desk where they'd remained hidden for the duration of the war. "The Boches didn't find these for a reason," he'd said. "I insist."

Georges-Henri had protested that he wouldn't need all of them, but his father had pressed the pouch into his hand. "You never know, mon fils."

Georges-Henri pulled out one of the coins and held it in the palm of his hand. He had more than enough to pay for his expenses and the return to Paris. He tossed the gold piece into the air and caught it again. That was it. He knew what he was going to do. Placing the coin carefully on the bed next to his clean shirt, he began to lather his face.

In the square below, the band was playing "*la Marseillaise*" and a crowd of villagers sang the words at the top of their lungs. Georges-Henri paused to sing along. His headache was gone.

On his way across the square to the chocolaterie, Georges-Henri stopped briefly at one of the market stalls where the vendor was selling small bouquets of lavender. He decided he would purchase one and present it to Bernard's mother. Maybe the old woman would forgive him for showing up.

"How much do you want for a bunch?" he asked.

"Ça dépend," the woman said. "Do you want to purchase a vase for it too, Monsieur?" She smiled a toothless smile. "I make them myself. Four francs total."

Georges-Henri nodded. He took out his wallet and handed over a five-franc bill. Hardly worth a *sou* since the war. "I'll give you this if you put it in that." He pointed to a ceramic vase that looked like a giant colorful insect with transparent wings.

"*La cigalle*. Excellent choice," the woman said as she accepted the money and shoved it into her apron pocket. Once she had placed the lavender in the vase, she held it up for him to see. "You hang this on the wall," she said. "*Comme* ça. Here in Provence, it is a gesture to make visitors feel welcome."

Georges-Henri took the vase from her. "*Merci beaucoup*." Patting the gold coin in his pocket to make sure it was still there, he bid the vendor au revoir and continued across the square.

Bernard was just turning the sign in the window to *FERMÉ*. Seeing Georges-Henri coming, he held the door to the chocolaterie open and waited for him.

"*Bonsoir*," Georges-Henri said.

Bernard shook his hand. "It is a happy day, *n'est-ce pas? Le jour de la victoire.*"

"Indeed," Georges-Henri said as he entered the shop. "Indeed."

Bernard closed the door and bolted it. Then he went to the window in front of the display of chocolates and pulled the curtains shut. The shop grew dark. Unbuttoning his chef's jacket, he slipped it off and hung it on a hook behind the counter along with his apron. His sweat-stained, sleeveless undershirt showed he had spent a long day working in the kitchen.

A mouth-watering scent of chicken roasting wafted from the apartment above. "We'll eat out in the garden," Bernard said, picking up a tray of pastries.

Georges-Henri followed him to the rear of the shop and out the back door where a long wooden table had been set with a brightly-colored cloth. A bouquet of flowers was in the center; four stemmed glasses, a bottle of rosé, and a plate of olives sat next to it.

Georges-Henri held up the bouquet he'd purchased in the square. "I thought perhaps your mother would like this," he said.

Bernard smiled. A peace offering. "*Pour faire la paix, hein?*" he said with a chuckle. "My mother will be pleased."

A child's cry came from the apartment above. Georges-Henri looked up at the open windows. Was that Odile?

"Bernard?" Marielle's voice came from the open door to the back stairway leading down to the garden.

Bernard set his tray of pastries on the table and looked up. "That's my signal to change this filthy undershirt that I've been in all day and keep the baby entertained until dinner." He smiled at Georges-Henri. "Have a look around the garden, *mon ami*. I'll bring her down." He winked. "We'll share an *apéro* and some olives and entertain her together." He turned and ran quickly up the stairs, taking two steps at a time.

Georges-Henri laid the lavender-filled vase on the table, plucked an olive from the dish, and popped it in his mouth.

The garden was surrounded by an ivy-covered wall and anchored by a lemon tree in one corner and a wood-framed chicken coop—*un poulailler*—in the other. A potager took up most of the area near the back. Georges-Henri could see rows of herbs, plus asparagus, leafy greens, cabbage, potatoes, and onions. A raised planter of strawberries was just beginning to spill ripening fruit over the side.

In the square, the band was playing a folk tune. He turned around at the sound of someone singing close by. Bernard was descending the stairs, half dancing, mostly bouncing to the music. His arms cuddled a curly-haired, giggling child who clung to his neck and kicked her legs. Odile.

Georges-Henri caught his breath.

When Bernard reached the bottom of the stairs, he said, "She likes music." He brought Odile closer. She wore a white cotton dress, her cheeks were pink, and her light brown hair glistened in the early evening sunlight.

Georges-Henri thought she was the prettiest child he'd ever seen.

"*Eh bien*," Bernard urged. "Say something to her."

What was it his sister Hélène always said to her children? Georges-Henri swallowed hard. "*Coucou.*"

Odile wriggled in Bernard's arms, then turned her entire body in Georges-Henri's direction.

He hooked her fingers with his index finger and said, "*Bonjour, ma petite.*"

Her eyes blinked, fear spread across her face, and she yanked her hand away as if she'd been burned. The next thing Georges-Henri knew she was shrieking at the top of her lungs, giant tears rolling down her chubby cheeks.

Bernard began to sing again, softly, next to her ear. *"Au clair de la lune, mon ami pierrot..."* The child snuggled into his neck and calmed.

"She has a loud cry," Georges-Henri said. At the sound of his voice, Odile raised her head and started bawling all over again. He felt his face redden. What to do? He pulled the gold coin from his pocket and held it in front of her nose. It glinted in the sunlight.

Bernard glared at him. "What are you doing? Don't you realize she..."

In his enthusiasm, Georges-Henri had forgotten the child couldn't possibly see it. *"Excusez-moi. J'ai..."* he stammered. But before he could pull the coin away, a small fist reached out and swatted it from his fingers. It fell to the ground.

Bernard's eyes grew wide. *"C'est vraiment étonnant!"* he said. "She's never done that before."

The two men stared into the little girl's eyes. There was a grayness in the pupil of her right eye, but the left eye was clear.

Georges-Henri bent and picked up the coin. He looked at Bernard who nodded encouragement, then held it close to Odile's face like he'd done before.

This time, she giggled and grabbed at it, but Georges-Henri quickly pulled it back. Odile's mouth formed a pout, her face screwed up, and she looked about to scream again.

Georges-Henri moved it to the side, closer to her left eye. She smiled and cooed.

Bernard pulled her hand away to stop her from trying to grab it. "Marielle!" he hollered. *"Viens tout de suite, chérie!"*

Marielle appeared at the top of the stairs. "What is it, Bernard?"

"Georges-Henri has discovered something wonderful. You have to see it."

Marielle came clacking down the stairs in her high-heeled shoes. When she reached the bottom, she didn't look at Georges-Henri. *"Bonsoir,"* she said softly.

Hearing the sound of her mother's voice, Odile opened her arms, kicked her legs, and reached out for her.

Marielle took her from Bernard and bounced her up and down.

Georges-Henri's heart melted as he watched them.

Marielle turned to Bernard. "What wonderful thing have you discovered, *chéri?*"

"Pas moi," Bernard said. "Show her." He nodded to Georges-Henri.

Georges-Henri's hand trembled as he held the coin up. "Odile," he said gently.

Hearing her name, the child turned her head slightly in his direction. He flashed the coin, hoping the sunlight would help her see it. Her little fist shot out and swiped the air, but she missed the coin completely.

"You see that?" Bernard said. "She has some sight. She's trying to seize it."

Georges-Henri held the coin closer to the left side of Odile's face. Same as before, she giggled and grabbed at it.

"It's her left eye," he said. "She can see with it."

Marielle's mouth opened. *"Mon Dieu*, Bernard!" She gasped and looked at her husband.

Bernard searched the garden for something to show to Odile. He picked up a sprig of mint and held it out to the child.

Odile didn't react. Instead, she turned her head at the sound of a hen cackling in the coop in the corner and let out a giggle.

They experimented with the flowers in the garden, and the fruit from the lemon tree, but the only thing that drew Odile's attention was the shiny gold coin Georges-Henri had brought.

"It's hers to keep," Georges-Henri said.

"*Non non.* It's too much. We can't accept," Bernard said shaking his head.

"I insist," George-Henri said.

Bernard's mother came to the top of the stairs. When she saw Georges-Henri, she put up her chin and turned to walk back inside.

Bernard gave Georges-Henri a sympathetic look. "*Maman,*" he said, "will take some time to win. Perhaps if she sees what you have brought for her…"

"What did he bring?" Marielle asked.

Georges-Henri pointed to the peace offering.

"It will take more than that to convince my mother-in-law," she harrumphed.

Odile yawned—a wide baby's yawn. She put her thumb in her mouth, and her head drooped forward.

"It's her bedtime," Marielle said. She looked at Georges-Henri. "Do you want to hold her?"

Georges-Henri's shoulder muscles tightened. "I would like that, but do you think she will come to me?"

Marielle whispered, "She's almost asleep. Sit down and hold out your arms."

He felt awkward. He'd only held his sister's babies once or twice. This was different. Odile was his child. He pulled a chair out from the table, sat down, and extended his arms in front of him.

Marielle leaned over. She was so close to him he caught a whiff of her perfume. The small gold cross she'd been given for her fifth birthday at the convent gleamed at the base of her throat. Ever so gently, she laid Odile in his lap. Then she backed away quietly, slid her arm through Bernard's and laid her cheek against his shoulder.

The sun was low in the evening sky, a soft breeze rustled the leaves of the trees, the band in the square played a jazzy version of Piaf's "La vie en rose," and Odile slept soundly in Georges-Henri's arms. He studied her curly hair and long eyelashes, smelled her sweet baby breath, and felt her warmth. He was in love.

Chapter Fifteen

After she'd lifted Odile from Georges-Henri's arms and taken the child upstairs to bed, Marielle descended the stairs and sat at the table next to Bernard.

They feasted on Madame Miniet's roast chicken with vegetables from the garden and finished with Bernard's chocolate pastries. Bernard poured generous glasses of rosé and toasted Georges-Henri who said he was genuinely happy to celebrate the Liberation with them.

Georges-Henri attempted more than once to catch Marielle's eye, but she ignored him. Curious about the chocolaterie, he asked if it had always been in the Miniet family. Madame Miniet's eyes brightened at the question, and she spent several minutes telling the story of how her late husband's father, Jacques, had founded the business in 1888 and she and Jacques junior had run it together for many years. Bernard piped in occasionally with tidbits about his growing up around so much chocolate.

The band in the square played louder as the evening went on, and conversation became increasingly difficult. Through it all, Georges-Henri was aware of Marielle sitting quietly. If she was listening to her mother-in-law and husband, he couldn't tell. He understood one thing--she was definitely ignoring him. Their eyes never met. It was as though he didn't even exist.

A day went by. Georges-Henri stayed in Les Moulins, hoping to have an opportunity to talk to Marielle and see Odile again.

Marielle remained out of sight.

On the second morning, Georges-Henri was seated at the café having a café crème and a croissant when he saw Bernard coming across the square toward him. When he reached the table where Georges-Henri was seated, he pulled out a chair and sat down. "Nice morning, eh?" he said. "I think I'll join you. He summoned the waiter and ordered a café crème. "The chocolaterie is closed for the day."

"No more chocolates left to sell?" Georges-Henri asked.

Bernard smiled. "We did well." He wiggled his fingers. "We had a steady stream of little visitors. Fingerprints and smears of chocolate all over the glass. It was to be expected." He chuckled. "My mother is cleaning the display cases."

The waiter brought Bernard's café crème. He plopped in a sugar cube and stirred. "I'm going to spend the day in the garden." He looked over at Georges-Henri and took a sip. "I'd welcome some company, if you would care to join me."

"I would like that," Georges-Henri said. Maybe he'd get an opportunity to see Odile and Marielle again.

Bernard took a sip of his café. "Are you enjoying yourself here in Les Moulins?"

Georges-Henri nodded. "It's so peaceful. I didn't realize there was anywhere in France that life had remained normal during the war."

Bernard tilted his head from side to side. "More or less normal. We had to make sacrifices like everyone else—food was scarce, supplies were difficult to get, especially the cocoa. Sugar was rationed. After I became involved with the Maquis, my mother had to improvise as best she could. She experimented making candies with fruits and nuts from the trees. There were days when the display cases were nearly empty." He took off his beret and scratched his head. "But she managed. It was important to her to keep up the spirits of the villagers, you know."

"She seems like a strong woman."

"She is."

Georges-Henri finished his croissant. "It was good to meet Odile," he said. "I'd like to see her again."

Bernard looked at him. "Marielle mentioned she needed to go to the hairdresser this afternoon. Perhaps she could leave Odile with us. We could take her to the park in her buggy. She likes to go for rides."

Georges-Henri smiled. "I would like that very much."

Georges-Henri was in the garden helping Bernard pick vegetables when Marielle came down the back stairs with Odile in her arms.

Georges-Henri took a deep breath. "*Bonjour*, Marielle," he said. She looked down, mumbled something to Odile, and handed the baby over to Bernard.

Odile immediately threw her arms around Bernard's neck and nestled into his shoulder.

"Are you taking her to the park, *chéri?*" Marielle asked Bernard.

"Oui," he said. "I've invited Georges-Henri to go with us."

Marielle patted Bernard's cheek. "Would you mind, *mon cher?*" she whispered. "I'd like to speak with Georges-Henri first. He can join you after...if he wishes." She'd acted as if Georges-Henri weren't in the garden with them.

Bernard kissed Marielle on the forehead. *"Pas du tout, chérie."* He lifted Odile in his arms and swung her over his head. She giggled. "Let's go play in the park, *ma petite chou,*" he said. She kicked her legs in the air.

Placing Odile in the buggy that was sitting by the back gate, he nodded to Georges-Henri. "We'll be on the bench near the pétanque players. *À tout à l'heure.*"

Marielle waited for them to leave. Then she turned to Georges-Henri and put her arms on her hips. "Why did you come here after all this time, Georges-Henri?"

Georges-Henri was taken aback. "Why do you think? To find you." He held out his hands, palms up. "It wasn't easy. I had no idea where you'd gone. I thought you and your parents..." He stopped, seeing the look of horror that crossed her face.

"My parents are dead," she said. "Doctor Yves shot them."

"I learned that from Joachim," he said. "I'm so sorry, Marielle. We, my father and sister and I, we had no idea what he was doing. If we had only known..."

Tears flooded her eyes. "What would you have done, Georges-Henri? Reported him to the police?" Her voice was shrill. "The police were in on it; I thought you all were. I couldn't trust anyone. I knew you didn't know I was with child, and I was afraid your father would come after me if he found out. So I ran...to the only place I could think of."

"To here...to the convent."

She nodded.

"Where I wouldn't know to look for you."

She looked at him. "How did you know to come here anyway?"

He shrugged. "You mentioned being adopted from a convent once. You have a slight Provençale accent. I put the pieces together finally. It was only when I talked to the Reverend Mother here that it was confirmed." He wiped his forehead. The sun was beating down, the air was hot, and the cicadas seemed extra noisy. Or was it his head that was buzzing?

Marielle turned around and pointed to the table under the canopy where they'd eaten dinner on the eve of Liberation Day. "It's a warm day, Georges-Henri," she said, "have a seat. I'll get us something cool to drink."

Georges-Henri went over to sit down. Sweating profusely, he took off his jacket and arranged it on the back of the chair next to him.

Marielle returned with two glasses and a pitcher of lemonade. She poured one for each of them and sat down across from him.

She was wearing a pale-yellow sundress; her hair was frizzy from the heat and humidity. He'd dreamed of the day when he'd be alone with her again. If only...if only it hadn't turned out like this. He took a sip of lemonade and said, *"Merci. C'est bon."*

Neither of them spoke for several minutes. Finally, Georges-Henri said, "Do you want me to leave?"

She nodded. "I'm happy here, Georges-Henri. I thought I'd lost everything. Bernard saved me. He loves Odile like his own. I don't want her to ever know he's not her papa. Do you understand?"

"I thought...I thought I could be part of her life somehow."

"I can't stop you from coming to visit on occasion, but you must abide by my request." Her eyes narrowed. "You are not, nor will you ever be, her papa."

"And if I do visit?"

"She will know you as *Tonton*." Uncle. "If you can't agree to that, then you will not be welcome in our home." Her brown eyes drilled into his.

Georges-Henri lowered his head. "I was hoping…"

Marielle rose. "The day she was born…" she quivered and let out a deep breath… "I wished I had died along with Maman and Papa. I didn't want to live anymore. If it hadn't been for my mother-in-law, Odile and I would both be dead. And you…" she put up her fist, "You were dead to me already."

"I…," he mumbled, "I thought we…"

"Please leave Les Moulins as soon as possible. There's a train to Paris departing in the morning. If you want to meet Bernard in the park, do so. Play with Odile." She wagged her finger at him. "Remember you are her uncle." With that she turned around and ran up the stairs to the apartment.

Overcome with emotion, Georges-Henri slumped in his chair and buried his face in his hands.

Chapter Sixteen

Georges-Henri wiped his eyes and sat up. Should he go to the park to meet Bernard? Or should he just leave Les Moulins? He shook his head. No. He had to see his petite Odile one last time before he left.

He rose from the table, passed through the rear garden gate, and followed a circuitous route through the narrow cobblestone streets of the village to the park.

A group of elderly pétanque players stood in an open area contemplating the placement of their *boules*. Across from them, Bernard sat on a bench watching. Beneath him on the ground, Odile was swinging her arms playing wildly in the sand.

A lump growing in his throat, Georges-Henri approached them.

"*Ah, te voilà!*" Bernard said, patting the bench beside him. "*Assieds-toi!*"

Georges-Henri took a seat. He looked down at Odile. "She's having fun," he said.

"She adores the sand," Bernard said. "I'm thinking of bringing some of it back to the garden and making a sandbox for her to play in."

Georges-Henri looked at him. "You love her, don't you?"

Bernard nodded. "I'm fortunate to have her and Marielle in my life," he said. "I never thought I'd have a family."

"Why is that?"

"I was wounded. Sniper fire in Corsica." He pointed to his groin and winked. "Not good for making babies anymore."

"Oh." Georges-Henri grabbed a handful of sand and sifted it through his fingers. "I wanted you to know I'm leaving on the morning train."

Bernard looked at him. "I had hoped you might stay the summer."

"I would have liked to, but I have to get back to my studies. I have a year to finish, then I hope to be a teaching assistant."

"Where?"

"The Sorbonne. I know a prof there who's going to help me get a position."

"Well, that's great." Bernard thought for a moment, then he picked up Odile and placed her on Georges-Henri's lap.

Georges-Henri nestled his cheek against hers. She didn't resist him. Instead, she wrapped her arms around his neck. "So, you know your uncle now?" he said, snuggling into her embrace.

Bernard's eyes widened. "Uncle?"

Georges-Henri winked at him. "She should call me *Tonton*, don't you think, Papa?"

Bernard swiped the corner of his eye and looked down. "So that's what Marielle wanted to talk to you about?"

Georges-Henri hugged Odile. "I want to come back to see her again. Maybe next year after I've finished my studies. I could spend the summer here." Perhaps, he thought, Marielle will have changed her mind about him by then.

"In that case, I have an idea," Bernard said. "There's a cottage up for auction not far from the village. It's badly in need of repair, but, if you were to buy it, I could help you fix it up in my spare time. I like to do woodwork."

"Interesting idea. If I stayed here an entire summer, I would need a place other than the hotel," Georges-Henri said.

"Want to see it?"

"Now?"

"*Pourquoi pas?*" Bernard rose. "I'll show it to you. If you like it, you can put in a bid. I don't think anyone else is interested. It's been available for some time."

Odile had fallen asleep against Georges-Henri's shoulder. Bernard took her from him and carefully placed her in her buggy. "It will be a nice walk. She'll get a good nap."

They took off through the streets until they came to a dirt road. "It's just ahead," Bernard said, carefully maneuvering the buggy so it wouldn't hit any bumps and awaken Odile.

The driveway led up the hillside to a patch of land next to a small lake. A small, vine-covered pink stucco cottage with Mediterranean-blue shutters sat under a stand of shade trees overlooking the valley below. The grass around the house was overgrown, and the place looked run down. Stone steps led to a front porch covered with blooming purple wisteria.

Georges-Henri stared at it. "This place is up for auction?"

Bernard nodded. "It's a small property, as you can see. The widow who lived here, Madame Bouchez, died last year. Her husband was killed in the Great War. They had no children, and no one has come forward to claim it, so the bank put it up for bid."

Georges-Henri walked up the front steps and peeked through a window. The interior was in need of repairs as Bernard had said, but it had a high wood-beamed ceiling and red tile floors. He could see a large stone fireplace in the front room, and what must be the kitchen in back. It looked inviting.

He went around to the back of the house where there were three sets of French doors and a wide veranda with a view of the lake. He sat down on a rickety old wicker rocking chair and watched a mother duck gliding over the water; her brood of ducklings paddled along behind her making ripples in the water. The sound of birds chirping in the linden trees above mixed with the ululation of early summer cicadas in the late afternoon heat. There wasn't a cloud in the sky. He imagined the bliss of walking out of his bedroom and sitting here on a summer evening.

Why not do this? Georges-Henri thought. He could spend his summers and breaks here. Bernard had said he would help with the renovation. He had enough gold coins with him to put in a bid.

He got up and walked around to where Bernard was waiting for him. "It's perfect," he said. "Where do I go to start the process?"

"The bank will be open until seven. We'll stop by on our way back to the village square."

"Is your offer to help with renovation still good?"

Bernard smiled. "Of course."

Georges-Henri shook his hand. "You are a fine man, Bernard Miniet."

The bank was located on a side street just off the main square. Bernard stopped in front of the entrance.

"I need to get back to the chocolaterie," he said. *"Bonne chance."*

Georges-Henri bid him au revoir and gave the sleeping Odile a gentle pat on the cheek. Then he entered the bank. There were no patrons. A teller looked up from behind the counter. *"Je peux vous aider,* Monsieur?"

Georges-Henri asked to speak to the banker in charge.

The man nodded. Just behind the counter was a glass door with the name Taschereau in bold lettering. The teller knocked lightly on the door and opened it. "Monsieur?" he said, *"Quelqu'un vous voir."* Someone here to see you.

Monsieur Taschereau rose from his desk. He was dressed in a dark suit, white shirt, and narrow black tie. A short, thin man, he wore a monocle which he held in place between his cheek bone and his right eyebrow. It made him look like he was permanently asking a question. "Oui, Monsieur?" he said, holding out his hand.

Georges-Henri introduced himself. "I wish to put in a bid for the cottage just outside town that is up for auction," he said, pulling out the bag of gold coins from inside his jacket pocket.

"In that case," Monsieur Taschereau said with a smile. "Please step into my office and have a seat."

Georges-Henri counted out all but three of the gold coins he had with him, and laid them on the man's desk.

"That should be more than enough," Monsieur Taschereau said. "I don't have another bid, so the place can be yours as soon as all the paper work is completed and signed."

"I'd like to do that today, if possible," Georges-Henri said. "I'm leaving Les Moulins on the morning train."

Monsieur Taschereau tented his fingers. "These things take time to prepare, Monsieur." He hesitated. "But this is a small village. We can agree to shake hands on it for now. I can forward the papers to you later. Does that suit you?"

"Yes indeed," Georges-Henri said. "In that case, Bernard Miniet will be my representative here in Les Moulins, if anything comes up. I assume you know him?"

The banker sat back and nodded approval. "A fine choice."

"I will be in Paris," Georges-Henri said. He took a piece of paper and wrote down his sister Hélène's address. "It's on avenue Mozart in the sixteenth. You can send the paperwork to me there."

They shook hands and that was that. They had a deal. Georges-Henri had purchased his *maison de campagne* in Provence.

Back at the hotel, he put one of the remaining gold coins in an envelope, addressed it to Bernard Miniet at the chocolaterie, and included a note telling him what had taken place at the bank. Seeing the banker's monocle had given him an idea, too. *The coin is for Odile,* he wrote. *Perhaps you can get her fitted with glasses by a specialist? I think she would like to be able to see your face.* And mine, too, he thought. He ended by saying he hoped Bernard would write to him and thanked him for all he had done.

The next morning, he left the envelope in the mail slot of the chocolaterie and boarded the train to Paris.

Paris
November 1950

Chapter Seventeen

Jacquie reread Georges-Henri's letter. He'd written no more about Odile. Who was she? There had to be a simple explanation. Maybe she was a child he'd gotten to know in the village. It would be just like him to befriend the locals. She rose from her desk chair, pulled on a sweater, and descended the stairs to the dining room. She would ask Hélène later.

There were only two places set at the table. Jacquie had expected at least Paul to join them for dinner, and perhaps Théo, Christine, and Charlotte, too. "Where is everyone?" she asked.

"My father has taken the children to a Christmas pageant as a special treat," Hélène said. "We are dining alone." She sat down at the table. "It will give us a chance to discuss some concerns I have..." she hesitated, "about recent events."

Jacquie took her usual seat at Hélène's right and wondered what Hélène was talking about. Had Théo tattled to his mother about what he'd seen the other night in the hallway? A simple kiss good-night. Nothing more. She could explain.

Hélène passed her a plate. "I thought we'd eat light since we didn't hold back on the pastries this afternoon at the tea room."

Jacquie forced a smile. An omelet with mushrooms. She hated mushrooms. "I'm really not that hungry," she said as she set the plate in front of her. "The pastries were good. Francine seemed to like them, too."

"If I were in her place," Hélène said, "I'd eat all I want from now on. She didn't say it today, but she weighed less than twenty kilos when she was liberated from Dachau." She took a sip of water from the goblet in front of her and picked up her knife and fork. "You and my brother seem to be getting on quite well," she said, changing the subject.

Jacquie detected a hint of something—was it sarcasm in her voice? "Georges-Henri has been very kind to escort me to plays and take me riding in the Bois de Boulogne."

"Has he told you about himself?"

Jacquie smiled. "Mostly he talks about existentialism. He's very enthusiastic about the subject he teaches. He gave me a book to read," she sighed, "but I find it difficult to understand."

"*En effet*," Hélène muttered. Indeed.

Jacquie picked up her knife and fork, pushed the mushrooms aside and cut off a piece of her omelet.

"I've been most pleased to have you as a guest in my house these past few months, Jacquie."

"And I have very much enjoyed being here," Jacquie added.

"Nevertheless," Hélène continued, "I'm sure you realize there are certain...expectations to be met."

Jacquie swallowed the bite of omelet. What was the woman getting at?

"As the mother of small children, I am concerned about them observing recent...how shall I say..., unfortunate demonstrations of adult behavior..." Hélène paused, her knife and fork in mid-air. "Let me put it this way, Jacquie, I've informed Georges-Henri that he can't stay here when he returns for the spring session."

Jacquie almost choked on her food. What had Georges-Henri done to deserve that?

"My father is in complete agreement with me," Hélène went on. "This infatuation with you, or whatever it is, will not be played out in this apartment. I have a responsibility to your parents."

Jacquie gasped. So that was it. Théo had tattled after all. The little brat. "I assure you, Madame, Georges-Henri and I have done nothing wrong."

Hélène's amber brown eyes bored into hers. After an awkward pause, she said firmly, "And that's the way we shall keep it."

"*Bien sûr*," Jacquie said with a slight bow of the head. She stared at the unfinished omelet on her plate and pushed it away, her appetite gone. Hélène had not used that tone of voice with her before.

Hélène put down her knife and fork, picked up both their plates, and rose from the table. "Let's move to the salon. I'll make us some coffee."

The salon was warm; a log crackled in the fireplace. Jacquie peered through the windows of the French doors into the garden. It had begun to snow.

Hélène came into the room carrying a tray with two demitasse cups and a small silver bowl filled with raw sugar cubes. She placed it on the coffee table in front of the sofa then sat down and patted the cushion next to her.

Still brooding over what Hélène had said, Jacquie sat in silence. This wasn't how this year was supposed to be going. She'd disappointed Hélène and gotten Georges-Henri kicked out of his own sister's apartment. What should she do?

Hélène poured coffee into one of the cups, placed it on a saucer with a small silver spoon, and handed it over. "There's something magical about Paris when it snows, don't you think? The children will be thrilled. If it doesn't melt, I shall take them to the Champs de Mars tomorrow morning to make a snowman."

Jacquie placed a lump of sugar in her demitasse and stirred. A pang of homesickness hit her. For the first time ever, she was going to miss the big Thanksgiving celebration with her family, the rowdy snowball fights afterwards with her cousins. They always ended up making angels in the snow.

"When will you leave for Munich?" Hélène asked, interrupting her thoughts.

"What? Oh…" Jacquie shook her head. "Sorry…" She took a sip of coffee. "My friends and I haven't decided exactly. Sometime during first week of December, I expect."

"How long will you be there?"

Jacquie shrugged. "It depends. A week perhaps."

"Have you made plans for *Noël?*"

Jacquie hadn't considered that the yearlong stay with Hélène and her family might mean not being included in holiday celebrations. "I…I don't know. With Claudine away…" Another pang of lonesomeness hit her. She missed Claudine already.

"You are welcome to accompany us to the château," Hélène said after a few minutes. "It will be just my father and me with the children." She took a sip of her coffee and added, "I expect Georges-Henri will remain in Les Moulins, as he always does."

Les Moulins. Jacquie stored that away. Perhaps she would send him a postcard from Munich, express regret for what had happened. "I would love to see the château," she said, trying to sound enthusiastic. "It must be magnificent."

"It is, now that the renovations are mostly done."

Jacquie cleared her throat. "Can I ask you a question, Hélène?"

"Of course."

"It's…it's about someone named Odile."

Hélène placed her demitasse and saucer on the coffee table. "*Ça alors,*" she exclaimed. "Really. How do you know about her?"

"Who is she?"

Hélène sighed. "Odile is Georges-Henri's daughter."

Jacquie felt as if she'd been punched in the stomach. "His daughter?"

Hélène rose, went over to a writing desk in the corner, and opened a drawer. Finding what she was after, she returned to the sofa. "Odile was not yet two years old when that photo was taken," she said, handing Jacquie a small black-and-white photograph.

Jacquie took it from her and studied it. A curly-headed child sat on the lap of a strikingly pretty young woman. Behind them stood a tall, dark-haired man with a mustache. "Who are the two people with her?" she asked.

Hélène picked up her cup and took a sip. "The child's mother, Marielle. And her husband."

"Her husband?"

Hélène sniffed. "A sad story," she said. "After the war ended, Georges-Henri searched for her, but by the time he found her she had married Bernard." She sipped her coffee.

"She didn't wait for Georges-Henri?"

"She thought he'd been killed." She took the photograph from Jacquie. "Odile is a sweet child." She hesitated, studying it thoughtfully.

"I have seen her only once. That was when I helped Georges-Henri settle into his country house."

The *maison de campagne* Georges-Henri's letter had referred to. "When was that?" Jacquie asked.

"The summer of 1947. I remember it well. I couldn't travel all the way from Paris with my two youngest, and asking Francine to watch them was out of the question. So I left them with my father and a nanny and took Christine with me. She was just seven at the time." She smiled. "Such a little mother she was to Odile, always watching over her so she wouldn't fall and hurt herself." She sighed. "You see, Jacquie. Unfortunately, Odile was born *aveugle*."

"*Aveugle?*"

"Unable to see."

Jacquie gasped. "She's blind?"

"She has limited sight." She handed Jacquie a second photo. In this one, the little girl wore glasses with thick round lenses. Next to her stood a smiling Christine with an arm draped protectively over the toddler's shoulders.

Jacquie was reminded of the comment in Georges-Henri's letter. Something having to do with Christmas preparations. "How often does he go there?"

Hélène shrugged. "He goes when he can. Summers and holidays mostly."

Just then, excited voices came from the foyer, interrupting their conversation. "Ah. My father and the children have arrived," Hélène said rising quickly from the sofa.

Jacquie handed the photos back to her just as Théo raced into the salon. "Maman," he cried, "it's snowing!"

Hélène helped him remove his wet coat and mittens.

Paul entered behind them. "A fitting end to our Christmas pageant, *n'est-ce pas, mes enfants?*"

Christine sat in a chair by the fire warming her hands. "Can you make us *chocolat chaud*, Maman?" she asked.

Hélène put the two photos back in the desk drawer and picked up the tray of empty demitasse cups. "*Mais, bien sûr, mes petits,*" she said.

Paul said he was tired and headed for his room; the children followed Hélène into the kitchen.

Jacquie rose from the sofa and quietly crept up the stairs to her own room. Sitting down at the desk and biting back her anger, she re-read Georges-Henri's letter. Why hadn't he told her about Marielle, that he had a daughter? He had a whole life she hadn't known anything about until tonight. What else, she wondered, had he been keeping secret? Maybe he had a girl in every port? How convenient for him that she had showed up in Paris. Right there in the apartment, too, so he could play Romeo to her Juliette. She wanted to spit in his face. The relationship was definitely over. She could never trust him again.

She stared out the snow-frosted windows and shivered. Claudine had been correct. Frenchmen were good-for-nothing philanderers.

Laughter floated up from the floor below. Everyone was still in the kitchen. She went over to the door and opened it. The hall was empty. She might have time to sneak down to Georges-Henri's room without being seen. All she would do was take a quick look at the photo next to his bed. She had to find out for certain whether the girl in it was Marielle.

"And what if it's some other girl?" a small voice inside her asked. She pulled the door closed, tiptoed quietly down the hall, and descended the back stairs to the former maid's room.

The hall was dark; she reached for the door handle and tried it. To her surprise, it wasn't locked. Her heart pounding, she slipped quickly inside.

The curtains were open, and the brightness of the moonlight shining on the freshly fallen snow outside cast a dim light over everything in the room. She could just make out the silhouette of a bed and a reading lamp on the nightstand next to it. She crept over and groped for a switch. One click, and the single bulb illuminated the space.

It was just as Claudine had described it—small and spare. A desk, a chest of drawers, a bookshelf, books piled on the floor next to the neatly-made bed.

Jacquie bent over to touch the duvet, caught a whiff of Georges-Henri's scent, and quickly stepped back. "Just find that photo, take a look at it, and get out of here," she whispered.

Claudine had told her it was in a silver frame on the table by the bed, but it wasn't there now. It didn't seem to be anywhere in sight.

The bed stand had a single drawer. She touched the small brass handle and pulled it open. Nothing but a pair of glasses, a pen and pencil set, and a pad of writing paper, the same kind he had written the notes to her on. No silver-framed photo.

Closing the drawer quickly, she went over to the desk. An old black typewriter sat on top next to a stack of paper. She pulled open the large center drawer. Supplies—scissors, paper clips, more pencils—all neatly arranged.

There were two small side drawers. Jacquie opened the one on the left. Nothing inside but a dictionary.

She reached for the drawer on the right when, just then, she heard loud footsteps. She paused, panic setting in. Telling herself to remain calm, she tiptoed over to the end table, switched off the lamp, slid to the floor behind the bed, and listened.

Several minutes went by; the apartment went silent. Jacquie rose. Without switching on the lamp again, she went over to the desk and opened the one remaining drawer as quietly as she could.

In the darkened room, a silver frame in the drawer reflected the pale snow light outside the window. Jacquie picked it up. She couldn't make out the photo, and she didn't dare risk turning on the lamp again. Sliding the frame quickly under her sweater, she closed the drawer, opened the door, and ran back up the stairs to her room.

It was the same girl she'd seen in the photo Hélène had showed her earlier. Marielle. Jacquie recognized the setting—the top of the staircase on avenue de Camoëns—with a view of the Eiffel Tower in the distance.

She slid the photo from the frame and turned it over to see if a date had been written on it. No writing, but something was taped to the back—a yellowed newspaper clipping.

The heading read *DEUILS*. Deaths. The third obituary was circled.

On apprend la mort de Marielle Miniet, pieusement décédée, à l'âge de 22 ans après une brève maladie, en son domicile à Les Moulins (Alpes-Maritimes), le 28 juin. Cet avis tient lieu de faire-part.

Jacquie gasped, tried to make sense of what she was reading. Marielle was deceased. A brief illness. She was only twenty-two years old. In Les Moulins, the same village where Georges-Henri was now.

She looked at the photo again. Tears flooded her eyes as she stared at the two young lovers coping, best as they could, in the midst of war. All the anger she'd felt dissolved. No wonder Georges-Henri couldn't talk about his other life. Hélène must have known. Maybe that's what she meant when she said it was a sad story.

Chapter Eighteen

Jacquie awoke with a start. Sunlight was streaming into her room through the lace curtains. Something wasn't right. Mornings were dark in Paris this time of year. Panic setting in, she pulled back the duvet and swung her legs over the side thinking she was late for class.

Seeing Claudine's neatly-made bed brought her back to reality. Claudine was in New York. It was winter break. She relaxed.

The high-pitched sound of children's voices came from downstairs. A minute later, the front door slammed shut. Hélène, Paul, and the children would be occupied playing in the snow for most of the morning.

Jacquie pulled on her robe and grabbed her shampoo and a bar of soap. Then she opened her bedroom door and went down the hall to the bathroom. It was a rare day that she could take a bath and wash her hair without having to make way for someone else. She was going to take advantage of it.

Back in her room after a luxuriously long soak, she towel-dried and combed her hair, put on some face cream and rouge, and applied a touch of lipstick. Then, dressing quickly in a wool skirt and heavy sweater, she picked up the silver frame and studied the photo. She wished she could ask Hélène about what had happened to Marielle, but then how could she do that without admitting she'd found the obituary? She heaved a sigh, grabbed her handbag, and ran down the hall to Georges-Henri's room.

After returning the frame to the desk drawer where she'd found it the night before, she descended the main staircase to the kitchen. A baguette sat on the counter next to a jar of blackberry *confiture*. She tore off a piece, slathered it with jam, and ate it quickly.

Outside, the snow glistened in the bright sunshine. A plan for the day was forming in her mind. First off, she'd take the Métro to the fifth, get off at the Cluny-La Sorbonne station, and stop by one of the bookshops on Boulevard Saint Germain to pick up that new book Georges-Henri had told her about—*Le Journal d'Anne Frank*.

Then lunch. She felt a pang of regret. Having lunch at Brasserie Balzar wouldn't be the same without Georges-Henri, but she was hungry for a steaming bowl of *soupe à l'oignon gratinée*. After lunch, she'd do some Christmas shopping. She made a mental list of gifts to ship to her family in New York—perfume and a silk scarf for her mother, a pair of soft leather gloves for her father. She'd get French berets for all the cousins, too. Everyone at home would find something Parisian under the tree this year.

An hour later, she was seated at Brasserie Balzar reading when she heard a low voice speaking English. "Well, I'll be...if it isn't Claudine's friend Jacquie, Georges-Henri's girl!"

Jacquie looked up. The Texan Georges-Henri had fixed Claudine up with to go dancing at the jazz club was standing above her with a wide grin on his face. She smiled.

"Duff? Right?" She held out her hand. "How are you?"

He shook her hand vigorously. So American. "Are you here all by yourself?"

She laughed. Wasn't it obvious she was alone? "Want to join me? I was just reading my new book."

He didn't wait for a second invitation. "What new book is that?" he asked as he sat down.

"Anne Frank's diary. It's just out in French. The English translation hasn't been released yet."

"Is it any good?"

She shrugged and closed the book. "Too early to tell. What brings you to Brasserie Balzar?"

"I was working in my office, getting ready for the new term, and I got hungry. What about you?"

"I like the onion soup," she said with a grin.

He winked. "Missin' Georges-Henri, hey?"

She shrugged again. "Well…"

He chuckled. "Understandable."

The waiter arrived with her soup and asked Duff if he wanted to order anything. "*Même que Mademoiselle*," he said, pointing to Jacquie's soup. "*Avec un verre de vin rouge, s'il vous plaît.*"

The young man nodded and left. "You're not having any vino?" Duff asked.

"I…I don't generally drink wine at lunch," she said. "Not in the habit yet."

"Didn't take me long to adjust. I'd say that's the best thing about spending a sabbatical here in Paris. Wine with lunch."

"How long are you here?"

"A year, but I'm thinking about extending my stay. They badly need teachers — lost a lot of the Jewish professors during the war."

His bowl of soup and glass of wine arrived. He thanked the waiter and ordered a *café express*.

"How come you don't have a Texas drawl in French?" she asked.

He laughed. "I didn't know I had a drawl in English? Do I?"

"Well, yes."

"Where are you from?"

"New York. Just like Claudine."

"Ah Claudine. When does she get back?" He picked up his spoon. "I'd like to take her out again."

"She plans to return after the New Year. Just in time for the next term."

"I hope she's having a good time."

"I haven't heard from her yet."

They both dug into their soup. Jacquie was enjoying herself. It was good to have company, and Duff was just the breath of fresh air she needed.

"Do y'all have any plans for break?" he asked.

She sighed. "I'm supposed to go to Munich with two girls I know from my art class. They want to visit Dachau concentration camp." She put down her spoon and took a sip of water. "I have to tell you. I'm having second thoughts about it. I met with a friend of my host family who was liberated from there. Her story was so depressing." She hesitated. "I'm not sure I want to see the place…especially around Christmastime."

His face became serious. "Then why go now? Make the trip some other time when you're ready."

"I sort of promised." She sighed again. "Besides, I really want to get out of Paris."

"Have you been invited anywhere for Christmas?"

She nodded. "My host family owns a château in Normandy. They've suggested I can go there with them, if I want."

He whistled. "A château, hey? Impressive. You're going, right?"

"I'm not sure yet. I'd like to see the château, but…"

"They're Georges-Henri's family, if I'm not mistaken?"

"Yes. But he won't be there. He's in…"

"The south. I know."

She looked at him. "You know?"

"Hell yeah." He leaned back in his chair, raised his arms, and linked his fingers behind his head. "He invited me to join him there for Christmas. He's got a cottage not far from a small village. Les Moulins, I think its name is. I'm fixin' to rent a car and drive down." He grinned. "Sunshine. Warm weather. Can't wait." He lowered his arms and sat back up. "Say. This is just a thought, but why don't you go with me?"

"Me?"

"Sure. Why not? A road trip will be fun. There's a lot of France to explore along the way. The châteaux in the Loire Valley, for example. I've been wanting to see Azay-le-Rideau."

"The one that's on the island in the middle of a river? There was a photo of it in my high school French textbook."

"The same. A real stunner. What do you say?"

Jacquie shifted uneasily in her chair. "But Georges-Henri wouldn't be expecting me."

Duff laughed. "True. We'll surprise him. I don't think he'll object. He's pretty taken with you."

"I...I don't know."

"Ah, come on. I'm safe. I won't make a move on you. It'll be an adventure."

"His sister won't approve."

He downed the rest of his glass of wine. "Do you have to ask her permission?"

"I guess not. She only hosts me when school is in session. I'm free to go where I please during breaks and holidays."

"Well, then, it's settled. I'll wire Georges-Henri to expect two guests for Christmas, but I won't tell him who's coming with me."

"Are you sure he'll be okay with it? My just showing up like that, I mean?"

He smiled. "In a New York minute."

Chapter Nineteen

At the end of the first week of December, Jacquie met Duff for lunch again at the Brasserie Balzar.

"I've made up my mind to accept your offer," she said as they sat down.

"Hot damn!" he said. "I thought you were going to turn me down."

She looked at him and added, "There's one condition."

His eyebrows lifted. "Oh?"

"No shared rooms."

He put up his hand. "I swear to God I'll be on my best behavior the entire trip."

She smiled. "And we divide all expenses. I insist."

His hazel eyes explored her face. "You're somethin', you know that, Jacquie?"

"How do you mean?"

"Independent."

She smiled again. "I guess you could say I am."

They agreed to leave Paris on the fifteenth.

That evening, Jacquie sat down at the dinner table with Hélène and Paul. Watching Paul pour them glasses of burgundy, she said, "I've decided to postpone my visit to Dachau until the spring."

Hélène looked up. "Oh? *Pourquoi?*"

"The weather," Jacquie said. "It's so cold now. I think it will be better to go when it's warmer."

Paul picked up his glass of wine and raised it in her direction. "Wise decision, *ma chère*," he said. "Germany is dreary enough this time of year anyway. I wouldn't go myself." He winked at her and took a sip. His eyes were so like Georges-Henri's. There was a sadness in them, even when he smiled.

"Will you be accompanying us to the château for Christmas, then?" Hélène asked.

Jacquie shook her head. "*Merci* for offering, but I've made other travel arrangements."

"Oh?" Hélène looked at her father. Their eyes met, and she smiled slightly.

Jacquie had the distinct impression they were relieved to get rid of their American boarder for a while.

Hélène dipped her spoon into her soup. "Where are you going, if I might ask?"

"Italy. My friends and I are planning to purchase train passes." It wasn't a lie. Several students from her art history class had made tentative plans to meet up in Florence to celebrate the New Year before returning to Paris for the start of the winter term. She was hoping to join them.

Hélène seemed satisfied with the answer. "I assume your parents know?"

Jacquie nodded. "*Bien sûr.* They are very supportive." That was also true. Her father had wired her extra funds to 'have some fun' during the holidays, and her mother had sent her a brand-new Kodak Pony camera for her Christmas present.

Chapter Twenty

On the morning of her departure, Jacquie kissed Hélène good-bye, picked up her bag, and said she was meeting her friends at the Gare de Lyon. In reality, she walked around to the end of the block where Duff was waiting for her in an aqua-blue cabriolet he'd rented.

"Told you this was going to be glorious," he said as he stowed her bag in the boot and held open the passenger-side door.

Jacquie climbed in and removed the scarf from her head. "This is a nice car," she said admiring the fine leather bench seat, and shiny wood steering wheel and dash. "What kind is it?"

"A Dyna Panhard," he said, "latest model. Gorgeous, isn't it? Just take a gander at that hood ornament. When we get to the south, we'll put the top down. That is, if the weather's warm enough."

She smiled. The 2-door car was indeed handsome, and his enthusiasm for it was contagious.

They drove out of Paris, passing though little suburban villages and into a winter-brown countryside dotted with small farms and churches, cemeteries with elaborate monuments, and an occasional road-side restaurant.

"I can't get over the difference in how it all looks," Jacquie said.

Duff nodded. "It smells different, too. Like the soil is really, really ancient."

Jacquie rolled down the car window. A blast of cold air hit her face and she quickly closed it again. "Brr," she shivered. "Hope it's warmer in the south."

After two hours of driving, they passed a country inn.

Duff sniffed. "Is that *frites* I smell?" He slowed, turned the car around, and pulled off to the side of the road. "I'm starving. Let's stop for lunch."

"Great idea," Jacquie said. "I think I might even have a glass of wine."

"Ah, the wine," Duff said approvingly. "I'm glad to see you've decided to adopt the French way of life."

"Why not? You're driving," she said with a laugh.

"Who said I'm driving after lunch?"

Chapter Twenty-one

D uff and Jacquie drove into Les Moulins late afternoon three days after they'd left Paris.

Jacquie rolled down the car window. A fierce wind was blowing, and the air felt bitterly cold. "I thought it would be warm."

They parked across from an old stone fountain in the center of the village square. "Georges-Henri warned me the weather could be like this," Duff said. "He called it a mistral."

"A mistral?"

He turned to face her. "The wind. Georges-Henri said it blows a lot around here in the winter. I guess we won't be putting the top down after all. Today anyway."

Jacquie looked at an eighteenth-century building across from them. The French tricolor flapping wildly in the wind over its front entrance identified it as the town hall, *la mairie*.

"Georges-Henri wired me to meet him in the center," Duff said. He looked around. "I don't see him, though. Let's get out and stretch a bit." He opened his door, climbed out, and went around to Jacquie's side to open her door for her.

She pulled her scarf around her head, grabbed the new camera her parents had sent her, and climbed out. The wind caught her scarf and she retied it.

A few villagers were busy arranging a Nativity scene next to the fountain. They appeared to be arguing over the placement of several brightly-painted terra cotta figurines.

Jacquie waited for just the right shot before she took a photo.

A woman was putting fresh evergreen branches at the base of the fountain.

"What are the figures called?" Jacquie asked.

The woman looked up at her and smiled. Wisps of white hair sprung from her scarf and framed her face. One of her front teeth was missing. "*Santons, Mademoiselle,*" she said. "*C'est la tradition ici pour Noël.*" She eyed Duff and the Dyna Panhard. "*Vous êtes visiteurs?*"

Jacquie nodded. "Oui. *Nous sommes américains.*"

The woman shook her head and went back to what she was doing.

Next, Jacquie aimed the camera at Duff who was examining the huge stone artichoke adorning the top of the fountain. He grinned at her. She focused and clicked. "It's a pretty village," she said. "How big do you think it is?"

He shrugged. "Not much more to it than what we see here, I'd say. Looks like it's just one long street surrounded by tall hills." He pointed to a large white structure with a pink-tiled roof and a carillon tower that dominated the hillside. "That looks like it's a monastery or convent."

The wind made eerie sounds in the village, sweeping debris around corners, rattling and clattering doors and signs. Despite that, the sky was bright blue, and the sun was shining. Jacquie took several more photos.

"Well, I'll be." She heard Duff's voice behind her after a few minutes. "Look who just came out of the chocolate shop over there."

She turned to see Georges-Henri making his way across the square. His pace was slow and uneven, his limp only slightly evident, and he wasn't using his cane. He carried a small green box tied with a white bow. Dead leaves and branches swirled around his feet.

Her heart skipped a beat. "You really didn't tell him I was coming with you?"

Duff raised the palm of his hand and shook his head. "Time for our big surprise!"

She gulped. "I hope you know what you're doing."

"Come on," he said. "He'll be thrilled."

Georges-Henri saw Duff first, nodded and smiled. Then he noticed her, and his face drained of color.

Oh God, she thought. So much for Duff's grand plan.

The two men shook hands. Jacquie snapped their picture.

"*Bonjour*, Jacquie," Georges-Henri said, turning to her. He leaned forward and air-kissed her cheeks Parisian-style.

Not exactly the enthusiastic greeting she'd anticipated.

"We ah…Duff and I thought…" she stammered.

Duff cut her off. "Let me explain."

Georges-Henri handed her the green box.

"Chocolates?"

Georges-Henri nodded. "When Duff wired he was bringing some-one, I assumed his girl…" He looked tentatively at Duff. "Are you two…?"

Duff chuckled. "I think he just said he assumes you and I are… you know."

Jacquie looked from Duff to Georges-Henri. She felt herself blush-ing. "Oh no! How amusing!"

Duff gave her a strange look. "Well, not exactly that amusing." Then he winked at her. "I'd better explain before he hauls off and punches me in the nose." He turned to Georges-Henri and spoke in a mixture of French and English. "Before you have a hissy fit, *mon ami*," he began.

Georges-Henri put up his hand. "What is this 'issy feet?" he asked in heavily-accented English. "I don't know this word."

Duff laughed. "Oh yeah." He scratched his head and looked at Jacquie who was watching him. "I don't think there's a direct translation in French."

"*Ne pas se fâcher*, Jacquie said, "not to get upset."

"Yeah. Thanks," Duff said to her. "Ne pas se *fâcher*," he repeated.

Georges-Henri nodded. "Duff's French is at times a foreign language to me."

"I've been told that before," Duff said with a sigh. "Anyway, I acci-dentally ran into Jacquie at Brasserie Balzar…"

"Ran into?" Georges-Henri asked with a concerned look on his face.

Jacquie laughed. The conversation between the two men was amusing. She wondered if it was always like that. She quickly provided a rough translation.

Duff nodded. "Yeah. That. Long story short. I asked Jacquie to come along on the trip 'cause I thought you would be happy to see her."

Jacquie opened the box of chocolates, peeked inside, and plucked one out.

Georges-Henri cleared his throat. "You're going to meet my friend Bernard, the chocolatier who makes those," he said, effectively changing the subject.

Bernard. The name Hélène had mentioned. Marielle's husband. Odile's stepfather.

Jacquie bit into the chocolate. "*C'est bon*," she said with a smile, but she felt a knot growing in her stomach. Georges-Henri hadn't said he was happy to see her.

Chapter Twenty-two

The sun was just setting when they arrived at the small pink stucco cottage.

Georges-Henri led Jacquie and Duff up the stone steps and hurriedly opened the front door for them. "Bernard named the cottage *La Pitchoune,*" he said, quickly closing the door and switching on a lamp. "It means 'The Little One' in Provençale."

"I think it's charming," Jacquie said, looking around. Two upholstered chairs sat in front of the large fireplace. A round wooden dining table and four chairs sat in one corner next to a china hutch.

"It's no château," Georges-Henri said as he took their coats.

Outside, the wind whipped the shutters and banged them against the sides of the house. The high, wood-beamed ceiling echoed the high-pitched and low-pitched whistling and howling. Jacquie shivered; the wind made her nervous.

Georges-Henri continued as if he hadn't heard anything. "There are only five rooms—this salon, which takes up the front half of the house, the kitchen there," he pointed to an arched doorway, "and three small bedrooms. I use one for my office."

"Oh dear," Jacquie whispered to Duff. Already, there was going to be a problem with the sleeping arrangements. She cleared her throat. "Perhaps, since you weren't expecting me, Georges-Henri, I should go to a hotel. I saw one in the village square."

Disappointment showed on Duff's face. He didn't say anything.

"Nonsense," Georges-Henri said. "You two will have the bedrooms. I'll sleep on the divan in my office."

"Are you sure?" Jacquie said.

"Let's get you settled," he said. "Then we'll go have something to eat at the local café."

He added a log to the smoldering fire in the fireplace, then led them through another arched doorway into the hall where the bedrooms were located.

An hour later, the three were seated inside a cozy dining room just off the main square. The place wasn't crowded. Only a few tables were occupied. A young couple ate at one. Across from them sat an older, white-haired gentleman with a small poodle at his feet. He raised his drink in their direction, wished them "*Santé*" then returned to concentrating on his meal.

"What is he drinking?" Jacquie asked.

"*Vin chaud*," Georges-Henri said. "Warm, spiced wine with cognac. It's traditional at Christmas time, especially when the weather is like this."

"I'd like to try it," she said.

"Me, too," Duff said.

Georges-Henri ordered three *vins chauds*.

"How did you wind up here in this village?" Duff asked Georges-Henri. "Somehow I can't see you picking this place out by yourself."

Georges-Henri glanced at Jacquie and cleared his throat. She held her breath and waited for him to answer.

"It's a long story," he said. "Now, shall we order? I recommend the daube, it's Provence's answer to boeuf bourguignon."

He never did answer Duff's question.

All night long, the wind howled and the shutters banged against the sides of the cottage.

Jacquie didn't sleep. It seemed to her the entire house was rattling. Once, she got up to look out the French doors. The lake in back was dark and churning. She placed her hands over her ears, but nothing would shut out the endless racket.

The next morning, the weather hadn't improved. Sleepy and irritable, she dressed quickly and found Georges-Henri in the kitchen making coffee.

"How do you stand it?" she asked.

He turned around. "What?"

"The wind. All that incessant clattering, tapping, roaring and rumbling."

He shrugged. "It will blow itself out soon. It always does."

"Always?"

He cocked his head slightly to one side and smiled. "It will be warm again. You will see." He handed her a bowl of coffee mixed with hot milk. "In a day or so."

He didn't buss her cheek as she'd hoped. Disappointed, she accepted the *café au lait* and went over to sit down at the wooden table which was draped in a cheerful blue, green and yellow tablecloth.

She took a sip and looked around the room. It was a well-organized kitchen. Pots and pans hung from the walls; spices and baskets of cooking utensils filled a tall rack. A gas stove sat in the corner at the end of the long countertop, and a huge white porcelain sink with a dark green tile backsplash was in front of the window. Above it all, hanging from the high wood-beamed ceiling, was a large rustic wrought iron chandelier.

The evening before, Georges-Henri had been pleasant, but aloof. She'd thought it was just shyness, perhaps because of Duff being there. Then again, he was acting the same way he had at the party the night before he left Paris without saying good-bye.

They had returned to the cottage after dinner. Georges-Henri had poured the three of them snifters of cognac, and they had sat in the salon listening to the new 78-rpm record Duff had brought Georges-Henri as a gift—the gypsy jazz of popular guitarist Django Reinhart.

Finally, when it had come time to say *bonne nuit*, Duff headed off to his room, but Jacquie had deliberately stayed back pretending to be interested in the books in the bookcase, hoping to buy extra time alone with Georges-Henri.

After some discussion about the latest work of Albert Camus, titled *La Peste*, Georges-Henri encouraged her to read it and she had picked it up to take it to bed. To her great disappointment, he had bid her *bonne nuit* without kissing her.

Now that she thought about it the next morning, there could be only one explanation for his giving her the cold shoulder—he blamed her for his sister kicking him out of the apartment on avenue Mozart.

"Hélène told me she made you leave," she ventured. "I'm so sorry. It was all my fault. We shouldn't have…"

"Nonsense," he said. "She didn't make me leave. I planned to come here as I always do for Christmas." He sniffed. "My sister can be a bit overpowering at times."

Jacquie got up and studied the cooking tools that hung on the wall. "Do you do a lot of cooking?" she asked.

"Some." Georges-Henri plucked a copper pan from a hook. "Bernard designed the kitchen when he did the renovation to the house while I was back in Paris. He's the one who likes to cook."

"He's the chocolatier?"

He nodded. "An excellent one, too. He's teaching the nuns at the convent how to make fine chocolates."

So that building overlooking the village was a convent. "Why?" she asked. "Can't they just buy chocolates from his shop?"

"It has to do with maintaining an occupation to sustain their existence. They are thinking of establishing a factory—*un artisanat de confiserie.*"

"You mean going into business for themselves? But wouldn't they be competing with your friend?"

"*C'est possible.*" He shrugged. "*On va voir.*"

She picked up an odd-looking utensil with a flared, jagged edge. "What is this used for?"

"I have no idea," he said with a chuckle. "In fact, I don't know what most of these are supposed to do."

She wondered if he meant that as a joke.

She watched him select a simple wooden spoon and spatula. Maybe now would be a good time to bring up the subject that had been bothering her. She cleared her throat. "You mentioned someone in your letter,

Georges-Henri. Odile?" He looked over at her. "I…I was just wondering who…"

Just then Duff walked into the room. He was wearing only a pair of pajama bottoms and an old white tee-shirt. He yawned and scratched his stomach.

"You look like you didn't sleep either," Jacquie said, trying not to show her frustration at the timing of his entrance.

His red hair was tousled, and there was a hole in his tee-shirt the size of two fingers. He grinned at her, dimples appearing at the corners of his mouth. "Morning to you, too, beautiful," he said. "How can anyone get any shut-eye around here with all that banging and rattling going on? Hell, it was as noisy as two skeletons dancing on a tin roof all night."

Jacquie laughed. "That's one way of putting it. Georges-Henri says the gale is going to blow itself out soon."

Duff went over to where Georges-Henri was standing by the stove cracking brown-speckled eggs into a bowl. "What are you making?" he asked.

"Omelettes," Georges-Henri said. "With truffles I found at the outdoor market yesterday." He held up a large, black lump and sniffed it. "They're in season now."

"That's the ugliest thing I've ever seen," Duff said. "Are you sure it's edible?"

Georges-Henri smiled. "Are you hungry?"

Duff rubbed his stomach. "As a horse."

Jacquie groaned inwardly. Truffles or not, she hated omelettes.

Chapter Twenty-three

After breakfast, Georges-Henri announced he was going out. "I'll be back later," he said pulling on his coat. He didn't invite Jacquie or Duff to go with him, and he didn't say where he was going.

"He doesn't want me here," Jacquie said to Duff after he left. I should just leave."

"Why?" Duff said. "We surprised him. That's all. He's probably got to get some food. I took a peek in his ice box last night. There's absolutely nothing to write home about."

"But he's not..." She wanted to say "the same affectionate man I know," but she caught herself. It wouldn't be appropriate to discuss something like that with Duff. Instead, she said, "I don't think he takes surprises very well. We should have warned him ahead of time I was coming."

"It's my fault," Duff said. "Hell. I thought he'd love it." He shook his head. "But what do I know? I'm just a Texas boy with a big heart and still a lot of learning to do where the French are concerned."

Jacquie felt edgy and out of sorts. Maybe it was the constant sound of the wind that had made her feel that way. She looked up and caught Duff staring at her. "Your big heart was in the right place, Duff. It's my fault just as much as yours."

"I…I'd better get dressed," he said awkwardly. He turned to go, then stopped. "Say," he said, "I was just wondering. Do you play cribbage?"

"Yes. Why?"

"I brought my board with me. How about a game while we wait for Georges-Henri to return." He grinned at her. "I'll warn you ahead of time. This ain't my first rodeo. I'm pretty good."

"Actually," she said. "I'm the champion cribbage player in my family."

"Well, I'll be. You're on. I'll be back in a jiff."

They spent the next two hours seated across from each other at the large table in the sitting room. A log crackled in the fireplace, the wind rattled the French doors, and the antique clock on the mantel ticked away the minutes. Still no Georges-Henri.

Occasionally, Jacquie looked up from her cards and caught Duff watching her. "I wish you wouldn't stare at me like that," she said.

"Why not? What else is there to look at?" He slapped a card on the table and smiled. "Besides, Jacquie, you're cute as a speckled pup, as my grandmother used to say. I like looking at you."

She ignored the comment and kept playing.

A few minutes later, he threw down his cards. "That's it. You win. I concede to the champ."

Jacquie rose from the table. "Looks like the wind has let up a bit," she said, staring wistfully outside. "Think I'll take a walk."

Duff yawned and stood. "Want some company?"

"Not really. The sky is clear and it's such a pretty color of blue. Maybe I can get some good pictures."

He darted a concerned glance at her.

"Okay. So maybe I've got a major case of shut-in-itis."

"Are you sure that's all?" He went over to where she stood and put an arm around her shoulders.

"Duff," she warned, pushing him away.

"Sorry," he said.

She went to her room to get her coat. Duff's putting his arm around her shoulders had unsettled her. She told herself he probably meant nothing by it. He was just being Duff. Or was that it? He *was* being Duff.

He'd been a little too affectionate since the day they'd spent exploring the Loire Valley on their way south. After visiting the castle in Azay-le-Rideau, they'd had a really nice dinner, with wine, and a lively discussion about the politics at home and opposing views about President Harry Truman.

Duff had a good approach to life. She liked that about him, even though he did get a little fresh sometimes.

She tied her scarf, pulled on her gloves, grabbed her new camera, and opened the French doors that led out onto the veranda. The back porch of the house was strewn with dead leaves and branches. A gust of wind sent them swirling as she stepped out.

She skipped down the stone steps to the water's edge and walked along the shoreline. The air smelled fresh and clean, and the small lake behind the house sparkled in the winter sunshine. A pair of ducks was foraging for food in the shallow waters, upended with their tails in the air. She smiled and snapped a photo.

A footpath led up the hillside to the convent. The complex was much larger than she had judged when she'd seen it the day before from the village square. She was reminded of Georges-Henri's comment about the nuns wanting to go into the chocolate business. She'd never heard of nuns doing something like that before. Surely the Catholic Church supported their effort.

The path was steep, and Jacquie occasionally paused to take pictures of the spectacular view. The lavender fields below were brown and dormant now, but she could imagine how they would look in the summer, and how heavenly the air would smell, when there were neat corduroy rows of purple throughout the valley. This was a beautiful part of France, even in winter. She hoped her photos would do it justice, even in black and white.

The footpath ended and Jacquie found herself in the quiet enclosed space of the convent garden. Topiary trees tightly clipped into neat mounds echoed the curves of the surrounding hills, and lush green and gray foliage bordered a flagstone path leading to a statue of a monk holding a small bird.

As she took in the beauty of it all, the bells in the carillon tower sounded. Three o'clock. She wondered briefly if Georges-Henri had returned to the cottage, but she wasn't in any hurry to get back. This peaceful walk was just what she needed.

After snapping a few more photos, she walked the short distance to the village square. At the café, the waiters were moving tables and chairs back outside. A good sign that the mistral was done. She felt suddenly hungry. She hadn't eaten since breakfast, and then she'd only picked at the truffle omelet Georges-Henri had made. She took a seat at one of the tables and ordered a *jambon beurre*, her favorite sandwich since she'd arrived in France.

From her vantage point, she could see the nativity crèche by the fountain. More santons had been added—three kings, a donkey, figures of shopkeepers and various other locals. It was charming.

The chocolate shop was just across the square. It was closed, as were all the shops. Only the café was open. It seemed odd. In Paris, the shops shuttered for two hours for lunch but they were always open by now.

"*Les magasins sont fermées?*" she asked the waiter when he brought her sandwich. "*Pourquoi?*"

"*C'est l'après-midi, Mademoiselle,*" he said. "In the afternoons, everyone takes a nap after a leisurely lunch." He smiled, put his palms together, tilted his head, rested his cheek against his fingers, and briefly closed his eyes.

Jacquie thought about that as she watched him hustle back into the restaurant. A nap sounded inviting just then, given the sleepless night she'd spent. She ate her sandwich, savoring the crisp baguette spread with unsalted butter and a thin slice of ham. When she had finished, the waiter brought her a *café crème*.

A thought occurred to her. "Where is the nearest church?" she asked.

The waiter pointed to a narrow street just off the square. "Place Saint-Michel," he said, "over there. Behind the mairie."

The spire was barely visible just beyond the roof of the town hall.

"Does the church have a cemetery?" she asked.

He nodded. "Oui." He explained that it was the only one in the village.

Jacquie finished her café, laid a few centimes on the table, and rose from her chair. Maybe she would try to find Marielle's grave.

The stone church was similar to the small churches they had driven past on the trip south. Every village in the country seemed to have one.

A cobbled pathway led around to the back. Jacquie followed it until she came to the graveyard entrance. She opened the iron gate and entered a maze of ancient raised tombs and headstones. Near the back wall, a figure, a man, stood in the shadows with his head bowed.

Jacquie froze when she realized who it was. She drew in a breath and watched as Georges-Henri knelt on one knee, kissed a sprig of holly, and carefully placed it on a headstone.

Panicking, she swung around but her heel caught on the stone path and she lost her balance and stumbled to the ground. Her camera landed with a loud thud against an ancient stone tomb.

She struggled to right herself and quickly picked up the Kodak. Other than a scratch, it was intact as far as she could tell, but her knee stung and it was bleeding. She bent to examine the damage. Her new nylon hose were ruined.

Georges-Henri was frowning at her.

"I'm sorry," she said, embarrassed. "I didn't realize you'd be here."

He came over to where she stood. "What are you doing here?" he asked.

Tears welled in her eyes. "Hélène told me about Marielle," It was a lie, but how else could she explain how she knew about the girl, or the fact that she had died? She couldn't explain she'd been snooping around in his room. "I thought I would try to find her grave."

He seemed confused. "Why?"

"I don't know. Perhaps seeing it might help me understand you better. You've been so…so distant."

He folded her in his arms. "I thought I explained in the letter I left you. It would be better…you would…if we didn't see so much of each other."

She stiffened. "Why not, Georges-Henri? Why shouldn't we enjoy each other's company?" A tear rolled down her cheek. "I thought we liked each other at least."

"For me, it was becoming more," he said. "I didn't mean to hurt you."

"You could have told me about Odile, at least. Since you mentioned her name in your letter. Did you think I wouldn't understand? That I was just a stupid, silly American girl in France for a fling and nothing more?"

"You are so young."

"I'm old enough to care that you lost Marielle, Georges-Henri. That you have a young child who needs you." She lifted her chin and looked in his eyes. "But, don't you understand? I need you, too."

His eyes were the color of old gold and soft as velvet. He kissed her, then he took her hand and led her over to the headstone where he'd been standing. "This is where my...Marielle is now," he said.

Jacquie stared at the grave. My Marielle, he'd said. She had to accept what the girl had meant to him.

"How did she die?" she whispered.

"Pneumonia," he said. "She became ill during the winter of forty-seven. I was in Paris. Bernard told me the doctor did everything he could..." His voice cracked, and a sob came from deep within him. "If only I'd told her..."

"What, Georges-Henri? Told her what?"

His eyes met hers. "The truth."

Paris
Fall 1946

Chapter Twenty-four

The city was still reeling from the aftereffect of the war when Georges-Henri returned in September for fall classes. Everything was scarce, rich and poor alike scavenged for food, and black marketeering was so common it wasn't even regarded as a crime.

The hunt for collaborators continued. Those identified were arrested, tried as war criminals, and sentenced to prison or death. Some were lynched on the spot.

At the Sorbonne, Georges-Henri found that many of the courses he needed to complete his studies had been postponed or completely canceled due to lack of instructors. The subject he was most interested in, and the one on which he hoped to write his thesis, was taught by Professor Jean André. To Georges-Henri's great relief, it was still on the list.

One day, a week into the fall term, Monsieur André approached Georges-Henri after class. "I think already you are intent on philosophy, *n'est-ce pas?* Might you be interested in teaching the subject one day?"

The professor's question surprised Georges-Henri. He responded, "I hope to. I have another year of studies, though, before I can qualify."

"*Ah bon?*" The professor rubbed his chin. "Unfortunately, we can't wait that long, young man. The shortage of teachers is severe, as you know. I have been unable to find an assistant which means I may be forced to cancel the course entirely." He pushed back his glasses. "My previous associate was sent to Auschwitz and, well... unfortunately, he never returned." He fetched a large volume from his desk and handed it to Georges-Henri. "I presume you have read Sartre?"

Georges-Henri took the book. "I admired *La Nausée* greatly. It's mainly why I became interested in the subject. I haven't read this one yet. It's his latest, isn't it?"

Monsieur André nodded. "I predict *L'être et le Néant* will become the most moralizing philosophy of the twentieth century. Consequently, I have decided to lecture from it exclusively this term."

Georges-Henri thumbed through the thick tome. At four hundred pages, it would take some time to get through. "I'll give it a read," he said. "*Merci.*"

"You'll do more than that, if you're interested in my proposal," the professor said. He tented his hands. "I'd like you to become my teaching assistant." He raised his eyebrows. "Now. This term."

Georges-Henri was taken aback. "Me?"

The professor nodded. "You will be learning right along with your students." He smiled. "My advice is to stay one chapter ahead of them at all times. I lecture on Mondays. You will hold small discussion classes, based on the current chapter being taught, on Tuesday and Thursday mornings for two hours each starting next week. If things work out, we'll add an additional class for you to teach next term."

That evening over dinner, Georges-Henri told his father and sister what had happened. "And, just like that, I'm going to teach at the Sorbonne," he said.

Hélène was cynical. "But how can they just make you a professor if you haven't even finished your studies?" she asked. "Won't you be breaking some rule of academia?"

"Professor André explained that I will be his assistant to start with. He said the school is trying to recruit professors from America to come here for a year on sabbatical."

"Well, it's wonderful news," his father said. "I'm proud of you, son."

Hélène sniffed. She had offered to let him stay in the maid's room of her apartment rent free for the year. "Will you earn anything?" she asked.

"Actually, there is a small stipend involved, but I have relinquished it."

"Why on earth did you do that?" she gasped.

He sighed. "Don't you see, Hélène? I'm getting a year's start in my teaching career, thanks to Professor André. He said he would arrange to have the course requirements waived so I can graduate early."

"I think that's wonderful," Paul chimed in. "The sooner he's earning a professor's salary, the sooner he'll be able to pay you room and board, Hélène."

She took a sip of her wine and harrumphed. "He should have at least accepted the stipend."

"Oh, Hélène," Paul said. "Don't be that way. We have enough for us all."

"It's just that I worry. With my husband gone…"Tears welled in her eyes. "I fear for all of us. The aristocracy is being targeted. Even those who resisted. Mirepoix, for example. There was nothing to incriminate him but his title. Nevertheless, he was tortured and narrowly escaped being sentenced to death. I hear stories every day. We are not safe, Papa. We can't trust anyone."

Her father rubbed his forehead. "I agree. I've heard the rumors." He patted her hand. "In time, it will be all right, *ma chère*. You will see."

"Did you ever hear what happened to Docteur Yves?" Georges-Henri asked.

"The butcher who promised to smuggle Jews to Argentina, but killed them for their valuables instead?" Hélène asked, her eyes full of fury.

Paul shifted in his seat and opened his mouth to say something.

Georges-Henri glanced at his father and shook his head. It would be best not to tell Hélène about Joachim's visit to the château. He wasn't ready to explain to her about Marielle and Odile.

Hélène blessed herself. "*Merci Dieu.* The monster went to the guillotine in May."

"Was there a trial?"

"Oui. And there was considerable publicity about it, too, as I recall. A Jewish woman, I believe her name was Rosen, claimed she had been shot and buried alive in quicklime but managed to escape."

Later, after dinner, Paul and Georges-Henri were seated opposite each other in the salon. A cool autumn breeze floated into the room through the open windows carrying the scent of logs smoldering in wood-burning fireplaces in the neighborhood.

Paul was quietly smoking his pipe and listening with his eyes closed to his favorite Mozart piano concertos.

Georges-Henri was trying to read, but he was having trouble concentrating. He was thinking about what his sister had said. Could the woman who testified at Docteur Yves's trial be Marielle's adoptive mother? Rosen was a common Jewish name. But how many Rosens would have given up all their valuables to Docteur Yves in exchange for passage to Argentina in 1944?

He tried to remember what Marielle's mother had looked like. He'd seen her once with Marielle, from afar. Marielle had never introduced him to her parents. "You're not Jewish," she had told him. "My father is very firm." She'd never mentioned how her mother felt. Odd, he thought, now that he knew the truth. Marielle wasn't actually Jewish, either.

He decided he would go to the bibliothèque the next day after classes finished. Hélène said the trial had received considerable publicity, and the execution had taken place in May. He would start with the Paris editions of *Le Matin* published during that time. Perhaps there had been wider coverage throughout France as well, though he couldn't recall seeing a newspaper anywhere in the provinces. Les Moulins didn't even have a *kiosque*, and no one seemed to care to talk about anything other than local gossip.

Marielle, he was certain, wouldn't have been aware of any publicity the trial had received.

He returned to the book in front of him. Professor André had explained the title straight away in his first lecture. It meant that man himself was *Being and Nothingness*. "Man is the being by whom nothingness comes into the world," the professor had said. Georges-Henri would need to have a better understanding of what that meant before he began leading the class discussions.

Paul interrupted him. "You haven't told Hélène about finding Marielle yet. Why is that?"

Georges-Henri lowered his book and raised an eyebrow. He'd had to tell his father about his discovering Marielle and Odile because, of course, he'd also had to explain the purchase of the cottage and the fact that he'd spent most of the gold coins his father had given him.

"I'm just not ready, Papa. I shall tell her in time. It's become complicated, as you realize."

Paul nodded. "I understand. It is probably wise. Your sister has enough to burden her at the moment. She's very worried about her financial situation, even though I've told her I will help."

"You brought the rest of the gold to Paris with you, then?"

Paul nodded. "I did indeed. I didn't want to leave it at the château."

"I hope you didn't place it in a bank."

Paul chuckled. "Of course not! No one can trust the financial institutions these days. But do not worry, Georges-Henri. It is in the place we agreed upon. It will not be discovered."

That night, Georges-Henri lay on his bed staring at the framed photo of Marielle and himself on his end table. He recalled how Marielle's scent had made him feel light-headed, the way she smiled at him with her lips partly open, teasing him to kiss her, and how they had laughed together... at the little things...before their lives had turned into a nightmare.

Now that he had the cottage, at least he would be able to spend his holidays with her and Odile in Provence. He leaned back into his duvet. The thought pleased him, even though he'd have to endure Marielle giving him the cold shoulder and, worse, Odile calling him *Tonton* rather than what she should rightly be calling him—Papa.

He put his hands behind his head and stared at the ceiling, trying to recall what Joachim Herz had told them when he'd come to the château searching for Marielle. Her mother had refused to flee Docteur Yves's office while her father confronted the man. Joachim had heard shots and presumed both Rosens were dead.

Georges-Henri's mind raced with questions. If Madame Rosen had survived that night, why hadn't she tried to find Marielle afterward? The Rosens had adopted their daughter from the convent in Les Moulins.

Certainly, Madame would have thought there was a possibility that Marielle would have gone there. Why hadn't she fled there herself?

He turned out the light. A nagging question remained in his mind: how would Marielle react, after all she'd been through, if she learned her mother had survived?

Chapter Twenty-five

It wasn't hard for Georges-Henri to find the news coverage of the trial in the library. The front page of the morning edition of *Le Matin* dated March 1946 showed a mug shot of the doctor with the bold headline: "*Le Mystérieux Charnier de la Rue Lesueur.*" The Mysterious Mass Grave of the Rue Lesueur.

The doctor's full name was Yves Félix Henri Lablais. He'd been caught because someone had recognized him at a Métro station in February and alerted police that he was still in Paris.

The trial had begun on March 19, and it had quickly become a circus. Docteur Yves maintained he'd only killed enemies of France as a Résistance fighter. The prosecution attempted to try him for all twenty-seven murders at once. There were dozens of witnesses. In the end, he was convicted of murder for profit of twenty-six people and imprisoned in La Santé where he was beheaded by guillotine on May 25.

Georges-Henri poured over the articles about the trial, searching for the name Rosen. He had a hunch that the one person who had survived, and, therefore, the one murder the doctor wasn't charged with was that of Marielle's mother.

In the end, he was right. He found Clara Rosen in a summary of the trial proceedings. He was surprised to also see Joachim Herz on the list of the key witnesses.

It occurred to him that Joachim might know where he could find Clara Rosen. It was a long shot, but worth trying. That night, he wrote to Joachim in Saint-Malo. On his way to class the next day, he posted the letter.

A month later, he received the response.

October 1946

Mon cher Georges-Henri,

I was very happy to hear from you and also to read the wonderful news that you found Marielle alive and well in Provence. I have often wondered what happened to her after we parted ways in Paris. It pleases me that she is happy, though I think you are a bit sad about the child.

As for the trial, yes, I was a witness. At first, I was reluctant to present myself. I didn't want to complicate things. In the end, though, I had to testify. I wanted to make certain the Butcher of Paris, as they called him in the press, would be sent to the guillotine. And he was.

I was as surprised as you must have been when you learned Clara Rosen had survived. Her description of what she went through, how her husband had bravely shielded her, was moving and brought many in the courtroom to tears. I personally don't know how she found the strength to tell her story. She is quite frail. You see, she was sent to Ravensbrück after she was found half dead by police in a street not far from the site of Docteur Yves's office. Until the very start of the trial, she called herself Clara Franck. Franck being her family name in Poland. As she told it, she decided to come forward at last as Clara

Rosen to seek atonement for her dear, brave husband who had given his life for her.

Marielle's name never came up during the trial. In my testimony, I was asked to describe only what I saw. I recounted what happened to my parents in the basement of DocteurYves's house, how I ran up the stairs chased by DocteurYves who had a pistol, and escaped while Monsieur Rosen blocked the doctor's way. Clara testified next. She didn't refer to Marielle, either.

Afterwards, I told her that Marielle and I had managed to get away and that Marielle had said she didn't want anyone to know where she was going. That seemed to be enough for Clara. Portant, she had tears in her eyes.

You asked if I know how you could locate Clara. Since the trial, I have had only one short letter from her. The address on the envelope was in Paris, in the nineteenth. I don't know if she lives there now, though that is where I am planning to send my response.

Enclosed is her letter for you to read yourself. In my answer to her, I shall include your address as well as an introduction for you in case, as you suspect, her daughter never told her about you. Please let me know if you do visit her. I hope you will. I think she will be greatly surprised, and pleased, to learn she has a grandchild. (I didn't tell her about the pregnancy.)

I trust I have answered all your questions. If there is something you wonder about still, feel free to ask. I hear from your father regularly. Please greet him for me.

Amicalement,

Joachim Herz

The letter from Clara was postmarked from Mouzaïa. Georges-Henri recognized the area. He'd taken one of Hélène's rescued pilots to a safe house there during the war. He recalled Le Parc des Buttes de Chaumont was nearby.

He opened the envelope and carefully unfolded the letter. It was short, less than half a page, and the handwriting was shaky. In it, Clara merely expressed that she was grateful for Joachim's friendship and she was pleased to have learned he had helped Marielle to escape. Nothing more.

Chapter Twenty-six

M onday the eleventh was a rainy, blustery November day, befitting the solemn mood of the date. It was L'Armistice, the day the country remembered its dead and injured from the Great War of 1914-1918.

Businesses were closed, schools shut, and the tricolor flew everywhere as if in defiance of history and the stormy weather.

Georges-Henri had the day off. With Clara's address tucked into his coat pocket, he took the Métro to the nineteenth arrondissement and got off at the Botzaris station. When he ascended to the street at the upper left corner of Le Parc des Buttes de Chaumont, the sky was gunmetal gray, and a light rain was falling.

The little village of Mouzaïa was named for a town and commune in Algeria. Detached two-story brick houses lined narrow cobblestone lanes. Georges-Henri noted that all the streets were named Villas — Villa des Lilas, Villa de Bellevue, Villa de la Renaissance. Gnarled vines tumbled over high walls, and heavy wrought iron gates protected the private gardens behind them from inquisitive passersby.

Few people were out. Georges-Henri met an elderly couple coming toward him. Both were dressed entirely in black. The man's empty right coat sleeve was neatly pinned to his shoulder, and he wore a victory medal on his lapel. Leaning against each other, they held a single umbrella to shield themselves against the rain and nodded to him as they went past.

Georges-Henri found Clara's address—number four—on Villa d'Alsace. Like all the other houses in the neighborhood, it had been invaded by creeping ivy. He peered through the heavy gate. The small garden looked like it hadn't been tended to for some time. Curtains in the second-story windows were tightly drawn; dead geraniums spilled from window boxes. A sign over the door read: *Chat Lunatique.*

He tried the latch, and the gate swung open with a loud creak. Keeping a sharp lookout for any sign of the crazy cat, he entered cautiously. Once inside, he closed the gate, climbed the crumbling steps to the front door, and lifted the heavy brass knocker.

No response. He knocked a second time, then a third. Nothing. The neighborhood was quiet. Raindrops tap-tapped gently on the overhang above the door. He hesitated, wondering what to do. One thing was certain. If he left now, he wasn't likely to return.

After a few seconds, he heard a sound, a muted shuffling. It came from inside.

"Madame Rosen?"

A curtain pulled back slightly in the narrow window next to the door. Two eyes framed in thick, wire-rimmed glasses peered out at him.

Georges-Henri took in a deep breath and said, "*Bonjour*, Madame. *Excusez l'intrusion.* I believe Joachim Herz sent you a letter about me. My name is Georges-Henri Delacroix. I would like to speak with you…about Marielle, your daughter."

The eyes took him in, then the curtain whipped closed.

Georges-Henri waited for what seemed like an eternity.

Finally, a dull metallic thud suggested a rusty deadbolt being unlatched. The front door opened just a crack.

"*Êtes-vous tout seul?*"

"Oui, Madame," Georges-Henri answered. Why was she wondering if he was all alone? Who did she think he would have brought with him?

She pulled back the door and peeked out as if to verify there was no one else around.

He smiled.

"*Allez, entrez,*" she commanded beckoning him in with her hand. "Make sure the gate is latched first."

Clara Rosen was a petite, soft-spoken woman with salt-and-pepper hair pulled back into a tight bun at the nape of her neck. She was rail thin, walked with a cane, and her black dress hung loose on her frame. From time to time, she covered a mouthful of bad teeth with her hand when she spoke.

"*Eh bien,*" she said, once he was inside the foyer, "hang your coat on the rack next to the door."

Georges-Henri removed his scarf and gloves, then slid out of his damp overcoat and hung it on the hook.

Clara motioned to him to enter the salon. The house gave off a musty scent.

"*Asseyez-vous,*" she said indicating for him to sit on an antique, brocade-upholstered loveseat that was tattered and worn.

She sat on a straight-backed chair opposite.

He looked around the dim room. A lamp on a small writing desk in the corner provided the only light, and an open book sat on a rectangular footed ottoman between them. No cat, crazy or otherwise, in sight.

"Now, Monsieur…Delacroix," she said, closely studying his face. "Paul Delcroix's son?"

"Oui, Madame. *Le connaissez-vous?*" Do you know him?

She cleared her throat, ignoring his question. "Joachim said you have seen Marielle recently?"

"Oui. In May, Madame," he said, wondering how much Joachim had told her in his letter.

Clara showed no reaction.

"I…I don't know where to begin," he continued awkwardly.

"Begin wherever you wish," she said in a low voice. "I have all the time in the world."

He tried to smile. "I realize Marielle never told you about me."

She clucked her tongue. "Oh, *mais* Monsieur. She did."

Had he heard that right? "She told you?"

She nodded.

"We were engaged. Did she tell you that?"

She looked at him. "I knew about the baby, too. Does that surprise you?"

He scratched his head. "Well, to be honest, oui."

She studied her hands. "My husband didn't know. She and I…it was our secret. She wanted to keep the baby." She looked at him. "Mind you. We didn't agree. Our plan was to wait until we were in Argentina to decide what to do. That night at Docteur Yves's…I…I decided it was best…for both of us…to just let her go her own way."

Georges-Henri's stomach churned at the woman's words. The coldness in her eyes, and the unemotional tone of her voice, explained why she hadn't tried to look for Marielle after the war. She hadn't wanted to find her.

"I know what happened," he said finally. "Joachim wrote to me about your testimony at the trial."

She took off her glasses. Her face was drained, and her eyes were clouded over. "I didn't expect to come forward, but I felt obligated after I read that Docteur Yves had been charged with murdering both my husband and me. You see," she wiped her glasses with her skirt, "as far as anyone knew, I was Clara Franck. My family was from Poland." She paused. "Drohobycz. None of them are left now. Out of over fifty people, I am the only one who survived the war." She shook her head. "I tried to find them afterward. My childhood friends, too. Everyone I knew there. Wiped out." She made a fist, and her voice rose. "Every single one of them. Murdered."

He nodded. "We don't have to discuss it if you prefer not to."

She leaned against the back of her chair and closed her eyes.

"Your daughter is alive, Madame," Georges-Henri said, hoping to soften her.

"So Joachim informed me," she said, opening her eyes. She put her glasses back on. "Would you like some tea?"

"That would be very nice."

She rose slowly, painfully, picked up her cane, and shuffled through an arched doorway. Beyond it was a small dining room. A china hutch, its shelves mostly bare, sat against the far wall and a crystal chandelier hung above an oval table covered with a crocheted table cloth.

Georges-Henri thought about what she'd said. There was no question the war had deeply affected her. She'd lost everything. But she had tried to find her family in Poland. Why hadn't she tried to find her daughter?

She returned with a tray and set it on the ottoman next to the open book. Georges-Henri watched her pour the tea into two china cups. The steam gave off the scent of oranges and cinnamon.

"Don't you want to know about the child?" he asked.

She put one of the cups on a saucer and handed it over. Then she took her own and sat back in her chair.

He waited for her answer.

Finally, she said. "It wasn't yours, you know." Her face was drawn and white.

Georges-Henri felt his pulse race, and a sickening knot form in his stomach. "What makes you say that?"

A half smile. "Marielle was raped by a German soldier."

Georges-Henri glared at her in disbelief.

Clara took a sip of her tea. "Actually, more than one of them..." Though her eyes were full of hate, the tone of her voice was flat, unemotional.

His hand shaking, he put his cup and saucer down on the ottoman. "Go on," he said, dreading what was coming next.

"She was stopped in the street one night." A shrug. "She thought she was going to be killed, but they let her go afterward. It wasn't long before she knew."

Marielle had never told him she was with child. He'd only learned that piece of information from Joachim after the war was over. "How do you know this is true? That she was..." He couldn't say the word.

She sat back in her chair. "You don't believe me, do you?"

He shook his head. Odile was his baby. He felt it. This woman was crazy.

"I don't blame you." She heaved a heavy sigh. "It's the story she told me. I wouldn't have been any more sympathetic if she'd admitted you were the father. I yelled at her, called her a whore. We argued terribly. I told her that if she had that baby after we were in Argentina, she wouldn't be welcome in our home ever again." She put her head in her hands. "In reality, I was no better than she was."

"What do you mean?"

She sighed again. "I never forgave him."

"Who, Madame?"

"Those eyes of his. Staring out all the time from that window." She looked up. "What right did he have to tell me what to do with my child? Our child."

This was absurd. Perhaps the woman really had gone mad in the concentration camp. "I…I don't understand. What are you talking about, Madame?"

She blinked. "Why, Marielle's father, of course."

"You knew Marielle's father?" he asked. "I thought she was an orphan you and your husband adopted?"

She sat for several seconds as if in a trance. Finally, she said, "I'm not sure why I am telling you this. I meant to go to my grave having never told a soul. Not even Marielle."

Georges-Henri felt a chill run down his spine.

"I was young, and adventuresome," Clara went on. "Paris in the 1920s was exciting. Dancing. Jazz clubs." A sparkle appeared in her eyes, then faded. "When we met, I fell immediately in love with him. He was so handsome, so debonair. We had such fun together." She sighed. "I knew he was married, but it didn't matter. I became his mistress."

"We took trips together, to the Côte d'Azur. On one such trip, our last, I discovered I was with child. He said I had to get rid of it. Then he told me he never wanted to see me again, and he left."

Her eyes grew cold. "I drove up into the hills, found a convent, and begged the nuns to allow me to stay with them until the baby was born. They said it was a girl. I told them I didn't want to see her. Then I returned to Paris."

Georges-Henri listened, his heart pounding.

"Years passed. I met and married my husband, Émile. We settled happily into an apartment in the Marais, but something was missing—we wanted to have a family.

"It became increasingly clear as time went by that we couldn't conceive. Émile was convinced it couldn't possibly be him." She clucked her tongue.

"One day, out of the blue, he suggested we adopt. I was surprised, but I agreed. I said I didn't want a newborn. I want a child a bit older, I told him, one young enough that we can raise in our faith." She finished her tea and set down her cup. "I was thinking of the child I'd abandoned. I had never told him about her. She would be five years old by then. Maybe there was a chance she was still in Provence.

"My husband readily agreed, so I told him about a convent I had heard of in the village of Les Moulins. The nuns, I said, were known to help find children for parents who wanted to adopt. He didn't question how I knew about it.

"We traveled south that spring and drove into the hills north of Nice. I had written to the Reverend Mother that we were coming and hoped to adopt the baby I had left behind. I didn't know if my child was still there, mind you, but I warned her not to divulge my secret.

"Émile was delighted with the darling girl the nuns called Marielle. He liked the name so we decided to keep it. The Reverend Mother assured me privately that all records up to the moment we arrived would be destroyed. The story we agreed on was that the baby was a foundling left at the convent gate in 1925. She kept her word. We took our daughter back to Paris and raised her as our own."

"You never told Marielle the truth?" Georges-Henri asked.

Clara shook her head. "She never suspected." She swept a loose strand of gray hair from her forehead.

Georges-Henri studied the woman's face. Other than the high forehead, there wasn't any resemblance that he could see between her and Marielle.

She rose, put their empty cups and saucers on the tray and disappeared into the back of the house.

The sun had set, and the salon was chilly. Georges-Henri got up to stoke a dying log in the fireplace. When the fire came to life, he picked up a box of matches and lit two candles sitting on the mantel.

Clara returned with a shawl wrapped around her shoulders. "The Parisian winter has arrived," she said as she sat down again.

Georges-Henri leaned against the mantel. "Did your husband ever learn the truth about Marielle?"

She pulled her shawl tightly around her and shook her head. "I couldn't let him ever find out."

Georges-Henri raised his eyebrows. "What about Marielle's real father?"

Her eyes narrowed and she wrinkled her nose in disgust. "*Ce fils de pute!*"

The expletive stunned Georges-Henri. He asked, "Is he still alive?"

She shrugged. "I never forgave him. It was a lesson for me. Don't let a man tell you what to do, I told myself. Never...ever...again, I vowed, would I allow that to happen. Then the war came..." She put her face in the palms of her hands. "Please leave," she said. "Now. And don't ever return."

Georges-Henri didn't know what to do. Finally, he left her in the salon, put on his coat and scarf in the foyer, and opened the front door.

A cat sat on the doorstep. Startled, it hissed at him and slipped through the door just before he closed it. He shook his head. *Le chat lunatique. Crazy. Just like its owner.*

The rain had quit. He lifted the latch, let himself out the gate, and stood in the dimly lit lane staring at Clara Rosen's house for a very long time.

He was trembling, but not from the cold. She'd asked if he was Paul Delacroix's son.

Chapter Twenty-seven

It was late when Georges-Henri returned to avenue Mozart. The trains were running on a limited schedule for the holiday, and the stormy weather had contributed to more delays. When he finally walked in, only his sister was up. Paul and the children were already in bed.

"Where have you been?" Hélène asked. "I was worried."

"Exploring. Anything left from dinner? I haven't eaten all day and I'm starving." He removed his coat. "Plus, I want to ask you a question."

Hélène nodded. "There is some soup. Potage Crécy. I made it this afternoon. And a baguette."

"Whatever you have. *Merci*, Hélène."

"Serve yourself a glass of wine while I heat it up." She turned to go into the kitchen. "I'll be right back."

When she returned with his meal, she poured herself a snifter of cognac and sat down at the table with him. "Now. You said you have a question?"

He picked up his spoon and stirred the soup. "Did Papa ever have a mistress that you know of?"

She looked at the ceiling and laughed. "Why on earth do you ask me that, Georges-Henri?"

"Because you're older than I am, Hélène."

Her neck stiffened. "Well, not that much older. We're not quite five years apart."

"I thought...sorry." He set down his spoon, picked up his glass of wine, and took a sip. "Please. You must remember something. Was he away from Paris often, for example? Did Maman and Papa argue a lot?"

"*Beh*, the only recollection I have from my really young years is when we went to the château for a time. There was an old donkey I adored named François."

"Do you remember when? Was it before I was born?"

"As a matter of fact," she said after a few seconds, "I couldn't have been older than four."

"Was it just you and Maman or did Papa go there also?"

"Just Maman and me. I remember Maman crying about something, and then we left Paris suddenly. I didn't understand what was going on, or why Papa wasn't with us.

"How long were you there?"

"I don't recall. Weeks. I remember asking for him. Maman cried every time I asked, so I quit asking."

"Didn't you wonder what he was doing?"

She shook her head. "I was too young to understand things like that." She paused as if in thought, then continued. "He came for us eventually. Maman seemed content to have him back, and we returned to Paris. Before I knew it, I had a baby brother." She took another sip of cognac and patted his hand. "In her delirium, years later when she was dying...I was about fourteen by then... Maman told me something of what had happened. He had taken a woman with him on his so-called business trips. She supposed she was his mistress. They'd gone to the south of France."

"I'm surprised she told you," he said.

"Her mind was in a haze. I think she believed she was talking to her sister Béatrice, not me." She sighed. "I haven't thought of that in years." She squinted at him accusingly. "You didn't answer my question. Why do you ask now?"

Georges-Henri drained his glass of wine and poured himself another. "He's never revealed much about himself to me."

Hélène thought for a moment. "It was common, you know, for men to have mistresses in the twenties." She clucked her tongue in disgust. "Papa was a good father. That's all I cared about. However he chose to lead his life wasn't any of my business." She shrugged and got up to clear the dishes. "By the way, I quite forgot. The concierge brought a letter for you earlier. She said it was delivered to the building next door yesterday by mistake. I left it on your end table."

Georges-Henri finished his soup and drained the second glass of wine. Then he bid Hélène *bonne nuit* and went to his room.

The letter was from Bernard. It was full of news about the cottage and the changes that had been made to it. Odile was doing well with the new glasses, too, he wrote. Thanks to Georges-Henri's generosity, they'd found a specialist who said he could help correct the vision in her one good eye.

Then, at the end:

We want you to come for Noël, Marielle, Odile, Maman and I. For the first time, we are making a chocolate crèche to put in the window of the shop. It will be spectacular. All the figures are completely made of chocolate in various shades.

And I, I am to be Père Noël in the village pageant. Odile is to be a little angel (which she is).

Georges-Henri felt a catch in his throat at the thought of Odile in an angel's costume. He read on.

Will you come? Your cottage is livable now. There is a nice big fireplace in the salon, and I have installed a stove and a small ice box in the kitchen. I will make sure you have cooking utensils, and a bed with a warm duvet, too. My mother has a friend who shops the marché for antique furniture. She's agreed to look for a table and chairs for you.

Georges-Henri read then reread the final sentence: *Marielle and I send our love.* He pinched the bridge of his nose. His eyes stung.

Before he turned out the light, he went over to his desk and wrote a note to Bernard saying he would depart when the fall term ended. Then, with a heavy heart, he lay down on his bed, but sleep never came.

All night, he thought about what Clara had told him. Had Paul Delacroix been her lover? And Odile. Was she his daughter, or a German bastard child? Marielle's last words rang in his ears. "You are not, nor will you ever be, her papa."

The next morning, Georges-Henri knocked lightly at his father's door. "Papa? Are you awake?"

He heard a shuffling sound, and then the door opened. Though he was getting older, Paul's eyes were clear, and they twinkled as though he were up to some mischief. "Of course," he said cheerfully. "I'm always up early, you know that." He tied his robe at his waist and pulled the door open wider. "Come in, *mon fils*. To what do I owe this unusual visit to start off my day?"

Georges-Henri entered the warm room. It had been a while since he'd been in there, but not much had changed. A large canopy-covered bed took up most of the space. The walls were covered in blue-and-cream striped wallpaper, a huge gold-framed painting hung above a wooden writing desk in the corner, and two comfortable brocade-covered armchairs flanked the fireplace. The mannequin known as Signalé sat by the closed French windows, as always posed as if staring out at the view of the Eiffel Tower in the distance.

"It's a gray day," Paul said as he glanced out the window. "At least the storm from yesterday is done." He went over to the glowing fireplace, turned to stand regally with his back to the fire, and raised his eyebrows, as if anticipating Georges-Henri's next words.

"Papa, I have learned some information recently that I'd like to ask you about."

His father nodded.

"Did you ever have a mistress?"

It had come out so suddenly that Georges-Henri surprised himself. "I mean, would you recommend it?" he stuttered, "If, after one is married, and…" He shrugged and smiled. "I…um…I thought you could possibly give me some advice on the subject."

"I'm not an expert," Paul laughed.

Georges-Henri looked at him. "So you never…"

His father picked up his pipe from the mantel and tamped down the tobacco. "I didn't say that, *mon fils*."

Paul lit his pipe and took a puff. Georges-Henri remained silent. The scent of sweet-burning tobacco filled the air. "I did have…one…"

he said finally. He studied his pipe. "A long time ago. It didn't work out." He glanced sideways at Georges-Henri. "I wouldn't recommend it. Too much trouble."

Georges-Henri faked a laugh. "Do you recall her name? What she looked like?"

Paul drew on his pipe again and stared into the fire as if remembering something. "She was a pretty young thing. But, alas, she dumped me for my best friend." He chuckled. "And, unfortunately, he got her pregnant."

"Not a good outcome. What happened then?"

"I don't know." He shrugged. "I imagine he learned a good lesson."

"And you?"

"I'd already made up my mind it wasn't worth it. I loved your maman."

"You never had anyone else? Another mistress, that is?"

His father shook his head. He went over to the Signalé. "This is my mistress." He smiled. "Look here." He beckoned to Georges-Henri to come closer. He shook the mannequin fiercely; it made a high-ringing sound like metal pieces hitting against each other. "Hear the chink of the coins?" His eyes twinkled. "The Signalé is our bank."

Georges-Henri smiled. "Are you sure it's safe? I thought you said you'd found a secure hiding place?"

"Bah! No one would ever think to look inside a tattered dressmaker's mannequin. Especially when it sits in an old man's bedchamber."

Georges-Henri studied his father for a moment. "You didn't say what the name of your mistress was, Papa. Surely you must remember?"

His father furrowed his brow. "Why is it important?"

"Just curious."

"Well, if you must know, her name was Nathalie."

Georges-Henri breathed a sigh of relief. "I was afraid you were going to tell me her name was Clara," he said with a nervous laugh.

His father's eyes grew big as saucers. His face drained of color, and he dropped his pipe.

Georges-Henri rushed to him. "Papa? Are you ill?"

Southern France
December 1950

Chapter Twenty-eight

Georges-Henri and Jacquie stood over Marielle's grave. The air was suddenly chilly, and Jacquie shivered. "What do you mean? If only you'd told Marielle what truth?"

He cleared his throat and checked his watch. "We should be getting back to the cottage."

She placed her hand on his arm. "Wait. Why won't you tell me more? What didn't you tell Marielle?"

"It is a long tale." He kissed the back of her hand. "And not a happy one."

"Because she died?"

He looked at her with sad eyes. "I want to show you something very special."

He led her along a gravel walkway lined on both sides by tall Italian stone pines. The sunlight, filtering through the trees, cast feathery shadows over the path. Jacquie slowed, lifted her camera and began fidgeting with the settings.

Georges-Henri waited while she snapped several pictures. When she had finished, she turned her camera on him and shot a close-up.

He frowned but said nothing.

The tall pine pathway led them to a quiet knoll where there were dozens of grave markers spaced only a few inches apart.

"This is what I wanted you to see," Georges-Henri said finally. "It's called *Le Jardin des Innocents*."

"The Garden of Innocents?"

"Oui. It's dedicated to all the abandoned babies who have been left at the convent gate over the decades. I wanted, in some way, to memorialize them. Most died before they were even given a name."

"You? You did all this?"

He nodded. "With Bernard's help, and the nuns who live here. We established this graveyard in the summer of 1947, six months after Marielle passed. Most had no identification. Often, they were simply left at the doorstep of the convent. Many had been born prematurely. For years, the nuns put the little bodies in cardboard boxes and buried them outside the convent walls. Until we began this effort, the graves remained unmarked and, sadly, forgotten."

He pointed to a marker in the far corner. "For example, Anne. Our first. We dug up her box and placed it in a handmade wooden coffin with a pink rose from the convent garden. Then the nuns arranged a proper burial service." He wiped his nose.

They sat on a wrought iron bench placed next to the grave. The marker took Jacquie by surprise. "Anne Franck? After the author of the book?"

"No. The book hadn't come out yet. This baby had been stillborn to a woman by the name of Clara Franck. Clara had arrived at the convent in 1925 seeking refuge. After the birth, she refused to know anything about the baby. She returned to Paris, and later married."

"Married the baby's father?"

"No. A Jewish man named Émile Rosen. The marriage remained barren until, one day, they decided to adopt. Thinking her baby would be still be living here in the convent, Clara had the idea that they could adopt the child, although she never told her husband she had had a baby before she met him."

"She didn't know her baby had been stillborn?"

He shook his head. "Apparently, no. Clara and Émile traveled to Les Moulins. It was only when they arrived here that she learned the truth."

Jacquie's eyes stung. "They didn't adopt after all?"

"There's more. Clara was told a healthy baby girl had been left at the gate around the same time as her baby had been born. The child was five by then and remained an orphan. Clara apparently seized on the opportunity. She insisted the records be altered to reflect that the child was hers. My guess is she donated a good deal of money to the convent too, because the Reverend Mother allowed them to take the child with them. As it happened, the documents were never altered or destroyed, and the originals remained stored, untouched for years, in the convent's underground vault."

"How do you know all this?"

He smiled and squeezed her hand. "I told you it was a long tale. Four years ago, I accidentally learned that the woman who adopted Marielle had had a baby here. She'd been involved in an affair with a married man."

"A mistress?" Jacquie could hear Claudie saying, "I told you that was what Frenchmen are all about."

"Oui. Unfortunately," Georges-Henri hesitated. "There's more. His name…" he paused again, "was Paul Delacroix."

Jacquie gasped. "No! Your father?"

He nodded. "Regrettably. In 1946, after I learned Clara was still alive and living in Paris, I went to see her." He tapped his index finger against his temple. "She didn't seem quite right in the head, mind you. Her husband had died during the war, and she had been in a concentration camp. She told me about a baby she had given birth to here in this convent, a baby she insisted she and her husband had later adopted."

"Marielle?"

He went on. "They adopted Marielle, yes, but she wasn't Clara's baby. She had lied to me. The summer after Marielle's death, Mother Marguerite and I spent hours poring over the massive number of records stored in the convent's vault. That was when we discovered the truth. Thankfully, an ancient nun was still living who remembered Clara and was able to confirm that Clara's baby had been stillborn. She told us she had assisted in the birth in 1925." He pinched the bridge of his nose. "I should have told Marielle I had found her adoptive mother, but I couldn't. I thought it best to let her continue to believe the woman who had adopted and raised her had died during the war."

"I don't understand. Wouldn't Marielle have wanted to see her mother, if she had known?"

He sighed. "Perhaps. Marielle had been through so much. I wanted to spare her more heartbreak. I couldn't tell her I knew Clara had made no attempt to find her after the war. It was obvious to me she didn't want to see her daughter again."

"Did you ever tell her mother that Marielle had died?"

"I wrote a letter. It came back to me in the post a month later. Someone had written on the front. Moved. Address unknown."

"That's all? You just left it at that? Didn't you even try to find her?"

He shook his head.

"How could you, Georges-Henri?"

He looked at his watch, stood, and pulled her to her feet. "We'd better get back to the cottage now."

Jacquie smoothed her skirt. She wasn't getting through to him. It was obvious this man had a hard crust. She would have tried to get Marielle and her mother back together. A mother and daughter reunited. She shook her head. The French culture was becoming more and more difficult for her to understand. Georges-Henri, especially so.

As they walked away, he pointed to a rose arbor in the corner. "I've arranged for a statue of Marielle to be placed in there," he said. "It's being done by a local artisan. And there will be a small plaque by the entrance dedicating the garden to her. Bernard and I are planning to have it all completed by next summer when the nuns inaugurate their first *Festival de Chocolat* to announce their new business."

"So that's why Bernard is teaching them to make chocolate."

He nodded. "It will help fund the upkeep of the garden. And allow new burials. The nuns are accepting bodies of children who are still being discovered in the battlefields and villages. Most, like these," he swept his eyes over the knoll, "died without ever being identified."

"How sad," Jacquie said wishing she could show more emotion. But it was the way she truly felt. Sad. It was clear Georges-Henri would never stop loving Marielle, and his vision with this cemetery was his alone. She realized at that moment that she'd never be able to share it with him.

The sun was low in the winter sky. They left the cemetery and walked back toward the main square. As they passed the fountain, a tall man exited the chocolaterie carrying a string shopping bag and a bottle of wine.

"Ah," Georges-Henri said, "We are just in time. There's Bernard just leaving for the cottage now."

Bernard closed the door to the shop and came toward them.

Georges-Henri introduced Jacquie.

"*Enchanté, Mademoiselle.* Bernard Miniet."

She took the chocolatier's hand. A large hand. Warm. His brown eyes radiated warmth, too. She liked him immediately.

"*Parle pas anglais, Mademoiselle,*" Bernard said with a shrug. "*Un mot ici et là. C'est tout.*"

Jacquie grinned at him. He spoke only a few words of English. She would be forced to speak French to him. Hélène would approve.

"*Où est Odile?*" Georges-Henri asked.

Bernard inhaled a breath. "*Malheureusement,* Odile has come down with a cold." He turned to look to the apartment above the shop; a light shone in the window. "*Ma mère* won't allow her to go out. She insists she needs to be put to bed early." He looked at Jacquie. "Since my wife died, we are very fearful of any illness."

Jacquie pondered what to say, but, in the end, she just nodded.

"You will come, anyway, won't you?" Georges-Henri asked, looking disappointed. "I want you to meet Duff."

Bernard lifted the bottle of wine. "*Bien sûr, mon ami.* I'll have a glass of burgundy with you, too, but I won't be able to stay long."

"Your chocolates are excellent," Jacquie said in French. "Georges-Henri gave me a box of them when I arrived. I'm afraid I've eaten them all."

Bernard smiled at her. "*Eh bien,* it's a good thing, then, that I've included *mendiants* in my shopping bag."

"His *spécialité,*" Georges-Henri added, "and my favorite."

"There's also a tarte au chocolat in here for later, *mon ami*," Bernard said, handing the bag to him.

When the three entered the cottage, Duff was sitting in the salon in front of a roaring fire in the fireplace. "There y'all are," he said in English. "I've been wonderin' what kept you." He rose from his chair and shot a dimpled grin towards Jacquie. "Looks like you found Georges-Henri."

"Indeed, I did." She set down her camera and took off her coat. "In the cemetery at the convent. Of all places."

Duff raised his eyebrows.

"Bernard doesn't speak much English," Georges-Henri warned.

Duff winked at Jacquie. "Do you think he'll understand my French?"

She laughed. "Not a chance with that accent."

Chapter Twenty-nine

The flames crackled and danced in the grate. Bernard whipped a cork-screw from his pocket, the kind vintners used, with a little knife attached, and deftly opened the bottle of burgundy. "I no can *rester* long," he said.

Rester, to stay. Jacquie smiled at his feeble attempt to put together an English sentence.

Georges-Henri went over to an antique china hutch, took out four wineglasses, and set them on the table. Bernard poured one for each of them.

"Odile is ill with a cold," Georges-Henri explained. "Unfortunately, our plans for the evening have changed. We'll have to wait until she's well enough to set out the crèche."

Duff lifted his drink. "To Odile. *À* Odile."

They clicked their glasses. "À la s*anté*! To health!"

Georges-Henri picked up the string bag Bernard had brought and carried it through the arched door. "Duff," he called from the kitchen a second later. "What is all this?"

"I got hungry," Duff said. "I couldn't help it. That empty icebox got to me." He winked at Jacquie. "When y'all didn't come back right away, I jumped in the Panhard and went for a little drive. I checked out the other villages around and found a few... er... items."

"I've got to see this," Jacquie said as she headed into the kitchen.

Georges-Henri was standing in front of a counter loaded with food. There were two baguettes, an entire ham, a bag of oranges, a huge round of cheese, dried sausages, and tins of paté and sardines. "He's bought enough to feed the entire village," he exclaimed.

Duff came through the archway followed by Bernard. "I thought, since it's Christmas," he said, "we ought to have enough fix-ins for a real Texas-size celebration." He turned to Bernard. "*N'est-ce pas*, Bernard?"

Bernard chuckled and raised his glass of wine. "*Pourquoi pas?*"

"That's not all I found," Duff went on. He grabbed Jacquie's hand and pulled her out the back door.

"What on earth?" she protested. "It's cold out here."

Georges-Henri and Bernard followed.

"Just give a lookie here." Duff pointed to a tall cut evergreen leaning against the wall next to the door. "I've found us a Christmas tree."

"It's huge. However, did you get it here?" Jacquie asked.

Duff laughed. "It took great finesse, I tell ya. I put the top down and drove with one hand on the steering wheel and the other holding the blasted tree against the wind." He held up two fingers. "Twice, it almost tumbled down the steep hillside."

She lifted a branch to her nose and sniffed the fresh pine scent. "What do we decorate it with?"

"There was this small shop in Le Cabrier. I think that was the name. I got some little metal candle holders that you clip on." He grinned and looked at Georges-Henri. "I guess that's a tradition around here?"

"It is," Georges-Henri said.

"I hope you don't mind, then?"

"*Non non. Pas du tout.* Odile will be thrilled."

"Oh, Duff," Jacquie said as they hurried back inside. "You really thought of everything. I feel bad that I don't have any gifts to put under the tree, though."

"No problem. I was going to propose we drive to Nice tomorrow." He draped his arm around her shoulders. She tried to pull away from him but he held firm. "We can do some sightseeing, shop, and have a bite to eat." He looked at Georges-Henri. "How 'bout it, *mon ami?* You want to go along with us?"

Georges-Henri's eyes focused on Duff playfully squeezing Jacquie's shoulders. "I...I wouldn't want to interrupt anything..."

Jacquie poked an elbow into Duff's ribs.

Duff winced and abruptly dropped his arm. "Sorry," he said.

"I like the idea," she said. "Odile might like a doll."

Bernard seemed to understand. He smiled. "Doll," he said in English. "*Elle adore les poupées.*"

"Then it's all set," Duff said. "Now, *mes amis*, let's eat."

Bernard didn't leave right away after all. He stayed to feast on the food, and afterward, he helped Duff and Georges-Henri haul the huge tree into the salon. It reached almost to the high-beamed ceiling.

They clipped the little metal holders to the branches and lit the candles.

"It's gorgeous," Jacquie declared, as she sat back on the sofa and sipped another glass of wine. This time a local rosé Duff had found at a wine shop during his afternoon shopping trip. "It all was so thoughtful of you, Duff. Wasn't it, Georges-Henri?"

Georges-Henri rubbed his neck and finally conceded that it was indeed.

It occurred to Jacquie that Georges-Henri had been gone all day, but he hadn't said anything to her about where he'd been or what he'd been up to. It was obvious he hadn't been preparing for their so-called party that evening.

After Bernard bid them *bonne nuit* and departed, Georges-Henri collected the wineglasses and went into the kitchen. He had been moody all evening, and Jacquie wondered if it was because Duff had paid a lot of attention to her—refilling her plate and wineglass, reminding her of the sights they'd seen on their trip south. She sniffed. Duff had been more attentive to her than had Georges-Henri.

With Georges-Henri out of the room, she seized the opportunity. "Duff," she said. "I want to get something straight between us."

He turned to her, wide-eyed.

"I would appreciate it if you...um...would back off a bit. I know you mean well, but..."

He put his hands on his hips. "I get it. You don't want Georges-Henri to have any competition? Am I right?"

"Not exactly. It's just that...did you have to be so...so...forward?"

"Forward?" He glared at her. "Ah, don't have a cow. I didn't mean anything by it. It's the way I am."

At that moment, Georges-Henri came back into the salon. He looked at Jacquie, who felt her face flush, and then to Duff who faked a yawn. "I'm one tuckered-out cowboy," he said. "It's been a great evening, Georges-Henri. I'm heading to bed." He gave a little wave and turned to go without looking at Jacquie. "See y'all in the morning."

Jacquie heaved a sigh. Maybe she shouldn't have said anything.

"We should put out the candles on the tree before they burn down much farther," Georges-Henri said, apparently oblivious to what had taken place just then.

"I'll do it." She rose from the sofa, picked up the long-handled black metal candle snuffer, and began working her way up from the bottom of the tree.

"You didn't say where you were all day," she ventured, concentrating on her task and keeping her back to him.

Georges-Henri remained silent.

"Duff and I played a game of cribbage until the mistral quit," she went on. "When you didn't return, I decided to take a walk and explore a bit." She glanced sideways wondering if he had fallen asleep. He was leaning forward with his elbows on his knees staring into the fire. "I think I got some good pictures with my new camera. I hope they turn out…"

She finished snuffing out the candles. The room was filled with smoke. Exasperated, she sat down again beside him. "What's bothering you, Georges-Henri?"

He looked over at her and sighed. "I'm sorry. I was just thinking about something."

"About Marielle?"

"*Non*."

"What then?"

"I received a wire earlier. From Hélène. Papa had a heart attack after they arrived at the château. She wants me to come to Normandy immediately."

"Is it serious? Will you go?"

"I don't know. Hélène will let me know. He has seemed quite well since the first one he had four years ago."

Jacquie tried to think of something sympathetic to say, but it was no use. Her view of Paul had changed since Georges-Henri had told her that afternoon about the mistress. She wondered briefly if Hélène knew. Somehow, she didn't think she'd approve. It occurred to her that Claudine would love hearing this juicy piece of gossip when she returned to France. She could hardly wait to tell her.

"What were you doing all day?" she asked. "You still haven't answered my question."

"I was arranging for Odile to attend a special boarding school for blind and partially blind children," he said. "It's close by, in Nice, so she can return here on weekends. Bernard is in favor of it. We believe it will do her good to be with children her age who have the same needs."

"How does Odile feel about it? I'd be terrified if I were in her place."

He looked at her. "Why does it matter how she feels about it? She's too young to understand what's good for her."

Jacquie tucked her legs under her and shifted her body so she could face him. "At six years old, I would think she'd at least have an opinion."

He stared into the fire. "Perhaps," he said finally.

"Who made the decisions for you when you were that age?"

"Papa, certainement."

"What about your mother?"

He shrugged as if the woman's viewpoint hadn't counted.

"Hum…I wonder what Simone de Beauvoir would have to say about that?" Jacquie mused. "Do you teach about her in your existentialist course?"

"An occasional reference," a quick wave of his hand as if he'd already dismissed the idea, "when her connection to Sartre comes up."

"Connection? She was his partner." Frustrated, Jacquie wanted to point out his equal, too. "You should make her book, *Le Deuxième Sexe*, required reading, if you ask me. Do you have any female students in your class?"

"A few."

"Well, then. I think you should do it. For their sake." She got up and stood over him. "And you should ask Odile whether she wants to attend that school in Nice. It's a new world, Georges-Henri. She should be given a say in her future."

It was the wine talking, she realized, but after reading de Beauvoir's new book, she couldn't help herself.

Minutes went by. Jacquie went over and stood by the window. A bright moon hung over the dark lake, casting a glow on the water.

"I'll do it," he mumbled under his breath after several long minutes.

Jacquie swung around to look at him. "What?"

"I'll add the book to the required reading for the spring trimester. I think Professor André will go along with that. He likes new thinking to challenge the students." He rose from the sofa and stood beside her. "But I have one request."

"What's that?"

"Will you come to the class one day and speak about de Beauvoir?"

"I…I don't know. I'm not really qualified," she said. "I've only just finished reading the book. What could I say?"

"What you said just now." He stared into her eyes. "I think you have a lot more to say about the subject."

Jacquie's pulse quickened. "Do you mean it?"

He wrapped his arms around her. She felt the tenderness of his breath gracing her cheek, the warmth of his body next to hers. "When I return to Paris," he said, "we will need to meet, of course, several times... for...lunch...at Brasserie Balzar." He kissed the top of her head and added, "to go over our discussion notes, of course."

"In that case, I accept," she said, nestling her face against his shoulder. "And will you consult with Odile about the school?" She looked up at him. "Please, Georges-Henri, promise me you'll ask her."

He played with her hair. "It will be up to Bernard. He is officially her father."

"But I thought...aren't you her father?"

He put his finger next to her lips. "That is a story for another day, chérie." He kissed her neck, then he kissed her again—a lingering, passionate kiss on the lips that took her breath away.

Chapter Thirty

When Jacquie went to bed that night, it wasn't the noisy mistral that kept her awake. She was in Georges-Henri's bedroom. The bed beneath her was his bed. His scent clung to the duvet. A mix of lavender and musk. Feeling his indentation in the mattress, she rolled onto her hip, fitted herself into it and tried to imagine his arms around her.

The house was quiet. Georges-Henri was next door, in the room he used as an office. Duff was in the third bedroom down the hall.

Nerves skittering, she rose and tiptoed over to open the door. Moonlight shone into the hall through the French windows. Walking quietly on the balls of her feet, she crept the short distance to the office door.

Touching the handle, she hesitated, took a deep breath, opened the door slowly, and poked her head inside. "Are you awake?" she whispered.

He lay on the narrow sofa reading a book in the light of a dim floor lamp. One arm rested behind his head against his pillow. A blanket covered his chest and legs. He looked up at her, concerned. "Jacquie? Is everything all right?"

"Can I come in," she said softly, "just for a few minutes to get warmed up? I...I'm cold."

He closed his book and put it on the table beside the sofa. Then he smiled and slid back his blanket, inviting her to join him.

She closed the door and tiptoed over to climb into his waiting arms.

"Are you sure everything is all right?" he asked again.

She rested her head on his shoulder, gazed into his eyes. "I was going to ask you the same."

He ran his hand across her cheek, then down her chin and neck. Her heart picked up speed as his fingers trailed over the shoulder of her nightgown and the bare stretch of her arm. Through his undershirt, she could feel his heart beating. Reaching up, he switched off the lamp. "*Bonne nuit, chérie,*" he said, settling back under the blanket with his arms around her. "Are you warm now?" he asked.

She cuddled against him. "Oui."

At the crack of dawn, Jacquie woke with a start. Georges-Henri was asleep, breathing softly against her forehead. She wished briefly they could spend the entire day cuddled like this. But Duff was down the hall; she couldn't risk being seen coming from Georges-Henri's room in broad daylight. Without wakening Georges-Henri, she slipped out of his arms and returned to the room next door.

His room. With his lingering scent. Feeling happy, she settled back into his bed, pulled the duvet up to her nose, and dozed off.

An hour later, a loud pounding at the cottage's front door woke her. She rose and put on her robe and slippers. Sunlight streamed in through the French doors. As she padded down the hallway, she could hear talking.

Duff and Georges-Henri were in the kitchen, both of them looking groggy and disheveled.

"What is it?" she asked. "Has something happened?"

"Another wire arrived just now from Hélène," Georges-Henri said. His voice cracked. "It's Papa."

"Paul?"

"He passed away last night."

She went to him and put her hand on his shoulder. "I'm so sorry," she said, gazing into his eyes. They shared an intimate moment before Duff interrupted them.

"We're driving Georges-Henri to the train station in Nice this morning," he said, explicitly clearing his throat. "We need to leave soon."

"I'll get my things together," she said, pulling her gaze from Georges-Henri's eyes. "I assume we won't be coming back here?"

"I don't know when I'll return," Georges-Henri said with a shrug. "Sorry."

Duff nodded and glanced at Jacquie. "Right. We'll figure out another place to stay after we drop you off at the station. I'll get my valise and meet you at the car in, say, half an hour?"

"I need to write a note to Bernard," Georges-Henri said. "We'll drop it in the box at the chocolaterie on our way."

Jacquie went to her room to pack. She was tempted to offer to go to Normandy with Georges-Henri, but reconsidered. She'd have to find some way to spend the next couple of weeks. Without Duff.

Paris
January 1951

Chapter Thirty-one

"Well, that's the story of my life since you've been away, Claudie," Jacquie said. "It's good to have you back."

"I can't believe so much has happened," Claudine said.

They were in their bedroom, lying on their separate beds and talking to the ceiling. Just as they had in early September when they began their year in Paris.

Claudine sat up. "What I want to know is…" she hesitated, "did you do it with Georges-Henri after all?"

Jacquie glanced over at her roommate. "We had a good cuddle the last night we were together in Provence." She sighed. "The next day he found out about Paul, and we all left. We never got to spend Christmas together, and I never met Odile."

"Wait. Back up. A cuddle? That's all? He's French! I don't believe you!"

Jacquie laughed. "We were in his office. On a sofa."

Claudine frowned. "So what? Don't tell me you didn't at least…"

"It was sweet. We fell asleep. She paused. I…I…"

"What? Tell me, Jacquie." Claudine's eyes were wide.

"It might have been a mistake. I was in the room next door. It was the middle of the night. Maybe it was the wine, but I sneaked into his room, and… Oh, Claudie, I probably shouldn't have…" She covered her eyes with her hands. "I haven't heard from him since." She swallowed hard. "He hasn't even sent me a note since I returned to Paris."

"Hum…Does Hélène know you were in Provence with him? Do you think he told her? If so, she would have put the kibosh on your relationship. Pronto."

Jacquie shook her head. "She thinks I was with my girlfriends in Italy the entire time. Which I mostly was, after…" She rolled over and propped her head on her elbow. "At the Gare de Nice, after we said good-bye to Georges-Henri and his train departed the station, I broke it to Duff that I was going to Italy and he could do what he wanted to for the rest of his holiday break."

"You did? Was he upset?"

"I don't think so. He acted as if it were no big deal. I think he anticipated it, actually."

"Why? I thought you said you two had fun together."

"The trip south was enjoyable. He rented a nice car. He has his good traits. But he can be just too…oh…you know, outrageous sometimes. He got mad when I asked him to back off."

Claudine giggled. "He's American after all. No secret agenda like these Frenchmen. He did say he was going to ask me out again, didn't he?"

Jacquie smiled. "He did. Do you really want to encourage him?"

"For some fun? Absolutely. Trust me. I am not going to fall for him. But," she added, "I'll take a Texan over a Frenchman any day."

Jacquie rose and looked through the frosted window. The sky was gray and a watery sun shone through the branches of the barren trees in the courtyard. She sighed. Compared to the brightness of Italy, Paris was drab in winter, muted. She swiveled around. "We should go dancing tonight, Claudie. How about it? It's time we got all poshed up and had ourselves some fun."

"Who will escort us?"

"We don't need an escort. We're modern girls. Besides, Hélène is so pre-occupied, she won't even notice if we go out. She spends hours in her father's room sorting through his things."

"The room with a view?" Claudine harrumphed. "I hope we will finally get to see it now that he's not...er...using it anymore."

"Right. That reminds me of something. Do you remember that mannequin Théo was so obsessed with?"

"The one he got me into trouble with? When he stole her pearls?"

"The very one." Jacquie could barely contain herself. "Welllll...the day I returned; Hélène was so upset she nearly knocked me over as she came rushing down the stairs. She had just found a fortune in gold coins stuffed inside it."

"Inside what?"

"The mannequin, silly. Her father had apparently hidden them there."

"No!"

"And listen to this...those gold coins spent the war stuffed into the legs of a desk at the château right under the Nazi's noses."

"No one ever discovered them?"

"Apparently not. The only one who knew was Georges-Henri and he kept the secret. Hélène was furious with him for that. And with Théo, too, because he had found the stash by accident and hadn't told her about it either. Remember that day when she dragged him from the table and he was yelling that the Signalé had a secret?"

Claudine laughed. "So that was what that was all about? Where are the coins now?"

"She put them in an old suitcase and took them to a bank. I went with her. Hah. She didn't think she'd be robbed if I was along. Just two women out doing errands. I still can't believe we were living just feet away from hidden treasure and didn't know it."

"Why didn't Paul put them somewhere safer after the war was over?"

"Apparently he didn't trust financial institutions."

"Sounds like my father," Claudine said.

"How is he doing?"

"As well as can be expected. He still has some trouble walking and speaking, but otherwise he's his old feisty self again. Mother hated doing everything for his business, especially handling the books."

"She should continue doing that," Jacquie said. "Men shouldn't be the only ones making the decisions. Women need to step up." She picked up the Simone de Beauvoir book and tossed it on Claudine's bed. "You should read this, Claudie. I'm going to need someone to share ideas with. I've been invited to speak to a class during the spring trimester." She crossed her fingers, hoping Georges-Henri's offer was still good.

"*The Second Sex?*"

"Uh-huh."

Claudine grinned, and her eyes twinkled. "Is it juicy?"

"Not that meaning, Claudine. The opposite sex...women. It's a philosophy, written by the partner, equal that is, of Jean-Paul Sartre, the existentialist. I spotted it in the bookstore one day and couldn't put it down."

Claudine thumbed through the pages. "It's in French," she groaned.

"Not out in English yet, sorry," Jacquie said. "But, even if you don't understand it all, I guarantee it will get you to thinking." She chuckled. "And it won't be long before you'll be encouraging your mother to learn everything she can about the business and to continue helping your father run it."

Claudine put the book on her end table. "I suppose you're right. She saved his butt, and I don't think he's even thought of thanking her."

Jacquie smiled. "Maybe he already knows she's his equal. It's a new world, Claudie. Now, about that jazz club. Where should we go?"

The Elephant Blanc in Montparnasse was crowded, and it smelled of sweaty bodies and cigarette smoke. A thick, blue-gray haze filled the air.

"I hope he's here," Claudine said scanning the mob. All of a sudden, her eyes lit up. "Oh, there he is." She poked Jacquie in the ribs with her elbow and waved. "Over there."

At the far end of the room, Duff was standing with a beer in his hand watching the dancers.

Jacquie groaned. "He looks like he's studying the girls as if he's choosing a rack of lamb at a *boucherie*."

Claudine laughed. "He spotted us. He's coming this way." She patted her hair. "Do I look okay?"

Head and shoulders taller than most of the crowd, the Texan swaggered toward them with a big grin on his face. "Well, I'll be," he said as he fixed his hazel eyes on Claudine. "Welcome back, honey."

Claudine grinned up at him, batting her eyelashes. "I'm still getting my land legs from being on the ocean for a week," she said.

He put one arm around her shoulders, and pulled her in for a hug. "It's sure nice to see y'all. You look terrific." His eyes shifted to Jacquie, and the muscles in his face tensed. "You, too, Jacquie. How was Italy? Did you have a good time?"

Jacquie heard the change in his voice. Distinctly cool. Not that unexpected, given how she'd treated him the last time she saw him. "It was lovely," she said. "How was your trip back to Paris?"

He shrugged. "I stayed in Saint-Tropez for a coupla days. Thinking about things. Ya know. Soaking up the sunshine. Then I drove straight through to Paris. Weather was lousy. Snow. Sleet. All of it. But the Panhard made it." He winked at Claudine. "You should have seen that car. What a beauty!"

Claudine beamed, still snuggled into his embrace. "I'm such a fan of cars of all makes. Perhaps you can rent it again and take me for a spin?" She glanced at Jacquie and cleared her throat. "Us, I mean. Were you here in Paris in time for New Year's, then?"

"Un-huh. A guy I know from the Sorbonne invited me to join him and some friends for the big *Réveillon* dinner at his girlfriend's family's house in Versailles. Huge crowd. Terrific food. Foie gras, oysters, smoked salmon, escargots, champagne. Must have been twenty-five people at the table."

The music started up again. Duff set his beer down. "Come on, sweetheart," he said pulling Claudine with him onto the dance floor. "Let's have a go at the tango."

Jacquie sighed as she watched them work their way through the throng of dancers. She crossed her arms and looked around, feeling suddenly lonesome and insecure and wishing she hadn't come.

"Would you care to dance?" a voice behind her asked.

She swiveled around. Dressed in a dark suit, white shirt, and dark tie, he was standing so close to her she could smell his scent. Her heart skipped a beat. "Georges-Henri? *Quelle surprise*! I thought you were in…"

He swept her into his arms and began to sway to the music. "I'm not good at dancing," he said, "but I wanted to see you." There were so many couples in the room that it didn't matter that they just moved together right where they were.

"I thought you would be back in Provence by now," Jacquie said. "Does Hélène know you are here?"

"No," he said quietly into her ear. "And don't tell her. I'm in Paris briefly to meet with Professor André. When Duff said you and Claudine were going to be here tonight..."

She pulled back. "Wait a second. Duff knew we were coming here? We only just decided an hour or so ago ourselves. Or, rather Claudine did." She narrowed her eyes. "Come to think of it, I was the one who suggested we go dancing, but she insisted we had to go to this club."

He smiled. "I've already said too much."

The music changed to an upbeat jazz tune. Using his left foot as a base, he swung his stiff right leg out like the pencil point of a drafting compass and spun her in a circle.

She laughed. "What do you mean you can't dance, Georges-Henri? That was perfect."

He shrugged. "Simple mechanics. *C'est tout.* Duff gave me the idea, but I didn't know if it would actually work."

"Are you staying with Duff then?"

"No. I've rented an apartment just off Boulevard Saint Germain not far from the university. When I return in the spring, that's where I'll live."

Jacquie felt a pang of guilt. She'd gotten him kicked out of the apartment on avenue Mozart. "Is that why you don't want Hélène to know you're here?"

"Partially. *En tout cas,* I can afford a place of my own now."

Jacquie thought about the gold coins and wondered if he knew his sister had deposited them in a bank.

When the music slowed again, Jacquie peeked over Georges-Henri's shoulder to see where Claudine was. She and Duff were dancing, foreheads together, swaying and talking. Despite what she thought about Duff, Jacquie liked that Claudine looked happy.

"What's your apartment like?" she asked Georges-Henri.

"It's small, above a bookshop. There is a restaurant next door and a boulangerie." He smiled and drew her close to him. "Walking distance to the Brasserie Balzar whenever we want *soupe à l'oignon*, too."

What did he mean by that? Whenever *we* want?

"Sounds perfect," she said. "When can I see it?"

He pressed his cheek close to hers for a second. Then he murmured into her ear, "Tonight, if you like."

Chapter Thirty-two

The bookshop was located on rue de la Parcheminerie, a narrow street in the fifth arrondissement not far from the Quai St. Michel. A sign over the door read: A. Padoue, Bouquiniste, Livres Anciens et Modernes

"My apartment is above the bookstore," Georges-Henri said as they descended from the taxi. He pointed to a balcony with a curved wrought iron railing on the first floor.

Jacquie tried to see into the bookstore's window. "It's so dark I can't see inside."

"You will like it. It's small and narrow," he said. "Very cozy. There are stacks of antiquarian books everywhere. Shelves filled all the way to the high ceiling. Monsieur Padoue, the owner, is eccentric, but you'll find him likable. He fought with the Résistance during the war. I rent the apartment from him."

Georges-Henri took her hand and led her to a heavy wooden door next to the bookshop's entrance.

She stepped into a darkened entryway. The space reeked of onions and garlic from the restaurant next door. Jacquie recognized the faint odor of something else. Urine. She'd grown accustomed to the stink that permeated the streets and back alleys of Paris.

"Careful," Georges-Henri whispered. "The steps are steep." They climbed a narrow wooden staircase.

When they reached the first-floor landing, there was barely enough room for the two of them to stand together. He pulled a key from his pocket, and unlocked the door. "*Le voilà*," he said, holding the door open for her.

They entered a small foyer. Georges-Henri switched on an antique brass wall sconce then helped her out of her coat and hung it along with his on hooks just inside the door.

The sitting room was sparsely furnished and smelled vaguely of lavender soap, the same scent she'd smelled in Georges-Henri's cottage in Provence. An antique brocade loveseat sat by the window. A crystal chandelier suspended from the high ceiling provided the only light. In the back of the apartment, Jacquie caught a glimpse of a tiny kitchenette and a wooden table and two chairs.

Georges-Henri stoked a log in the cast-iron fireplace and it came to life. Then he went into the kitchenette and returned with two snifters of cognac. He handed one to Jacquie.

"When I come back to Paris in the spring," he said, "I'm going to ask Hélène to lend me a few more pieces of furniture."

Jacquie sat on the loveseat, tucking her feet under her. "You might add some rugs. The floor is cold." She looked up. "I like the chandelier."

He joined her on the sofa. Just close enough to touch his shoulder to hers.

"Where do you sleep?" she asked.

He pointed to a narrow space above the kitchenette. "Up there...in the *grenier*." He smiled. "It's only large enough for a small bed."

"A loft? Really? However do you get up to it?"

"There is a spiral stairway hidden in the back corner of the kitchen." He paused. "I'll show it to you later..." he paused, cleared his throat, and added, "if you want."

She felt herself blush. "Have you heard how Odile is?" she asked, changing the subject. "Did she get over her cold?"

"I assume she has recovered. Bernard would have contacted me if she had gotten worse."

"So you missed spending Christmas there?"

"Unfortunately. But I plan to make it up to Odile when I return. I have a very special surprise for her."

Jacquie sipped her cognac. "You do? What is it?"

"I have arranged for her to have a dog. A specially-trained one that will help her see. There are people in Belgium who train dogs to help the blind avoid getting into dangerous situations. Odile's will be delivered by a trainer after my return."

"What about the school you're planning on sending her to?"

"I thought about what you said, about asking her. You made me realize something."

"What is that?"

"She may be too young to leave home, especially so soon after her mother's death."

"So you asked her then? If she wanted to attend the school, that is?"

He shook his head. "*Non*. Maybe I'll ask her eventually." He shrugged. "We'll see." He put his snifter on the coffee table and turned to face her. "Jacquie, there's something I want to talk to you about."

She felt her pulse quicken. "If it's about what I said about Simone de Beauvoir, you don't have to invite me to speak to your class. I understand."

He put his finger to her lips. "*Écoutes, chérie*. It's not about that. My offer still stands. I just want to ask if you will consider something else."

She blinked. "What?"

He took her hand in his and played with her fingers. "I need you," he said.

She glared at him, glanced up at the loft. Had she heard him correctly? What kind of girl did he think she was?

"What do you mean, Georges-Henri?"

He went on. "I know you have another year left of school, and I'm asking if you could possibly consider spending it here in Paris instead of going back to America."

She swallowed hard. "That's impossible, Georges-Henri. I am expected to return to New York in June."

"That's just it. Professor André has made a generous offer. In the fall, I will have a full teaching assignment. We could be together, you and I. You could finish your studies...and..." He reached up and caressed her cheek.

Jacquie pulled away and rose from the loveseat. Her skin felt hot where he had touched it. What was he asking? "This is all so sudden. I couldn't possibly consider..."

"I am leaving at the end of the week, and I won't return until the start of the spring term. I don't expect an answer from you before then."

She went over to the window. A heavy rain beat against the pane. Her heart was doing the same in her chest. He seemed so different. Had his father's death affected him?

Georges-Henri rose and went over to stand close to her. "I love you, Jacquie," he whispered.

She sucked in a breath. "We hardly know each other."

"The night you came into my room…I couldn't get it out of my mind after I left the next day. The loneliness I felt after we parted. I realized then how much I need you."

She'd given him the wrong impression. Why, oh why, had she thought it was a good idea to go to his room? Feeling dizzy all of a sudden, she stood and held on to the edge of the loveseat to stop from falling. "I think the cognac has gone to my head," she said. "I should be getting back to the apartment. It's late."

"I'll drive you," he said.

"That won't be necessary. I'll take a taxi."

"There aren't any this time of night."

He put his arm around her, but she pulled away. All she wanted to do was escape. She went into the foyer and snatched her coat from the hook by the door. Her hand shook as she turned the doorknob.

"Jacquie," he pleaded. "Wait."

"I…I need time to think about what you said, Georges-Henri."

Before he could stop her, she flung open the door, forgetting that the landing was tiny, and the steps were steep and narrow.

Chapter Thirty-three

Jacquie lay on her bed with a cold washcloth covering her forehead. Her right eye was swollen shut, and she had a pounding headache. She lifted the cloth and peered at Claudine who was sitting on the edge of her own bed staring at her. "Do you think I'm going to have a shiner?"

"Doesn't look good," Claudine said, shaking her head. "You're going to be wearing sunglasses for a while. Rain or shine."

Jacquie groaned. "What am I going to tell Hélène?"

Claudine heaved a sigh. "Yes, my friend, that's definitely going to be a problem. She'll have a fit when she sees your face."

"I know. Trouble is I can't tell her where I was."

Claudine rose from her bed, took the washcloth from Jacquie, and went over to rinse it in the sink.

"Tell me," she said as she carefully replaced the cloth over Jacquie's swollen eye. "What happened last night? Where exactly did you and Georges-Henri go anyway? Did you get mugged?"

Jacquie heaved a big sigh. "He took me to see his new apartment."

"He has an apartment? Here in Paris?"

Jacquie nodded. "It's in the Latin Quarter. He rented it recently so he'll have somewhere to live when he returns for the spring session. We had a cognac. Talked about what he needed to do to make the place more livable. It was rather nice, just the two of us sitting on the loveseat talking. That is, until he suddenly became serious."

"As in, he started kissing you. Right?"

Jacquie bit her lip. "Claudie, he asked me to consider staying in Paris another year to finish my studies. He said he wanted us to be together."

"Let me get this straight. He was suggesting you stay with him rather than going home to New York?"

"Uh-huh."

"Wow. Now that is a surprise. Where did he get the idea he could propose something like that, and you'd agree to it?"

"I know. He's always been so reserved and shy. It seemed out of character."

"I suppose he said he loves you, too?"

Jacquie nodded. "Yes, actually, he did."

"Like I thought." Claudine shook her head in disgust. "Frenchmen. All they want is to get a girl to go to bed with them. What did you do to give him the idea that you might be interested in an arrangement like that?"

Jacquie sighed. "I might have given him the wrong impression."

"Ah, how is that?"

"Remember how I told you about the cuddle we had that night in his cottage in Provence?"

"Oh no."

"Yes. He may have misunderstood."

"May have? You didn't make it clear to him last night that you aren't *that* kind of girl?"

"I was caught off guard. I didn't know how to react, Claudie."

Claudine stared at her.

Jacquie explained about the panic attack she'd had, and the bad fall she'd taken in her haste to get away from Georges-Henri. "I forgot about the landing and the narrow steps," she said. "It was dark. I tumbled nearly the entire length of the staircase before I managed to catch myself. I banged my head against the wooden banister. At least that's what I thought it was I hit. I'm not sure. I think I knocked myself out for a second or two. I barely remember Georges-Henri carrying me back into his apartment and then bringing me here."

"You should have wakened me when you got here."

"You were sound asleep. I didn't want to upset you on your first night back in Paris."

"I feel bad. It was my fault. I only thought we were meeting Duff at the club. I had no idea he would bring Georges-Henri along with him. If only I'd known, I'd have warned you. I'm sorry."

"It's okay. I wouldn't have done anything differently if I'd known he was going to be there." Jacquie held the washcloth away from her face and squinted at Claudine with her one good eye. "Out of curiosity, how did you manage to contact Duff so soon after your return to Paris?"

"It was a coincidence, really. While you were getting ready to go out, I sorted through some mail that had come for me while I was in New York. There was a postcard from him."

"Duff sent you a postcard?"

"Uh huh. From Saint-Tropez."

"Really?" Jacquie felt a twinge of regret for having deserted him like she did.

"He wrote that I should let him know when I arrived back in Paris," Claudine continued. "He included the phone number of his apartment building so I could contact him. I immediately ran down to the foyer and used Hélène's phone. It was a terrible connection. Static. I couldn't even tell if the person I talked to understood any of my French. I hoped it was the concierge, or at least someone reliable." She looked over at Jacquie. "I didn't know for sure if he'd gotten the word until I saw him. It was such a lovely surprise." She sat back in bed and hugged her knees to her chest. "And what a wonderful evening we had. We're going out again before classes begin next week."

"So now you're in love with him, I suppose."

Claudine laughed. "Duff? You've got to be kidding me. I mean, he's charming and fun all right, but love? Ha!"

Jacquie clicked her tongue.

"Seriously, Jacquie," Claudine said. "What are you going to do about Georges-Henri? You're not considering his request, I hope?"

"No. Well. I don't know."

There was a knock at the door.

"Who is it?" Claudine called.

There was no answer.

Jacquie groaned. "Oh, shoot. It's Hélène."

"Let me handle this," Claudine whispered. She put on her robe and went over to open the door.

Jacquie heard a male voice next. "Is she awake?"

When Claudine hesitated, he added, "Please. I need to speak with her."

Claudine closed the door and turned around. "It's Georges-Henri. He looks terrible. Do you want me to tell him to go away?"

Jacquie's head felt like it was going to explode, but she rose from her bed and put on her robe. "No," she said, "I have something I want to say to him."

He stood in the hall, a long-stemmed red rose in his hand. "How are you?" he asked. The stubble on his chin told Jacquie he hadn't shaved.

She lowered the cold cloth to reveal her swollen eye. "*Regarde-moi*, Georges-Henri. How do you think I am?"

He winced. "*Je suis…désolé…Je…*" He shook his head.

His eyes were sunken and sad, and he looked so thoroughly miserable, her heart melted. She took the rose from him and held it to her nose. "I was the one who misjudged the steps," she said. "It's not your fault. I should have been more careful."

"If I upset you…"

"You did. There's been a huge misunderstanding, Georges-Henri." She looked down the hall to assure herself Hélène and the children were not within earshot. "That night in your cottage…I just wanted to spend some time alone with you. One thing just led to another, and…"

He nodded. "I didn't think the worst of you for it."

"Nevertheless, you just assumed I would move in with you next year." She felt her face flush. "Don't you even realize what that implied?"

He shrugged. That infuriating Gallic shrug. As if to ask 'what's the problem with that?'

"Well, let me tell you, you clueless French ass."

From inside her room came a "whoop!" Claudine had been listening.

Jacquie pulled the door closed behind her and continued. "Where I come from girls, decent girls that is, don't *live* with men if they aren't married to them." She crossed her arms in front of her and glared at him.

"I didn't expect you to stay with me. You ran out of the apartment before I could explain what I had in mind." He paused and waited for her to acknowledge.

"Ok. Explain." She tapped her toe impatiently. "I'm listening."

He remained calm. "I asked Hélène, and she agreed to extend your stay another year if you wish. And your parents concur, of course."

"She did?" He was assuming a lot.

He nodded. "She says she enjoys having you here and wouldn't mind your staying on. When I told her how I feel about you, she softened. I think she has suspected it all along."

"Oh." Jacquie cleared her throat. "What about your wanting me to spend the summer with you and Odile in Provence? Can you explain to me how you thought that would happen?"

"I plan to put you up in the hotel in the square. It's a very comfortable hotel. I've stayed there myself." He scratched his temple. "It's in a good location directly across from Bernard's chocolaterie."

Had he really considered all this ahead of time, or was he making it up as he went to get himself out of hot water?

"Well, that doesn't change anything. I'm going home to New York in June. Period."

He looked stunned. "*Eh bien.* In that case, I withdraw my request. You are under no obligation to give me an answer, Jacquie." His voice cracked. "I shall hope to see you spring term, but should you decide you don't want to see me or speak to my class about Simone de Beauvoir, you are under no commitment to do so."

With that he turned on his heel and left her standing in the hall clutching the stem of the single red rose.

Paris
January 1951

Chapter Thirty-four

The month of January produced days on end of dreary weather. A cold rain tumbled from the sky, punctuated by episodes of sleet and hail. A strong wind blew, reminding Jacquie of the mistral in Provence. And of Georges-Henri.

On those rare days when blue sky and sunshine appeared, Jacquie took the Métro to the Bois de Boulogne. Enjoying the fact that her father was not around to caution her she might fall and break something, she would rent a horse and ride as she wished—galloping through the park, jumping hedges. All the while, trying to get thoughts of Georges-Henri out of her mind.

Saturday evenings, when Claudine had her standing date with Duff, Jacquie would put on her warm fur coat and leave the apartment alone to attend the theater or to go night-clubbing. She loved having the freedom to go out all by herself. In jazz clubs and all-night cafés, she mixed with the young expat crowds until the early morning hours. Then she would return to the apartment happily humming "La vie en rose." The song had fed her romantic dream of falling in love in Paris long before she'd even arrived in France.

Jacquie's world was being transformed by her year abroad. France was the place where she could become herself. She could read what she wanted, wander wherever she wished, and discover new ideas.

Sundays, she and Hélène would often visit museums. They never talked about Georges-Henri.

Try as she might, though, he was never far from her thoughts. She was surrounded constantly by reminders of him. The apartment on ave-nue Mozart, for example. Every evening at dinner, there was the empty chair next to her, the chair he had sat in the first time she'd met him. Then there was the Sorbonne where he would return for the spring term, and the Brasserie Balzar. As many times as she went there to eat by herself, she always felt his presence.

"He's not even in Paris now, but I can't get him out of my mind, Claudie," she had confessed one night.

"Understandable," Claudine said. "You two were pretty close."

Jacquie went on. "I want to be my own woman. Independent. Just like Simone de Beauvoir says in…"

Claudine interrupted her. "You're taking that silly book too seri-ously," she harrumphed. "I don't see what the big deal is all about. Beauvoir pooh-poohs femininity. That doesn't mean you should, too."

"Just read the chapter on the Independent Woman, Claudie. You'll understand better what I'm talking about. She concludes girls can't win."

Claudine chewed her lip. "Why? Because they have an inferiority complex? That's pure horse pucky, as Duff would say. You know what I think, Jacquie? I think you miss Georges-Henri, but you won't admit it."

Chapter Thirty-five

On a Sunday afternoon in mid-March, Hélène was homebound, caring for all three children who were in bed with bad colds. Claudine was out with Duff. Restless, Jacquie took the Métro to the fifth. The sun was out, and people were browsing the antiquarian book stalls that lined the banks of the Seine.

Jacquie was drawn to a stall run by a grisly old codger in a black beret. He wore a green wool scarf around his neck, his tweed coat was shabby, and his boots were scuffed and spattered with mud. He greeted her with a smile and a twinkle in his eye. "Searching for something in particular, Mademoiselle?"

"Do you have anything by Simone de Beauvoir?" she asked, trying to make her schoolgirl American French less noticeable. It was something she'd been determined to work on all winter, but no matter how much she wanted to sound like a Parisian, the locals always seemed to revel in exposing her.

"I've just read *Le Deuxième Sexe*," she said, choosing each syllable carefully.

"Ah, *bon?*" He nodded. "You are an American who reads French, *alors?*"

So much for thinking she could fool a Parisian. She smiled. "Oui, Monsieur."

"Did you know Simone writes her books in green ink?"

"I believe you are making fun of me, Monsieur."

"*Mais non, Mademoiselle!*"he protested, his eyes wide. "*C'est vrai.* She comes to my bookshop sometimes to write or edit her manuscripts. She prefers green ink."

"Really?" She still didn't believe him.

His hazel eyes twinkled. "*Je vous assure, Mademoiselle.* Simone lives in the *quartier.* Her apartment isn't far from here, on rue de la Bûcherie." He pointed in the direction of the Quai Saint Michel. Jacquie noticed his fingers protruding through the ragged fingertips of his knit gloves.

"You should come visit my bookshop one day, Mademoiselle. Unfortunately, Simone is out of town so you won't have *la chance* to meet her. She and Sartre are away at the moment. In Africa." He paused to titter and shook his head. "Such a pair of lovers, those two…"

"*Votre librarie--où est-elle, Monsieur?*"

"*Mais,* it's right here in St-Germain. Rue de la Parcheminerie." He extended his hand. "Antoine Padoue, bouquiniste."

Jacquie took his hand in her own soft leather gloves. His name sounded familiar. And the street. Suddenly, it dawned on her why. Georges-Henri's voice played in her head. 'Monsieur Padoue…eccentric…I rent the apartment from him.' This man was Georges-Henri's landlord, the owner of the bookshop below his apartment. What else had he said about the man? That he'd fought with the Résistance during the war. She touched her forehead, recalling the night she'd tumbled down the steps in her haste to get out of the apartment. Had Padoue known about that?

"*Heureuse de vous connaître, Monsieur,*" she said. "I shall stop by your bookshop one day." She turned to leave.

Monsieur Padoue put up his hand. "*Attendez,* Mademoiselle. You were looking for something by Simone?"

"Oui, Monsieur."

He put up an index finger. "Ah. I have just the tome."

She watched as he searched through a pile of books at the back of the stall, all the while mumbling to himself. "Ah! *Le voilà,*" he said finally, emerging with a small bound volume. He brushed the dust off and handed it to her.

She took it from him and read the title. "*L'invitée?*"

"Simone's first novel," he said proudly. "Written several years ago now. An enjoyable story."

Jacquie plucked her coin purse from her bag. "*C'est combien,* Monsieur?"

"*Pour vous, rien, Mademoiselle. Un cadeau.*"

"A gift? Mais, Monsieur, this is very generous of you, but I can't accept."

He smiled and said in English, "I hope you to visit my shop soon."

"*Merci beaucoup, Monsieur.*" She tucked the book under her arm, gave the old bouquiniste a little wave, and walked away wondering if Georges-Henri had known that Simone de Beauvoir was a regular visitor to the bookstore below his apartment.

Cher Georges-Henri,

Regarding your request for me to address your class on the subject of Simone de Beauvoir, I respectfully decline as I am occupied with my own classes at the moment, as well as my plans to return home to New York in June.

I do have a suggestion for you, though. Consider the following:

Jacquie stopped writing, pausing in mid-air with the new pen she'd bought, one with green ink. The tone of the letter was all wrong. Too stiff. Snotty, even. She tore the page from her notebook, crunched it in her hands, and began again.

Cher Georges-Henri,

I hope you are enjoying your

No no no. She didn't hope he was enjoying anything. New page.

Cher Georges-Henri,

I met your landlord by accident recently. I was out strolling along the Seine on a pleasant Sunday afternoon in March when I stopped to browse the books in the bookstalls. I don't know why but Monsieur Padoue's bookstall caught my attention. He and I began to chat. I asked if he had any books by Simone de Beauvoir, and he told me he knows her. You can imagine my surprise when he said she comes into his shop sometimes to write. And she writes her manuscripts in green ink! Hence, my new pen, which I purchased today at a stationery boutique on my way home from class. I am hoping it will inspire me.

I have been considering your request to speak to your class, but I fear I am too occupied with my own studies at the moment to do any justice to it. Therefore, I shall have to decline your invitation.

I do have a suggestion for you, however. There is a specific chapter, which I consider the most significant in de Beauvoir's entire book. It's entitled "The Independent Woman." In it, she sums up the advantages men enjoy. For example: freedom to go wherever they wish, do whatever they want. This, she claims, puts them in a favorable position.

You might point this chapter out to your students. The problem, as de Beauvoir explains it, is that, women (as girls) are conditioned by society into accepting a passive, dependent, objectified existence in order to conform to stereotypes imposed by men.

I am convinced she is right. A woman can be beautiful, feminine, and smart at the same time, n'est-ce pas?

Jacquie paused writing. Had she gone too far? Would he even under-stand what she was trying to say? She tore the page from her notebook, signed it *Cordialement,* folded it carefully, placed it in an envelope, and wrote Georges-Henri's name on the front.

It was a nice day, the leaves on the trees in the Latin Quarter were just beginning to bud, and the warmth of the spring sun after the cold win-ter months felt good. Jacquie headed for the Latin Quarter and Monsieur Padoue's bookshop.

The shop's window displays featured Simone de Beauvoir's work. She looked up to Georges-Henri's apartment. To her surprise, the French windows were open and the curtains were fluttering in the breeze. Was he already in Paris? The last thing she needed was to run into him there, of all places.

She hurried to open the door of the shop. The bell jangled, and the musty odor of old books filled her nostrils, reminding her of the antique stores she'd visited with her grandmother in New York when she was small.

A young woman sat on a stool behind the desk. She was pretty, with a curly head of auburn hair. Jacquie guessed she was no more than eighteen years old. In front of her was an open, oversized book of ancient maps. She appeared to be repairing the pages.

A fluffy white cat sat on the edge of the desk, moving its tail back and forth, watching her. There were no other customers in the shop.

Jacquie cleared her throat. "*Bonjour.*"

"Feel free to browse, Mademoiselle," the girl said. She didn't look up from her work.

"Is Monsieur Padoue here?" Jacquie asked, looking around. The shop was just as Georges-Henri had described it. Books piled everywhere, floor to ceiling.

"Not at the moment," the young woman said, peering at her over wire-rimmed glasses.

"When do you expect him back?" Jacquie persisted.

"If you need help finding something, perhaps I could..."

Jacquie held up the letter and said, "Actually, I had hoped Monsieur could deliver this to his tenant in the apartment above the shop. His name is Georges-Henri Delacroix."

The young woman carefully put down the tool she was using. "Monsieur Delacroix is no longer renting the apartment, Mademoiselle. I am."

Jacquie furrowed her brow. "I...I don't understand. He's supposed to return to Paris soon...for spring term at the Sorbonne."

The woman waved her hand. "Monsieur Padoue will be back soon. You can ask him."

Jacquie stared at her. "Do you know what happened? With Monsieur Delacroix, that is?"

"No. I came to Paris looking for employment. I am from a small town near Toulouse." The girl grimaced. "I couldn't wait to get out of there. Anyway, I was walking down this street, and I saw a sign posted in the window." She pointed to the front of the shop. "Monsieur Padoue was looking for an assistant. I walked in and applied. The apartment above the shop had just become available." She grinned. "I am to attend the Polytechnique starting in April so it was a perfect situation for me. I have a job and a place to live. Monsieur Padoue is a very generous soul."

Jacquie smiled, wanting to be happy for the girl, though her heart was sinking. Where was Georges-Henri? "I'll just look around a bit until Monsieur Padoue returns," she said.

"As you wish, Mademoiselle." The girl went back to her repair work.

The cat moved to a sunny corner next to the window.

Jacquie was in the back of the shop, seated in a comfortable chair reading, when she heard the front door open and the bell jangle. She rose to her feet and peeked around the corner to see Monsieur Padoue removing his scarf and coat. He hung them on a rack by the door but he didn't take off his beret.

"There's someone waiting for you, Monsieur," the girl said.

"Oh?" Padoue looked toward the rear of the shop.

Jacquie came forward to greet him. "*Bonjour,* Monsieur Padoue," she said with a smile. "As promised, I've come to see your shop."

He took her hand. "*Soyez le bienvenu, Mademoiselle.*"

She held up the book she had been reading. "While I was waiting for you to return, I found a treasure, too."

His eyes twinkled. "*Le Sang des Autres.* Simone's second novel about the Résistance. Excellent choice, Mademoiselle."

She opened her handbag. "This one I pay for."

He chuckled.

"I also came to deliver a note to Georges-Henri Delacroix," she added, "but your assistant told me he no longer rents the apartment above."

She paused. When there was no reaction, she continued. "I understood he was planning to return to Paris in April."

The bookseller nodded.

"What happened? Do you know?"

"I do not, Mademoiselle." He lifted his beret and scratched the top of his head. "One day a letter came saying he had changed his mind. The apartment wouldn't be needed after all." He shrugged.

"No explanation? Or forwarding address?"

He shook his head. "*Non*."

How odd.

Jacquie paid for the book and bid Padoue and his assistant au revoir with a promise to return to the shop soon.

Finding a bench with a view of Notre Dame across the river, she sat down to think. The wind was cool, and the only sound was an occasional car driving along the quay. A few feet away, a *clochard* lay fast asleep in the shade of the riverbank, his wine bottle lying next to him.

Jacquie sighed. She felt sad, though she couldn't think why. After all, she had been the one to put a stop to the relationship with Georges-Henri. Guilt, perhaps, for how she had handled it. Up until now, she hadn't even given a thought about the impact it might have had on him. She stared at the envelope in her lap wondering if she should have apologized for her behavior in the note. Perhaps.

She sat there until the sky began to darken and the headlights of the cars driving by illuminated the quay. Taking one last look at the shadow of Notre Dame across the dark waters of the Seine, she got up and headed for the Brasserie Balzar. She had promised to meet Claudine and Duff there for dinner that evening. Claudine had said it was to "celebrate."

As she walked toward the restaurant, Jacquie didn't feel at all in the mood for celebrating.

Chapter Thirty-six

The Brasserie Balzar was noisy and crowded, and the air was thick with cigarette smoke. Waiters in white aprons threaded among the tables with platters held high.

Jacquie found Claudine and Duff canoodling in a booth along the silver-mirrored wall. The two were so wrapped up in each other that they didn't even notice her approaching. Feeling envious, she cleared her throat. "Sorry I'm late."

They pulled apart, faces flushed.

Duff rose from his seat. "Great you could make it, Jacquie." He kissed her on each cheek and held her chair. He looked over toward the bar and gave the young man behind it a signal.

Claudine was all smiles. "We told the waiter to hold the champagne until you arrived."

"Champagne?" Jacquie said. She shot a quick sideways glance at Claudine's left hand. No ring. "What are we celebrating?"

"Duff has some absolutely terrific news."

He slid into the booth again. "Yep! When y'all sail back to New York in June?" He paused dramatically. "Well, I'm fixin' to go with you."

"Really?" Jacquie said. That was the news? "I thought you were thinking about spending another year in Paris?" She glanced at Claudine. "What, or who, changed your mind?"

"Come on, tell her the rest, cowboy," Claudine said, patting Duff's hand.

"You go ahead, darlin'," he said.

Claudine beamed. "Duff here has been offered a position at Columbia University."

"Yep," Duff confirmed. "Full professor in the Sociology department. Starting in August." He put his arm around Claudine's shoulders and pulled her in close to him. "Claudie here is going to help me find an apartment."

"Isn't it exciting?" Claudine said. "We'll be together in New York."

"It is, indeed," Jacquie agreed, thinking that an engagement might be the next thing the three of them would be toasting.

By the time they had finished their glass of champagne and ordered dinner, Jacquie's mood had improved.

"We should plan a little trip before we all leave France," Duff suggested.

Claudine agreed. "There are some places we said we were going to visit but haven't yet," she said looking at Jacquie. "For example, Dachau?"

"I did say I would make that trip when the weather got better, but I'm still not sure I want to go."

"We could combine it with a stop in Strasbourg," Claudine suggested. "I've been wanting to see Alsace."

Duff traced an outline of France on the white tablecloth. "Let's say we leave right when classes end in May. If we drive east through the Vosges mountains," his finger moved over the table, "cross the border into Germany here at Strasbourg, get a quick look at Dachau, then head south through Switzerland, which I've been wanting to see, by the way, we could easily make it back here in time to catch the boat."

"I like it," Claudine said. "It's a perfect way to end our year here."

"Me, too," Jacquie chimed in. "We should definitely do it."

Duff poured them each another glass of champagne and lifted his glass. "To our end-of-year voyage," he said.

Claudine turned to Jacquie. "Do you think Georges-Henri would be interested in going with us?"

The question took Jacquie by surprise. "Why?"

Claudine laughed. "Well, he and you just might…"

"Forget about that, Claudie," Jacquie said. "You've had too much champagne already."

Claudine shrugged. "Maybe."

Jacquie looked at Duff. "Speaking of *your* friend," she said.

He suppressed a smirk. "Georges-Henri?" he said. "That friend?"

She ignored him. "I need to get a note to him." She opened her handbag and took out the envelope. "I owe him a response as he asked me to speak to his class next term." She waved the letter in the air. "Problem is, I went to deliver it today to his new apartment in Saint-Germain, and he seems to have moved out already."

Duff furrowed his brows. "Moved out? What do you mean?"

"I asked the man who rented it to him, the owner of the bookshop below, what had happened, but he didn't know."

"That's strange," Claudine said.

Jacquie agreed. "It is. He said he planned to live there when he returned to Paris for the spring term. Duff? Do you know anything about this? Have you heard from him?"

"Not a thing," he said. "I thought he'd be back in Paris by now, but I haven't seen him. Want me to check his office? I could leave your note there." He paused. "Unless, you want to deliver it personally."

"No no." She shook her head. "Would you?" She handed the envelope to him.

He put it in his inside jacket pocket. "Sure. No problem."

"Are you absolutely certain you don't want to invite Georges-Henri to join us on our road trip?" Claudine asked.

Two days later, Jacquie was seated at a table in the corner of the back courtyard.

"Jacquie?" Claudine called from the open French doors that led from the salon.

Jacquie stood and waved. "I'm back here, Claudie."

"Duff's here. He wants to talk to you."

A minute later, Claudine and Duff joined her in the garden.

"It's such a lovely day," Jacquie said, "I've been out here all afternoon trying to write."

Duff leaned over to peek at what she had written. "Green ink, hey?" He whistled. "What are you working on, beautiful? A novel?"

She quickly closed the notebook. "Oh, just some silly poetry. I felt inspired."

"Is it romantic, I hope?" Claudine asked.

Jacquie smiled. "Perhaps." She looked over at Duff. "Claudie said you wanted to talk to me?"

He sat down at the table. "I've just come from a meeting at the Sorbonne. All the teaching assistants for the spring term were supposed to be there." He frowned. "New rules and all that. Georges-Henri should have been there, but he wasn't." He scratched his temple. "I was surprised, too, because he normally doesn't skip meetings like the rest of us are known to do."

"Did you go to his office?" Jacquie asked.

He nodded. "I went directly there after the meeting was over. It was obvious he hadn't arrived yet. His desk was clean. A young woman, a new teaching assistant I hadn't seen before, was lugging a big box in the door. She said her name was Valery and that she had just arrived from California. I helped her carry her stuff over to the vacated desk next to Georges-Henri's."

Claudine was staring daggers at him. He gave her a sideways glance and cleared his throat. "Anyway, I told her I was looking for a friend of mine, the guy who occupied the other desk in the office. She said she hadn't seen him yet, but she was anxious to meet him."

"Do you still have my letter then?" Jacquie asked.

He smiled. "No. Before I left, I put it on Georges-Henri's desk. Right in the center so he couldn't miss it."

"Thank you," Jacquie said. That was that, she thought. End of saga. But she couldn't help wondering whether Georges-Henri would acknowledge he'd received it.

Claudine nudged Duff's arm. "So was Valery the California girl pretty?"

He grinned. "Um. Yeah." Then he punched her arm and added as an afterthought, "Not as pretty as you, *ma belle*."

Claudine laughed. "You failed the test, but I adore you anyway, you big Texas hunk."

The sound of children's chitter-chatter filled the air.

"Here she is, Maman. Out here in the courtyard." It was Théo. Christine and Charlotte came running down the garden path behind him, followed by Hélène still wearing her hat and coat. She seemed distracted.

"Ah, there you are," she said. "We've just come from the park."

Duff stood. "Madame," he said with a polite bow of his head.

"Nice to see you again, Duff," she said, pulling off her glove and taking his hand.

Charlotte tugged on her mother's coat. "Can we have a treat now, Maman?"

"Oui, *chérie*," Hélène replied, "after you three have gone upstairs and changed into clean clothes." She turned to Jacquie.

"If you have a moment," she said, "I'd like to speak with you." She glanced at Claudine. "Privately, that is."

Claudine raised her eyebrows and gave Jacquie a look as if to ask, "What now?"

Jacquie rose from the table, and followed Hélène inside.

The children ran ahead and disappeared up the stairs.

"What is it, Madame?" Jacquie asked. "Is something the matter?"

Hélène closed the doors to the salon, then turned to her. "It's about Georges-Henri. I've just received a letter from Les Moulins."

Nice, France
March 1951

Chapter Thirty-seven

All Georges-Henri remembered was that there had been a thick fog that morning. The day before, he and Bernard had decided to drive to Nice to pick up a shipment of couverture chocolate for his shop. They also intended to purchase a new frock for Odile for her upcoming first communion, which they planned to celebrate before he left for Paris.

They had departed Les Moulins early in the morning and traveled only a few kilometers from the village when it happened. The road was slick. Bernard missed a turn. The car slid close to the edge, then tipped dangerously. For a heart-stopping moment, they hung over the cliff before plummeting backward into the steep ravine below. Afterward, Georges-Henri recalled briefly thinking about Jacquie and Odile before everything went black.

The next thing he knew, he awakened in a hospital room in Nice and learned the devastating news. Bernard was dead. He'd died instantly.

Bernard, who had been the anchor for Odile after Marielle passed away, had taken on the burden of running the chocolaterie almost single-handedly and raising Odile by himself. Madame Miniet, Bernard's aging mother, was no longer able, or willing, to help him in the shop.

Through the fog of morphine, Georges-Henri was still trying to process what had happened when the door of his hospital room opened and a nurse appeared.

"You have a visitor," she said.

"Who?" he mouthed. His throat was dry, and he had little strength. He tried to sit up, but he couldn't manage on his own.

The nurse leaned him forward and stuffed a bolster behind his back. He felt a sharp pain and looked down at his right leg, the same leg that had been crushed in the labor camp during the war. The doctor said it might have to be amputated.

The nurse held a straw to his lips and waited for him to take a sip of water. "Mother Marguerite is here," she said. "She's waiting to see you."

"La Mère Abesse?" he rasped.

"Oui. From the convent in Les Moulins."

He looked toward the door.

"I'll show her in," the nurse said, "but she can't stay long. You need to rest."

Mother Marguerite filled the doorway, and her habit swooshed against the tile floor as she entered the room and came to stand by his bed. "My child," she whispered taking his left hand in hers.

Tears filled his eyes.

"I am told you will heal," she said. "In time, God will give you the strength to go on."

He studied her face, which seemed to glow in its white wimple frame.

"I am here," she continued, "because Madame Miniet came to see me. She wanted to discuss the future of the chocolaterie without Bernard." She made the sign of the cross. "As you know, he was teaching our order to make chocolates so we could establish our own confectionary business."

He blinked.

"Madame Miniet has decided to turn over the entire operation of the chocolaterie to the convent. She insists she can't run it by herself, and she plans to spend the years she has left with her sister in Eze." She paused to make sure he understood. "Georges-Henri, there is something you and I need to discuss. Are you feeling up to it, or should I return later?"

He stared at her, trying to focus his eyes. "Water," he said.

She picked up the glass and held the straw to his lips for him to take a sip.

"*Merci,*" he said, trying to clear his throat. "Please. Continue."

"Madame Miniet is not willing to care for Odile now that Bernard is gone," she said. "She has asked if the child might be allowed to stay in the convent." She hesitated. "It would have to be temporary, of course, until a suitable situation is found. Perhaps adoption by a good family would be the best solution."

He furrowed his brow. He couldn't allow that to happen. "Odile is my daughter," he said.

The Reverend Mother's head bowed slightly. "Madame Miniet told me there was some question about that."

He grimaced.

She went on. "She said she had learned the truth from Marielle when she was on her deathbed."

The truth? He held his breath.

The nun went over to stand by the window. "Marielle had apparently lied about being attacked by Nazi soldiers during the war. You see, she was trying to resolve her circumstances on her own because she thought you were dead. It became complicated when you turned up."

Georges-Henri recalled that painful day in 1946 when Marielle had ordered him to leave Les Moulins. "You are not, nor will you ever be, her papa," she had said.

Voices echoed in the hallway; someone knocked on the door of a nearby room. Then all grew quiet again.

Mother Marguerite fingered the ornate filigree cross that hung from the silver chain at her front. "Now that Bernard is gone," she went on, "Madame insists the child is your responsibility. She wants nothing to do with her."

Georges-Henri could not control the choked sobs that escaped from his lips. How could the woman be so heartless?

The nurse came back into the room with a syringe. "I'm afraid you will have to leave, Sister," she said. "It's time for Monsieur's medication."

Mother Marguerite bowed her head. "Please let me know when he is able to continue. We have more to discuss." She touched Georges-Henri's forehead gently and left the room.

The nurse injected a syringe of morphine, and Georges-Henri felt himself drifting into a deep sleep.

When he opened his eyes next, the room was glaringly bright, and he blinked several times to focus. Turning his head slightly, he saw the Reverend Mother sitting by the window writing.

Recalling their earlier discussion, he tried to sit up.

The nun looked up. "Ah, you are awake." She breathed a sigh of relief. "Should I call the nurse?"

"No." His voice was no more than a rasp.

"Are you quite certain?"

He nodded. "No morphine." He needed a clear head.

She rose to help him sit up, then she held the straw so he could take a sip of water.

"What day is it?" he asked.

"The last Thursday of March."

A feeling of panic swept over him. He should have been back in Paris by now. His classes were set to begin soon.

The nun sat down and folded her hands into her habit. "We need to talk about Odile," she said after a few minutes.

He nodded, and she went on. "The child has been given her own room at the convent. We try our best to read to her to cheer her up, but it is of little use. She seems lost. You see, we couldn't allow her to bring her dog."

Georges-Henri groaned. Poor Odile. She had become inseparable from the specially-trained Belgian Malinois who'd come to live with them to help her see. She'd named him "Gaullie" after Charles de Gaulle, the leader of the Free French Résistance during the war.

"Where is...dog?" he asked.

"Madame Miniet said something about giving it to a man who grows lavender in the valley. When she brought Odile to us, along with a trunk packed with clothes, she said the child wouldn't let go of the animal. The dog put up a terrible fuss and had to be dragged away."

"And Madame Miniet?"

"She has left for Eze. I have her sister's address, if you wish."

He shook his head. Bernard's mother had disliked him from the beginning. She'd only tolerated him because he and Bernard had become close. A hard woman, Madame Miniet. His heart ached thinking about what Odile was going through. He had to get well for her sake. He was all she had now.

"I have put all this in a letter I am writing to your sister in Paris," the Reverend Mother said. "Is there anything you would like me to convey to her? I shall post it today before I return to Les Moulins."

As best he could, he told her to add that Hélène needn't rush to Les Moulins. "She has children," he said. He asked also that Professor André at the Sorbonne be alerted that he wouldn't be available for the spring term.

Then he thought of Jacquie. "*S'il vous plait, ma Sœur*, may I have paper and a pen?"

Georges-Henri stared at the ivory letter paper on the tray in front of him and picked up the pen. What could he say to Jacquie? Please come to me, my darling? I love you and need you?

It was no use. He set the pen down and closed his eyes, remembering the last time he had seen her—the morning after her fall at his apartment. She had told him she had made up her mind. She was returning to New York at the end of the term. A sinking feeling came over him. Her year of study would be over in another month. She would be leaving France soon after that, and he would never see her again.

He looked at his bandaged right side. Maybe it was better if she didn't see him like this. He was just a shadow of a man now. A cripple. He tried to move his injured leg. He'd survived the war. Now he might lose it in a car crash.

He picked up the pen again and wrote two words: À *Dieu*. Goodbye. Forever. Then he folded the paper and wrote a large "J" on the outside. That was it. It was over for them. He brought it briefly to his lips, kissing his love for her a fond farewell. Then he closed his eyes and waited for Mother Marguerite to return.

When the nun came back into his room, the sun was just setting, and hazy light filtered through the window.

Georges-Henri handed her the folded piece of paper. She took it from him.

"Will you do something else for me?" he asked.

"*Bien sûr*. How can I be of help?"

"Could you bring Odile to see me?"

She raised an eyebrow.

He went on. "I should ask her what she wants now."

The woman nodded approval. "A fine plan."

"Has she been told about Bernard?"

She hesitated. "Actually, I think not. Madame Miniet said the only thing she'd told her was that there had been an accident involving her papa and you and that she would have to go live in the convent for a while."

"She doesn't know?"

She nodded. "I believe that is the case."

"I want to tell her myself," he said. "In a few days. If you would be so kind. Bring her here." He needed time to think what he was going to say.

Chapter Thirty-eight

Georges-Henri gazed longingly out the window. It was the kind of day he couldn't resist. Blue sky, bright sunshine, the scent of flowers and fruit trees in blossom filling the air. Later, he planned to ask the nurse to take him outside in his wheel chair. The fresh spring air would do him good.

The door opened a crack, and he heard a small voice. "*C'est ici?*" Then a "Shush" followed by a whisper. "Remember. We have to be quiet. He may be sleeping."

Mother Marguerite peeked into the room.

Georges-Henri smiled and nodded. "*Entrez*, Mother Marguerite," he said. Then he called out Odile's name.

The little girl emerged from behind the Reverend Mother's habit. "*Tonton?*" she whispered. She searched the room for him.

"Oui, *chérie.*"

Odile's head moved toward the sound of his voice. She let go of the nun's hand but stood frozen, as if wondering what to do. "Where are you, *Tonton?*"

He waved to her. "Over here. Can you find me?"

The child smiled then felt her way to the edge of the bed. He held out his left hand and helped her climb up next to him. She put her arms around his neck and stared into his face. Her eyes, so close to his, looked huge through the round correction lenses she wore. "*Tonton,*" she whispered, "are you sleeping?"

He hugged her. "*Non, chérie.* See?" He widened his eyes. "I am awake."

Odile smiled. "I don't have to whisper anymore?"

Mother Marguerite chuckled and set a parcel wrapped in plain paper and tied with a string on the bedside table. He had asked her to bring it from his house.

He thanked her. It was a gift for Odile he had purchased previously and he had planned to give it to her on Easter Sunday, the day she was to have made her first communion.

Georges-Henri smoothed the little girl's hair and gently touched her brow. "I'm so happy to see you."

"Do you have Gaullie?" she asked. Her mouth formed a moue. "They took him away."

Georges-Henri's heart sank. He glanced over at the nun. "He's not here, *chérie,*" he said softly, "but I promise we'll go find him as soon as I get well."

"What about Papa? Why can't he go get him? I think Gaullie is missing me."

Georges-Henri looked over at the Reverend Mother's sympathetic face. "Please leave us," he said. "Odile and I need to be alone."

Mother Marguerite bowed her head and left, closing the door quietly behind her.

"Now then," Georges-Henri said, untying the string and pulling a small stuffed bunny from the parcel the Reverend Mother had brought. "This is for you."

Odile reached for the gray-brown toy, stroked its soft body and felt its floppy ears.

"It's a bunny," he said.

She examined the pink nose and stubby tail. "Her name is *Bisou*," she said matter-of-factly.

"Oh?" he asked.

She nuzzled the precious gift. "Because I am going to give her lots of kisses." She thought for a moment. "And when we bring Gaullie home, I'll introduce her to him."

Georges-Henri felt the back of his eyeballs sting. How was he going to tell this sweet child about Bernard?

"How would you and Gaullie like to come live with me in my house after I get out of the hospital?"

She concentrated on playing with the toy, not appearing to have heard him.

"Odile?"

"Gaullie and I live with Papa," she said in a small voice. "And Mémé."

"Mémé has gone to live with her sister now," he said.

The girl shook her head. "She's just visiting for a while. That's why I had to go to the convent."

So that was how Madame Miniet had explained it to her. This was getting complicated.

Odile looked at him and frowned. "She said you had an accident. Is that why you are here?"

"Oui. Your papa and I were on our way to Nice."

"Is he in this hospital, too?"

"No, *chérie*," he said.

"Where is he then?"

It pained Georges-Henri to say it. "He's with your maman."

She thought about that for a moment. "But Maman's in heaven."

"And that's where your papa is now, too."

He watched her as she processed the information. Then, a horrified expression crossed her face. "But I want Papa here," she cried.

He gently patted her cheek. "Sometimes things happen, *chérie*, that we can't change."

"Like when maman went to heaven?"

"Yes."

"Will I be able to visit Papa like I do Maman? In the garden at the convent?"

"That would please him, I think."

She looked thoughtful.

"I talk to Maman sometimes when I go to see her." A look of sadness. "She never answers, though. Do you think Papa will answer me if I talk to *him*?"

He didn't know what to say to her. His chest hurt. Finally, he said, "When you come to live with me, we will visit them together."

She put her arms around his neck and laid her head on his shoulder. "Then it's all right, *Tonton*. Gaullie, Bisou, and I will live with you."

Georges-Henri rested his chin on the top of her head. He wondered if she would, in time, learn to call him Papa.

Le Havre, France
June 1951

Chapter Thirty-nine

Jacquie contemplated the ship in the port. The *De Grasse* was set to depart the next morning for New York. She sighed. Duff, Claudine and she would be on it. Duff and Claudine were at the hotel now repacking their trunks and trying to fit in all the souvenirs they'd purchased on the road trip.

The harbor was filled with liberty ships, military ships that had been refurbished for tourists. She'd been on one a year ago, coming to France for her first time to spend her junior year abroad.

It had been a magical year. She'd dreamed about France long before she ever crossed the ocean. Paris, and the French language, had only existed in her imagination before that.

In actuality, she had experienced a country that was reeling from a devastating war. Food hadn't been plentiful. Water closets had taken some getting-used-to. Streets were being renamed after military heroes, and plaques were everywhere commemorating Résistance heroes who had died fighting the Nazis. In so many ways, she'd been a witness to France's recovery. She now knew the real France, not the imagined one of her youth. Despite the austerity, she'd loved everything about it.

She was a different person now from the girl who had set sail from New York a year ago. She smiled to herself. Although, she didn't care if she ever had to eat another mushroom omelet again.

A ship's horn sounded pitifully forlorn in the harbor.

She'd been lucky to live in the sixteenth. Hélène's genteel apartment on avenue Mozart, with its well-worn antiques, cold, shared bathroom, and lovely courtyard had become her home.

She found a post box and slipped the postcard she'd written to Georges-Henri into the slot. She'd only sent her address in New York, written "Farewell" in large letters, and signed her name. There was nothing else to say.

The thought of him made her legs go suddenly weak. She sat down on a bench nearby. Breathing in the fishy, industrial smell of the harbor, she recalled the day she had met the shy, handsome brother of her host. She'd just arrived in Paris. Late for dinner, he had taken the empty chair next to her.

She felt a pang of sadness. They had attended the theater together, ridden horses in the Bois de Boulogne, and shared many lunches of *soupe à l'oignon* at Brasserie Balzar. He had seemed so easy to talk to.

A seagull swooped down and landed next to her bench. The graceful bird balanced on one webbed foot as it looked at her first with one sharp eye and then the other. The two of them stared at each other until the bird flew off. She watched it as it soared far out over the harbor, gliding in a wide circle with its wings spread, then flapping wildly in ascent, to be carried along on a second crosswind. Chee! Chee! Chee! She heard its cries rise and fall across the water as she finally lost sight of it.

She had been certain she was in love when Georges-Henri had kissed her the first time. She shivered, still recalling that night in the darkened courtyard where, barefooted and in her robe, she had accidentally discovered him seated at the table smoking a cigar.

Was it love? Or was it just Paris? She'd never really know now. She would go home to NewYork and never see him again. It was farewell forever. He'd as much as said that in the note he'd sent.

She put her face in her hands. She couldn't shake the image of him lying in a hospital bed, injured. Did she really want it to end like this, to leave France without seeing him one more time?

She rose from the bench and started back toward the hotel. She knew what she was going to do.

The lobby was in chaos. Steamer trunks and valises were scattered everywhere. Arriving travelers were checking in; those departing checking out. Bellhops in uniform scurried around, pushing carts filled with luggage and overflowing garment racks. Travelers sat in comfortable chairs sipping drinks and chatting. The general atmosphere was one of excitement mixed with nervous anticipation.

Jacquie walked past a couple kissing in the corner and ascended the staircase to the suite she shared with Claudine and Duff.

"How are you going to pack all this in one trunk, darlin'?" she heard Duff ask as she opened the door.

The large oil painting of Sacré-Coeur Claudine had purchased during one of their excursions to Montmartre sat next to her trunk alongside a miniature replica of the EiffelTower and a huge pile of books.

"I'll find room, big guy," Claudine said, poking him in the chest. "Don't worry."

Duff put his hands on his hips. "And what about that cuckoo clock from Munich? How are you going to fit it in?" He guffawed. "Maybe you can wear it on your head as a hat."

"Very funny," Claudine snorted. "I thought it would go nicely in your suitcase along with that one-kilo wheel of Swiss cheese you bought in the Alps."

He shook his head. "We're going to need another trunk."

Jacquie watched the two, jealous of their easy relationship. "You can have my extra," she said. "I managed to fit everything into one."

"You did?" Claudine asked. "I'm in awe. How did you do it?"

Jacquie laughed. "Well, first of all, I purchased a smaller painting in Montmartre than you did."

"If I'm going to hang it over the fireplace in my first-ever living room," Claudine harrumphed, "it has to be large."

"And I shipped all my antiquarian books home a month ago before we took off for our road trip."

"Smart girl," Duff said with a wink.

Claudine held her chin and sighed. "I should have done the same thing. My trunk is going to weigh a ton."

Duff just shook his head. "I'm not volunteering to carry it for you."

"Let's get out of here for a while," Jacquie said. "Go to a café for a glass of wine. I have something important to tell you."

Once they were seated at the Café du Port, glasses of burgundy on the table in front of them, Jacquie spoke. "I'm not going on the *De Grasse* with you tomorrow," she said.

"What?" Claudine said. "I don't think I heard that right."

"I said I'm not sailing tomorrow."

Claudine and Duff stared at her wide-eyed.

"I've decided to change my passage to depart from Marseille. I checked the schedules. There's a liner leaving from there to New York via Barcelona at the end of June." She swallowed hard. "It will take me a little longer to get home, but I've made up my mind. I'm going to go visit Georges-Henri in Les Moulins."

"Well, hallelujah!" Duff declared, raising his glass of wine in a toast.

"Oh my God!" Claudine exclaimed. "Are you kidding? Really?"

"It's not what you think," Jacquie said. "I just want to see him before I go home."

Chapter Forty

The steam locomotive chugged through the lush countryside pulling the train closer to Nice. A heady scent of lavender fields in bloom permeated the air in the compartment. Enchanted, Jacquie gazed out the window at the sea of purple passing by. After nearly twenty hours, she had reached the South of France.

She regretted that she hadn't brought her camera. Packed away in her trunk, it was on its way to New York with Duff and Claudine. She checked her watch. Two more hours. Sighing, she returned to her reading.

She had been so busy with all the activities before she left Paris that she hadn't had a chance to get to the Simone de Beauvoir novel she had purchased from Monsieur Padoue's bookshop. A fascinating love story, it was keeping her entertained throughout this long journey.

Just as she was finishing the last few words, the train pulled into the Gare de Nice-Ville and screeched to a halt. The novel's ending caught her by surprise. Tasting coal grit in her mouth, she stared out the window for a moment thinking about it. Then she stood, smoothed her wrinkled skirt, collected her valise, and stepped onto the platform. She felt as if she were covered in soot.

According to a map of the city posted in the station, the hospital was within walking distance. It was a warm morning, and she set out, glad to have the opportunity to stretch her legs. The air smelled fishy and briny, the scent of the sea.

A large building, the Hospital Saint-Roch looked as if it had been built in the last century. Jacquie stood at the entrance, sucked in a breath, patted her hair into place, and entered.

At the main desk, she asked the receptionist for Georges-Henri only to hear he had been released from the hospital.

"Can you tell me where he went after he was released?" Jacquie asked.

"*Non non, Mademoiselle,*" the woman insisted, "We are not allowed."

A nervous panic seized Jacquie. "Can you at least say if he was all right?"

The woman stared at her. "He is no longer here, Mademoiselle. *Voilà. C'est tout.* That's all I can tell you."

Frustrated and worried, Jacquie wandered outside and down the street. A haze in the air filtered the daylight and colored the façades of the green-shuttered apartment buildings rose-gold.

What should she do now? It had occurred to her during the trip that she didn't really know for certain Georges-Henri was still in the hospital. She had just assumed because there hadn't been any word about him since the Reverend Mother from the convent had written to Hélène.

The only possible solution was for her to go to Les Moulins. Someone there, surely the Reverend Mother herself, would know where he was.

A lone taxi sat idle in front of the hospital. Jacquie approached the dozing driver and tapped his shoulder through the open window.

"Do you know the village of Les Moulins, Monsieur?" she asked when he opened his eyes.

"Ah, oui, Mademoiselle," he said, sitting up and yawning.

"Can you take me there?"

He looked at her strangely. "I can take you, Mademoiselle, but it will be *cher*." He rubbed his thumb and third finger together. "*Le gaz, vous savez. Ça coûte.*"

She sighed. "*D'accord*," she said with a shrug.

He adjusted his beret, got out of the driver's seat and opened the rear door for her. "*À votre service, Mademoiselle.*"

He tossed her valise on the rear seat, and she slid in beside it.

"*Allons-y!*" he announced, and off they went.

Later, Jacquie remembered it as the trip from hell. A narrow, two-lane highway led into the steep hills north of the city. The taxi driver, a Corsican he'd informed her, drove like a maniac, taking the dangerous curves at break-neck speed. She was jostled about and barely able to stay on the seat. At one point, they rounded a bend and came perilously close to the edge of the cliff. Jacquie looked down the sheer drop to the valley below and closed her eyes, thinking about Georges-Henri's accident.

Finally, the taxi pulled into the sun-drenched village. "Les Moulins, Mademoiselle. *On arrive enfin*," the driver shouted as if it had been a major feat to get there.

Jacquie said a silent prayer of thanks, paid the driver, and stepped out of the car, her legs shaky from the experience.

The fountain in the center of the square was bubbling and sur-rounded by flowers. Far different from the Christmas crèche scene and barren trees she had taken pictures of in December.

She looked across the square to the chocolaterie. A sign in the door read *FERMÉ*. The display in the shop window was empty, replaced by a photo of Bernard surrounded by flowers and lit votive candles. Poor Bernard, she thought.

Silently thanking her parents for the extra funds they'd wired for her trip home, she picked up her valise and walked across the square to check in at the hotel. She needed to wash off the grime from the trip and change her clothes before she saw Georges-Henri.

A little voice in her head asked, "What if he's not here?" She shoved the thought away. Where else could he be?

A half hour later, she set out for Georges-Henri's cottage, remembering the dirt path as if she'd been there just yesterday.

The landscape reminded her of one of Cézanne's paintings. The sky was azure, the hills blue-green, and the valley below a deep violet.

Georges-Henri's small pink stucco *maison de campagne* was as picturesque as a painting, too. What was it he had called it? *La Pitchoune*. Provençal for 'little one.' As she approached, she breathed a sigh of relief. The Mediterranean-blue shutters were flung open. He was here after all.

Had she done the right thing by coming unannounced? Sucking in a deep breath, she stepped onto the wisteria-covered front porch and rapped on the front door.

There was no answer. A slight wind whispered in the trees, and the whir of the cicadas intensified in the stifling heat of the afternoon.

She knocked again, then peeked through the open window. "*Allô?* Georges-Henri?"

No response. She tried the door handle. It wasn't locked. Feeling like Goldilocks, she let herself in.

The interior of the cottage was light and airy, yet cool and comfortable. Nothing much had changed furniture-wise since she and Duff had visited. She flung her purse on a chair and took off her headscarf.

"*Allô?*" she called. Still no response. She took a deep breath and told herself to calm down. He was likely to walk in the door any minute.

She wandered over to the table where some postcards were fanned out next to a blue ceramic vase filled with sunflowers. To her surprise, the cards were from Duff, written during their recent road trip. He hadn't told her he'd sent them.

She picked one up. It was a painting of the huge Gothic cathedral in Strasbourg. He'd written on the back that he, Claudine, and she were traveling before they sailed home to New York in June. No details.

The next one was a plain card posted from Munich. *Well, we visited Dachau camp*, Duff wrote. *Can't say how I feel. Stunned. Appalled might be a better word. Made me want to get out of there as soon as possible.*

Jacquie recalled the smell of the white-washed room with drains, and the oven, the crematorium, the sense of emptiness and loss, a ruined Munich under reconstruction. Afterwards, she had felt nauseous. She still had trouble sleeping at night.

A third postcard showed a photo of a castle in the Swiss Alps. Duff had merely written *Breathtaking!* but she knew it had been his favorite part of the entire trip.

As she put the postcard down, the bells in the carillon tower chimed, reminding her of her visit to the convent cemetery in December. She wondered if Georges-Henri thought about Marielle every time those bells chimed.

She wandered down the hall to Georges-Henri's office and rapped on the door. No response. Expecting to see his desk, books, the sofa where they'd cuddled that night, she opened a crack and peeked in.

The room had been transformed into a little girl's room. A stuffed bunny sat on the canopied bed and there was a small antique rocking chair and an armoire painted white.

Jacquie closed the door quickly. Perhaps it was wrong of her to have come after all. Odile must be living with him now. She hadn't considered that. In the letter the Reverend Mother had sent to Hélène, she'd written that the child would be staying in the convent.

Panicking, she headed back to the salon to collect her purse, but a noise on the back veranda stopped her. She heard the kitchen door open and a woman humming softly. Grabbing her bag and scarf, she hurried to the front door, but it was too late.

A round little woman with wiry, graying hair and rosy cheeks appeared in the kitchen doorway. When she saw Jacquie, she abruptly stopped humming.

"*Mais, qu'est-ce que vous faites là, Mademoiselle?*" the startled woman asked, suspicion written all over her face.

The fear and paranoia the war had caused hadn't gone away.

"*Pardon, Madame,*" Jacquie said, realizing the alarm she'd caused the woman by entering the house unannounced. "I'm looking for Georges-Henri," she said.

The woman furrowed her brow and scrutinized her. "*Ah oui? Pourquoi, Mademoiselle?*"

An unmistakable sweet fragrance filled the room. Lavender. The basket the woman carried was filled with fresh cuttings tied with twine.

"*Je m'appelle* Jacquie." She smiled, adding that she was a friend. "*Je suis une amie.*"

The woman's violet-blue eyes matched the color of her apron and the lavender in the basket. She appeared to relax. "*Ah bon? Enfin, oui,*

Mademoiselle." She pointed toward the lake behind the house. "*Il est là. Au bord du lac.*" He's out there. By the lake.

"*Merci,*" Jacquie said. She'd forgotten about the lake. Of course, he'd be there on a hot day like today. It should have been the first place she checked. She opened the front door to go outside.

"*Non non,*" the woman said, pointing to the kitchen. "*That way. Attention au chien!*"

Chien? Dog? Suddenly Jacquie remembered Georges-Henri telling her he was arranging for Odile to have a guide dog. Oh dear. She thanked the woman, went to the back door, and cautiously opened it. No dog in sight.

Georges-Henri was seated in a wheelchair on the bank overlooking the water. He wore a white linen shirt and a wide-brimmed straw hat. His back was partially to her, but she could see he was reading a book. A light blue blanket covered his lap.

Suddenly, behind her, there was a low growl followed by a series of ferocious barks. She whirled around to see a large dog, a Malinois, with pointy ears leap from the veranda and head straight for her. Its lips were curled and its teeth bared.

A curly-haired little girl behind him screamed, "Gaullie!"

Jacquie stood perfectly still, telling herself to remain calm. Her family had had dogs when she was growing up. She knew what to do.

Out of the corner of her eye, she saw Georges-Henri twist in his chair.

The housekeeper came running from the side of the cottage.

"Gaullie," Jacquie cooed in a soft voice as the dog approached her. She let it sniff the back of her hand, then her canvas espadrilles. "You must be Odile's new friend," she said. "It's nice to meet you."

The canine stopped, cocked its head to one side, and looked at her thoughtfully with its soft brown eyes. The harness it was wearing swayed back and forth.

The housekeeper kept saying "*Mon Dieu*" over and over again, and the curly-haired little girl continued to call the dog's name repeatedly.

Finally, the dog gave Jacquie's hand a quick lick, then turned and ran back to the girl, its long, furry tail waving in the air.

Drawing in a sigh of relief, Jacquie glanced at Georges-Henri.

He had moved his wheelchair around and was staring at her.

She shrugged, and smiled sheepishly.

He didn't react.

The girl took hold of Gaullie's harness, and allowed the dog to lead her toward Jacquie.

"You must be Odile," Jacquie said, squatting as she approached.

"Who are you?" Odile asked, coming up close and squinting at Jacquie through round, bottle-glass thick lenses.

My God, Jacquie thought. The little girl's stunning eyes were the same unusual color as Georges-Henri's—gray with little flecks of gold.

The dog's long black nose burrowed in next to Odile's face, both heads just centimeters away from Jacquie's.

"Gaullie thinks you are pretty," Odile said. She patted the notched collar of Jacquie's belted cotton shirtwaist dress, straining to see it up close. "And your frock is yellow, just like mine."

"My name is Jacquie. I am a friend of your…" Before she could say more, the little girl threw her arms around Jacquie's neck.

Feeling her heart melt, Jacquie held her. "I think you are pretty, too, Odile," she whispered.

"Odile," the housekeeper called, "*Viens à la cuisine pour ton casse-croûte.*"

The child relaxed her arms, and Jacquie stood.

"You can come to the kitchen and have a snack, too," the girl offered. "Marie-Madeleine made petits fours."

"That sounds wonderful," Jacquie said. "Why don't you go ahead? I'll be there shortly."

Odile nodded. "*Allons*, Gaullie," she said, seizing the harness. Seeming to understand, the Malinois gave out a little "woof!" and took the lead back to the house.

Jacquie watched them until they were on the veranda. Then she turned and moved toward Georges-Henri. With his straw hat, he reminded her of a photo she had seen of the artist Cézanne, beard and all, taken in Aix not far from where she was now.

"What are you doing here in Les Moulins?" he said when she was a few feet from him. "I thought you would be halfway across the Atlantic with Duff by now." He glanced back toward the cottage, his gray eyes glaring at her. "Or is he here with you?"

She shook her head, puzzled. "Why would Duff be here?"

He shrugged. "He sent me postcards of your road trip together. I assumed he would be with you." His voice sounded petulant.

"Well, we did have a good trip," she said, "but he's not here."

He removed his hat and laid it on top of the book in his lap.

He was sulking. Suddenly it dawned on her. Of course, that was it. He was jealous.

"Georges-Henri," she said firmly, "Duff was never with me."

"He wasn't?"

This was getting irritating. She shook her head. "Never for a minute. Claudine and Duff are together now. They seem pretty serious. He's sailing home to New York with her to teach at Columbia University this fall." She took in a deep breath. "I changed my passage so that I could come to Les Moulins to see you before I left. I'm sorry I didn't warn you I was coming."

He was silent. She wondered if he had understood what she'd said.

"If I had known, I would have told you not to come," he said finally.

She gasped, her heart sinking. "But why?"

"I wouldn't have wanted you to see me like this. It would be better if you leave now, Jacquie." He turned his wheelchair around with his back to her.

The endless chirruping of the cicadas grew louder.

A lump formed in the back of Jacquie's throat. She covered the short distance between them and came to his side.

He stared out at the lake, ignoring her.

"I thought it would be a nice surprise," she said. "We hadn't heard anything. I was so worried about you. I didn't even know if you were still in the hospital in Nice. I went there first."

"I was released only recently."

"Are you well then?"

He shrugged. "Well enough. They didn't have to amputate my leg."

She stretched out her hand and touched his arm, her heart pumping. "It doesn't matter. Don't you understand? I came here because I care about you."

He lifted his head to gaze up at her. "The doctors won't tell me for certain if I'll ever walk again."

She held his gaze.

Finally, after what felt like an eternity, he took her hand and pulled her down to him.

She closed her eyes as his lips brushed her left cheek, then the right. The third time his kiss was more tender and very close to the corner of her mouth. His beard tickled her chin.

"You shouldn't have come," he said.

"I couldn't leave France without seeing you."

"When do you sail?"

"We have a week."

Aboard the *De Grasse*
September 1952

Chapter Forty-one

The sky was bright blue, and the sea a beautiful mixture of teal and aquamarine. On the deck of the liberty ship approaching the coast of France, Jacquie leaned against the railing and hummed "*La Vie en Rose.*" The ship's horn sounded a long, forlorn blast as the port of Le Havre came into view.

She looked up at the twin red funnels billowing out black smoke, her thoughts on that day at the end of June over a year ago when she'd bid au revoir to Georges-Henri and Odile in Les Moulins. Odile had begged her to stay. Georges-Henri hadn't done the same, much to her chagrin. Instead, he had continued to insist they could not be together until he could walk again.

"As if that would have mattered to me," she mumbled to herself.

There had been precious little opportunity for them to be alone during the week she'd spent in Provence. As much as she had grown fond of the little girl, Odile being around all the time had been a challenge.

Breathing in the tang of salt in the air, salt and something vaguely fishy, she recalled the day she and Georges-Henri had had a picnic lunch together by the lake. Odile and Marie-Madeleine had gone to a neighboring town to market, leaving them alone.

It was a beautiful afternoon. They had fixed crusty baguettes with butter, thin slices of *jambon*, a local goat cheese, and fruit. She had sat on a blanket on the ground beside George-Henri's wheelchair basking in the warm sunshine as he read aloud to her from a book by Honoré de Balzac.

"'The snowy sparkle of the moon is on thy lovely brow. Heaven's azure centres in thine eyes.'" He had paused at that point, looked at her and smiled. "'Thy lashes fall like starry rays.'"

She caught her breath now as she remembered what happened next. Touched by his tender look, she had stood and climbed into his lap, careful to not put her weight on his still-healing leg. Removing his straw hat, she pressed her lips to his.

"Your beard tickles," she teased.

Giving into the moment, he kissed her slowly and deliberately. Then, just as abruptly, he pulled back. "*Je suis un homme qui n'est pas...n'est pas... complet*," he said. Not whole? What did he mean?

"The wheelchair doesn't make any difference," she said.

"*Quand même*." Even so. The shrug and the look of doubt on his face told her he didn't believe her.

As the week went on, it became clear he was unwilling to make a commitment. She had wondered if it would always be that way with him.

On the day of her departure, he hadn't even offered to see her off. His parting embrace, on the cottage's veranda, had been touching. He held her for a long time, as if bidding her goodbye for the last time. She'd gone alone to Marseille, stood on the ship's deck watching the coast of France disappear. Weeping.

In all the months since, he had written her just once and that was to tell her he planned to return to Paris to resume his teaching in the fall. She pulled the saved letter from her bag and reread the last part.

Now that Odile has recovered enough to travel, she will go to Paris with me.

I have enrolled her in a special boarding school where she will study Braille, and Gaullie will be allowed to stay with her. He, too, will receive additional training. I plan to rent a room nearby so I can be an attentive father to her. (Oui, she calls me Papa now.)

You should know, Jacquie, that going to the school was Odile's choice. She was very excited to make the decision herself.

There had been no explanation about what it was Odile had recovered from. She was pleased, though, that he had remembered her insistence about Odile being old enough to be consulted about her life. She wrote back, but he had never responded.

It was Claudine who had suggested she return to Paris for her graduate studies. During a special dinner they'd held to celebrate her and Duff's engagement, Claudine had pushed the idea.

"I would love to," Jacquie said, "but I don't know if it will be the same. Maybe I just had rose-colored glasses on when we were there. Staying in the apartment on avenue Mozart would be out of the question."

"Why is that?"

Jacquie sighed. "They say you can't go back again."

"Poppycock," Claudine said. "You know Hélène would give you back our old room in a heartbeat. I'm sure of it. She adores you. All you have to do is ask."

"Yes, but what about Georges-Henri?"

"What about him? Wouldn't you want to see him again?"

"Well, maybe, but it seems clear he doesn't feel the same about me. I doubt that he would want to see me."

"Hog wash. You know you still love each other. You even speculated as much. Remember?"

Jacquie had done that once. During a conversation the two women had over a bottle of wine.

"If you don't go back," Claudine persisted, "you'll never know for certain. So what if he'll be in a wheelchair for the rest of his life? You can handle that."

Duff weighed in on the subject at that point. "He's just worried about not being man enough. Well, I'm tellin' you. That's a bunch of horse *merde*." He made her and Claudine blush at what he said next. "A certain part is all it takes for sparks to fly."

After that conversation, Jacquie had decided to apply to the Sorbonne after all. Georges-Henri notwithstanding, she had begun to realize how much she missed France. She resolved to do it for herself. She was accepted and would begin an advanced program of graduate studies in Fine Arts in October.

With the encouragement of Claudine, she'd written the good news to Hélène and politely inquired about the possibility of renting her old room in the apartment on avenue Mozart.

Hélène wrote back that she had taken the children to the château for the summer and they planned to stay on in Normandy for the school year. Théo, she noted, was delighted with his new puppy. In the fall, Hélène was to oversee the re-opening of the local *école élémentaire* which had been mostly destroyed by a bomb in the aftermath of the invasion of 1944. Christine and Théo would be among the first pupils to attend. The apartment was closed up now, but Jacquie would be most welcome to stay in it as long as she wished. Hélène had even sent the key via special delivery.

"What? Hélène offered you Paul's old room? The room with the view? I'm jealous," Claudine had said when she'd told her the news.

Knowing it wouldn't take much convincing, Jacquie had suggested she and Duff spend their honeymoon in Paris. "I'd give up the room for you," she had said. The couple had agreed immediately. Their wedding had taken place the week before she sailed so Jacquie could be Claudine's bridesmaid and the couple planned their honeymoon for the following April.

As the ship pulled into port, the mood on deck was jubilant. People cheered and waved their hats wildly in the air as they docked.

Jacquie strained to see a familiar face in the throng of people waiting to meet the boat. She'd wired the details of her arrival to Hélène but hadn't known how to let Georges-Henri know. It was a long shot, but she held out hope that Hélène would have gotten word to him, and he'd be there in Le Havre to meet her.

"You read too many romance novels," she chastised herself. But still...

Her heart skipped a beat at the sight of a wooden wheelchair similar to the one Georges-Henri used. She raised her hand to wave, but lowered it immediately, disappointed. Not him after all.

Between the noise of the crowd and the incessant rock, rocking of the ship at anchor, the wait seemed interminable.

"Are you meeting someone?" a voice behind Jacquie asked. She turned to see a young woman with blond curly hair. They'd been introduced at dinner one evening. Jacquie remembered her radiant smile. Her name was Cynthia. "Yes. I hope so, anyway," she answered. "And you?"

"My fiancé. I haven't seen him in several months. I'm so excited. We are to be married in Paris."

"Congratulations!" Jacquie said, feeling jealous.

Finally, the passengers were allowed to begin disembarking. They moved forward a few feet. Jacquie pushed her suitcase along with her foot.

Cynthia suddenly began waving frantically. "John!" she called. "That's him," she exclaimed pointing to a tall young man in an American soldier's uniform brandishing his cap above his head. "Isn't he cute?"

Jacquie shielded her eyes from the bright sun to see him. The man's tousled rust-red hair and dimples reminded her of Duff. "He's very handsome," she said.

"He's stationed here temporarily to help with the recovery effort. We'll stay in Europe until he's needed somewhere else." She grinned. "Not a bad assignment."

"Indeed," Jacquie said, continuing to scan the crowd for Georges-Henri.

They reached the end of the ramp. Cynthia dropped her suitcase and ran into her fiancé's arms. He swung her around, kissed her passionately, then, still keeping one arm around her shoulders, he picked up her suitcase, and they walked off together.

Jacquie sighed. All around her, couples were embracing while others pushed and shoved, eager to get off the boat.

"Move ahead, Mademoiselle," urged a man from behind.

"*Oh, pardon*," she said, stepping aside.

As the crowd thinned out, she lingered near the bottom of the ramp, continuing to search the faces on the dock. For the first time since she'd left New York harbor she felt like crying. Of course, he wasn't there to meet her.

"Silly me," she muttered as she started to walk through the port's drab maze of corrugated iron warehouses on her way to the Le Havre train station. Not for the first time since she'd begun her journey, she wondered whether he'd found someone else. Someone more like Marielle.

Passing the post box where she had mailed the postcard to him the year before, she sat down on the bench next to it and took off a shoe to rub her aching feet. There was a hole in her nylon stocking where her big toe had worn through. Just like the hole he had left in her heart.

Quashing her disappointment, she allowed herself to enjoy the excitement of being in France again. The city she loved most was just two hours away. She adored everything about Paris—the cafes and the bistros, the open spaces of the Bois and the Luxembourg gardens…and the bridges and the bouquinists along the quais. She couldn't wait to see it.

"I shall have a terrific year regardless," she said aloud as she put her shoe back on and rose from the bench. She didn't need Georges-Henri or anyone else to make that happen.

At the Gare, she bought a one-way ticket to Paris.

Chapter Forty-two

G are Saint-Lazare was bustling with activity. Jacquie walked along the platform, inhaling the familiar smells. Strong coffee. Cigarette smoke. Warm croissants. Oh, it was so good to be back.

Though she knew he wouldn't be there, she eyed the crowd on the platform, hoping to see Georges-Henri. Foolish thought. He couldn't even remotely have known she'd be on this particular train.

A lineup of Citroën 2CVs waited at the taxi stand in front of the station. She went to the first in queue and signaled to the driver. He was the picture of a Paris cab driver—black beret, wiry mustache, beady brown eyes—and he smelled of sweat. A cigarette dangled from the corner of his mouth.

The cabbie jumped out of the taxi, took her suitcase, opened the rear door for her to climb in, and scurried back to the driver's seat.

"*Vous allez où*, Mademoiselle?" he asked as he put the car in gear and pulled away.

"*Le seizième*," she answered. "Avenue Mozart."

"*Américaine?*" He turned his head slightly and grinned at her with a mouth full of brown-stained teeth.

Of course, he'd detected her accent. She'd have to work on that now she was back.

"Oui, Monsieur," she answered politely. "New York."

"*Ah bon?* First time in Paris, *n'est-ce pas?*"

Sneaky. He was testing if he could get away with the more lucrative longer route.

Oh well. It was a warm day, and what did it matter how many times they crossed the Seine? "*Non,*" she said, "but I'm not in a hurry."

He smiled. "*Bon. Alors, vous allez retrouver laVille Lumière, Mademoiselle.*"

La Ville Lumière. The city of light. She peered out the open window while he drove at a crawl through the tree-lined boulevards. Mothers pushed baby carriages. Lovers walked arm in arm, laughing, stopping to embrace. There seemed to be a new optimism about the place. People of all ages filled the terraces of outdoor cafés chatting over an afternoon *aperitif*.

They passed the Champs de Mars, the large public space between the Eiffel Tower and the École Militaire in the seventh. The cabbie slowed to a stop to let her get a good look at the view. "*La voilà!*" he exclaimed. "*La Dame de Fer.*"

Seeing the Iron Lady never grew old. Jacquie thanked him before he could launch into a lengthy history lesson.

At the Trocadéro, they finally crossed into the sixteenth. Seeing the open-air market reminded her of the times she and Hélène had meandered the stalls, buying fresh produce and cheeses. Her favorites were the peaches and sweet cherries when they were in season. She made a mental note to go shopping as soon as she could.

The apartment's ice box would be empty. Even when Hélène was there, she never had much of anything to snack on except for a left-over dry baguette in the bread bag hanging behind the kitchen door and a jar of fruit preserves on the counter. Claudie had complained about that a lot. Hélène only purchased what she needed, and she always prepared dinner with fresh ingredients purchased the same day. Jacquie planned to do the same.

Her next thought was about the apartment. It would need airing out after being closed up all summer. Hélène had written that all the furniture was covered in sheets, but she should feel free to remove them and make herself comfortable.

The driver suddenly pulled to an abrupt stop. "*Voilà*," he announced. "*Nous sommes arrivés. Avenue Mozart. Numéro vingt-huit.*"

Glancing up at the building's façade, Jacquie was surprised to see the French doors flung open in Paul's old room—the room that was supposed to be hers for the next year. Had Hélène returned?

She paid the cabbie and slid out of the back seat. "*Bon séjour*," he wished her, tipping his beret and smiling.

When the taxi had pulled away, she picked up her suitcase and walked to the heavy wooden entrance door. Using the key Hélène had sent, she let herself into the apartment.

A bouquet of fresh flowers sat on the table in the foyer, and the apartment smelled good, as if someone had been cooking. How nice, she thought. Hélène had come to welcome her to Paris.

"*Coucou! Hélène?*" she called as she set down her handbag and her suitcase then removed her scarf.

No sheets covered the furniture in the salon, and all the windows were opened wide to let in the fresh air. The entire room was perfumed with the fragrance of the roses outside in the courtyard.

She peeked into the dining room and paused, recalling the evening she had first met Georges-Henri. He'd taken his place at the table next to her at dinner. She remembered thinking he was sad. Now that she knew more of his story, she realized why.

Noises came from the kitchen. Someone was moving around, rattling drawers.

"Hélène?"

A cupboard door closed.

She stopped. "*Bonjour*? Hélène? *C'est* Jacquie."

Nothing. She froze and called out, "*Qui est là?*"

She was about to turn and run when a figure appeared suddenly in the open doorway.

She jumped, startled. It was Georges-Henri.

"Oh! It's you!" she exclaimed. She felt her face flushing. "I didn't expect you to be here."

Dressed in a white shirt and black pants, he was tan from being in the south of France. She took in a breath. He was even more handsome than she'd remembered.

"Your hair is longer," he said with a gentle smile.

"And you have shaved your beard," she said.

He held her eyes, staring at her.

Shy, still.

"How did you know I was arriving today?" she asked.

"Hélène."

She shot a quick look behind him. "Is she here?"

He shook his head. "Just me."

"Is Odile with you?"

"In Paris, oui. She and Gaullie have settled in at the boarding school."

"I was so pleased when you wrote you let her decide on that for herself."

He shrugged. "It wasn't my decision. She was very definite."

He stepped into the room and came forward with only a slight limp.

"No wheelchair!" she exclaimed.

There was a flicker of a smile in his eyes. "I tossed it in the lake."

"You didn't!"

He took her hands in his, leaned in and bussed her right cheek. "Actually, no," He bussed her left cheek. "In the end, I gave it to the convent." Then, Parisian-style, his lips returned to linger just a little longer against her right check again. "Some of the nuns are very old. It will be put to good use."

Her pulse raced. She breathed in his familiar scent, lavender and musk, examined the delicate streaks of gold around his pupils. "You look well," she said.

He returned her stare. "And you. You look beautiful."

He bent his head and kissed her fingers, sending electric tingles through her.

"I thought we'd have a glass of champagne to celebrate your return," he said. "Would you like that?"

She nodded, unable to speak.

He led her into the dining room where a bottle of Moët et Chandon sat in a tall silver cooler on the sideboard.

She watched him expertly uncork the bottle. "We met in this room. Do you remember?"

Filling two crystal glasses, he handed her one. "Two years ago. A lot of water has flowed under the Pont Neuf since then."

A lifetime, she thought. She lifted her glass. "I wrote you from New York. Did you receive any of my letters?"

He took a sip of his champagne, studied her face. "I received all of them."

"You did? That's strange. Did you write back? I only had one response from you the entire time."

He scratched his temple. "*En effet*, Jacquie, I wrote to you once a month." He bit his lip. "I didn't post any of them, though."

"Why ever not?"

"They were…"

She moved closer to him. "Were what, Georges-Henri?"

"*Billets doux*," he muttered. "I tried to write how I felt about you after you left Les Moulins…the words I should have said then but couldn't."

Love letters? She hadn't anticipated that. She swallowed a big gulp of champagne.

He refilled her glass. It was so quiet in the apartment she could hear the champagne's soft fizzing.

He stared into his glass. A look of anguish crossed his face. "Then… when she…"

She? Who was he talking about?

"What is it, Georges-Henri?" Jacquie put her hand on his arm.

"Let's go into the salon," he said. "I have something I want to tell you."

She was trembling. This was it. Forget the finger kisses and the champagne. He was going to tell her it was all over between them. He'd fallen in love with someone else.

Carrying her glass, she forced herself to follow him into the salon.

He waited for her to sit in the Louis XIV chair, then sat facing her on the loveseat by the open French doors.

She gripped the thin arms of the chair and waited, a sickening feeling growing in her stomach.

"I don't know how to begin," he said, leaning back and crossing his legs.

She wanted to tell him to just get it over with. "When did it happen?" she asked, a bit too abruptly.

He looked at her and took another sip of his champagne. "I know I should have written to you about it. I tried to. But I just couldn't bring myself to put it in writing."

What could be so difficult about dumping a girl for someone else? She finished off her second glass of champagne in a single gulp. Maybe she could see this conversation through without crying. Maybe.

"It happened so fast."

She stared at him, wishing for another glass of champagne.

"The month after you left, Odile and I walked up from the cottage to visit Marielle and Bernard's graves in the convent cemetery." He lowered his head. "She had been asking, begging me, over and over if we could visit her maman and papa. I agreed to go because Gaullie wasn't allowed on the convent grounds, and, despite her threats to do so, she couldn't see well enough to go there by herself.

"I was able to use the pair of crutches the hospital sent home with me, though the steep uphill trail made the progression painfully slow for us both. Finally, we visited the graves and then Marielle's statue in *Le Jardin des Innocents*."

"How did Odile react to all of it?" Jacquie asked. She remembered him telling her he was planning to have the statue in the garden dedicated in Marielle's memory to all the abandoned babies.

"Odile had been complaining earlier that morning that her head hurt, but I didn't think anything of it. Then, while we were visiting the garden, she started rubbing her eyes and said, 'My head really hurts bad, Papa.' It was the first time she called me Papa."

Jacquie smiled. "That must have meant a lot."

He sighed. "Oui, but I only realized later the extent of her desperation. By the time we returned to the cottage, it was evident something was really wrong. It wasn't seeing the graves that caused it. She was burning with fever." He closed his eyes.

"She grew worse," he went on after a few seconds. "Marie-Madeleine became very anxious. She went for the village doctor. He thought it was just a severe case of measles. But, by the next day, Odile was in severe pain and soaked with sweat. We took her to the hospital in Nice."

"What was the matter with her?" Jacquie asked. His face had become pallid. This wasn't about his meeting someone new after all. He was truly in pain.

"It wasn't measles; it was poliomyelitis."

"Oh no! Polio? Here? In Provence?"

He rubbed his neck. "We don't know how she contracted it. She was put on a respirator to help her breathe, but the doctors couldn't offer much hope." He set his empty glass on the coffee table in front of him, leaned forward, and held his head in his hands. "I was frantic," he said, fighting back a sob. "I told them she couldn't die. My daughter couldn't die."

Jacquie rose from her chair, set her empty glass next to his on the coffee table, and went over to sit next to him on the loveseat. "But she is all right now, isn't she, Georges-Henri? And she's here with you in Paris, too." She rested her cheek against his shoulder.

"For ten days," he went on, as if he had not heard her. "I sat by her bedside, holding her hand, talking to her. Finally, one day, she opened her eyes. The doctors pronounced her out of danger two weeks later. Except, there was the damage."

Jacquie gazed at him. "Damage? What do you mean?"

"The disease attacked the muscles in her legs. They said she might be crippled and that we should hope for the best. I asked her over and over again to wiggle her toes for me. She tried and tried, but she couldn't."

Jacquie's heart sank. "I'm so sorry," she said.

"Then came the sad day when they clamped the steel braces on her small legs." He looked at her with tears in his eyes. "She cried. She thought she would lose Gaullie because she couldn't walk anymore."

"It must have been terrible for you."

He nodded. "It has taken a lot of work—both of us–swimming in the lake, walking every day." He lifted his leg, badly injured during the war and then cruelly crushed in the accident. "In the meantime, I slowly mended, too." He drew in a breath. "Odile and I, we became strong together."

"Does she still wear the braces then?" Jacquie knew some of the polio victims at home in the United States never walked normally again.

He looked into her eyes. "On one leg, yes—the most severely damaged. She hates it, calls it 'that *merde* thing'. Says she's going to throw it in the Seine someday." He chuckled. "I don't doubt that she will, too."

She caressed his war-scarred cheek then slid her arms around his neck. Suddenly, the only thing that mattered to her was to be in his arms again.

He drew her to him, his kiss crushing her lips.

"Do you even realize how much I missed you?" he said softly.

"I think I do now."

Chapter Forty-three

Church bells announced the six o'clock hour. *L'heure bleue*, that magical time between day and night. Outside in the garden, birds chirped and a cool breeze rustled the trees.

Georges-Henri rose from the loveseat and held out his hands to Jacquie.

Not entirely certain her legs would support her, she took his hands and allowed him to pull her upright.

He wrapped her in his arms again. His face was flushed; his eyes bright.

"Kiss me here," he said, indicating the spot where a kiss would be welcome.

She bussed his cheek.

"Now here."

Their lips met. And continued to meet.

"Would you like to see your room?" he asked finally. "It has a spectacular view."

"So I'm told," she muttered.

He put an arm around her waist, she laid her head against his shoulder, and, together, they walked down the long hallway.

"Claudie and I once tried to peek inside. Do you remember? You caught us before we could even have a look in the door."

"I do remember." He pulled her close to him and kissed her again.

"Is the mannequin still in there?" she asked.

"No."

"What a relief!"

They both laughed.

The setting sun filtering in through the windows cast a warm glow on the gold-framed paintings in the hall. Renoir. Dégas. Scenes of the family's château. Jacquie recalled how she had loved looking at those paintings when the apartment was quiet and everyone was out.

They came to the end of the hall. Georges-Henri stopped and ran his hands over Jacquie's bare arms, sending shivers through her. Then he opened the door. "*Et voilà*," he said.

"Oh my," she exclaimed as she entered.

The high-ceilinged room was decorated in soft colors. The walls were a pale celadon green, as were the antique armoire and a matching carved-wood rococo bed covered with soft cream linens. An ornate mirror hung above the sculpted fireplace opposite, and an elegant sparkling crystal chandelier hovered above it all.

She swung around to face him. "It's so elegant. So…so romantic."

His eyes gleamed. "I hope you won't ever want to leave."

Her trunk had been placed at the foot of the bed, and a fresh bouquet of pink roses in a porcelain vase sat on the nightstand alongside a stack of letters.

Curious, she walked over and fanned through the envelopes. There were about a dozen of them, all addressed simply to "J."

"Are these the letters you wrote to me?" she asked.

He nodded. "You can read them now." He cleared his throat. "No. I don't mean that. Not now," he mumbled. "I..." he looked at her. "Whenever you wish, *chérie*."

She grinned at him and strolled to the open French windows. A slight breeze tickled the sheer linen curtains, carrying with it the scent of the river. From the street came the sound of traffic driving over the cobbles, impatient drivers beeping their horns, and a general hum from the packed bars and outdoor cafés.

Georges-Henri came up behind her. She felt his warm breath on her neck. Taking her hand, he brought it to his lips, gently turned it over, and planted a kiss into her palm.

"My heart is in your hands now," he said.

Their eyes locked.

"There is no one else then?"

"Only you, *amour*."

The Eiffel Tower loomed in the distance, its iron latticework silhou-etted in the pale peach-pink and pastel blue of the evening sky.

"It is such a perfect view. I could stand here forever," Jacquie said softly.

Georges-Henri kissed her neck. "My father always said there is only one perfect view. And that is of the woman you love."

ABOUT THE AUTHOR

MJ Roë lives in Southern California. Her lifelong passion for La Ville Lumière and for all things French has fueled her novels and given her the opportunity to visit the city many times. She has worked in France as a business and marketing executive and previously taught French and creative writing.

The author's previous novels have won awards at the Paris Book Festival, the London Book Festival, and the Los Angeles Book Festival.

This is her first novel written under the pseudonym MJ Bachman.

MJ and her Golden Retriever Paris

ACKNOWLEDGMENTS

When I began writing this story, I had just read an excellent book by Anna Sebba entitled *Les Parisiennes: how the women of Paris lived, loved and died under Nazi occupation.* The book is well researched. What struck me the most, however, and what inspired me to write this story was the account of an unknown American, a twenty-year-old student in her junior year of college, who went to Paris on a study-abroad program run by Smith College in 1949-50. Her name was Jacqueline Bouvier, the same woman who was destined to become First Lady of the United States.

A decade later, I was a great admirer of Jackie Kennedy, and a star-struck French student who dreamed of studying in Paris myself. During the sixties, student exchange programs to Europe flourished and young women were encouraged to follow their dreams. Adding to that, the rise of mid-century feminism presented a new atmosphere in the postwar period, one that infected young women like me with a sense of independence. When I landed at Orly Airport for my own study-abroad experience, and saw the Eiffel Tower for the first time, I fell in love.

A verbal bouquet goes to the Rancho Bernardo Writers Group in San Diego for their critique in the early (pre-pandemic) days of this story creation, and a warm thank you especially to Connie During, Rob Ruenitz, and my husband Denny for the thorough and thoughtful feedback they gave me as beta readers. Last but not least, I would like to thank Annie Mydla with Winning Writers, who critiqued my manuscript and provided detailed and constructive comments.